Empty Heart

Wildcat Wizard Book 10

Get deals and new releases notifications first via the newsletter www.alkline.co.uk

Brr

Being married is a lot like toast. It's hard, but very enjoyable. Plus, you get to smother butter and marmalade all over your favorite thing in the world.

I smiled at Penelope as we disembarked from the plane, pleased to stretch my legs. As we walked across the airfield, I breathed in deeply of the damp early summer air. You know you're home when it's summer but cloudy and there's a fine drizzle that you think will hardly get you wet but soaks you through to the skin. I loved it.

A fortnight on a beach in a posh resort on a small island in the middle of the ocean had left me feeling antsy. If it wasn't for copious amounts of sex and more food than I was used to, I'd have gone out of my mind. Wizards aren't designed to relax in their swimming trunks, they need lots of clothes with pockets, and something to get angry about.

I was unsettled the whole time, expecting something awful to happen. For an utterly ridiculous series of events to unfold that would see me running around like a nutter blasting bad guys, and stressing about Penelope, my new wife, getting hurt.

Nothing happened, so I spent the entire two weeks on edge waiting for it to happen, and when it didn't, I became convinced that somehow the world had ended and the inhabitants and guests on the island were all that remained of humanity.

Seems that was wrong too, as the bloody plane was rammed, same as on the way out. It was obvious planes were now much smaller, or they believed every passenger had shrunk to the size of a small child with extraordinarily stumpy legs.

But we were home, it had been an awesome fortnight even with all the stress of it being lovely and nothing happening, and I was now a married man.

"You okay?" asked Penelope as we followed the line of passengers and entered the building only to stop and queue—definitely home.

"Sure. Pleased to be on terra firma, and back in Blighty."

"Me too. I'm all for taking it easy but you can have too much relaxation."

"Wow, it wasn't just me then?"

"Arthur, are you serious? Do you think I didn't notice you were out of your mind with boredom?"

"Huh? I thought I hid it well. And there were some very nice times." I grinned as I pinched her bottom. She squealed then reddened as people turned to see what the commotion was.

"Behave," Penelope whispered.

A man turned and stared at me, then Penelope. "I wish I had a nice bum I could pinch," he said, then winked.

"Um, okay, right," I said, flummoxed.

"I wish someone would pinch my bum," said a woman in her seventies three people ahead.

"That's disgusting," said a smartly dressed woman in her thirties. "Women have rights now, you know? We aren't living in the sixties. That's sexual harassment. Men!"

"Well, I'm a woman," said the old lady, "and I wish someone cared enough to pinch my bum."

It got weird. Half the people in the queue began discussing if it was okay to have their bums pinched, whilst the other half moaned about the lack of affection they received. Brits weren't like this, we stood silently in queues, grumbling under our breath whilst maintaining an orderly line.

Finally we made it inside the building proper and went to collect our bags. Ours came out first, and that was when I began to freak out a little.

It doesn't matter who you are, for some inexplicable reason I am yet to understand, every single person's bags are the last ones to come around that circular carousel. It's a law or something.

So as I retrieved our luggage and we walked towards the customs area, I panicked.

This was going well. Was this how it would be now I was married? Everything would work out fine, nothing bad would happen?

I hoped not.

Bit Rude

"I don't like your beard," said a tiny customs official in an oversized hat as we strode through the "Nothing to Declare" lane. I felt nervous, skin tingling, palms sweaty, the same as I always did even though I knew I had nothing I shouldn't. His words totally flummoxed me.

"Um, okay. Bit rude though, saying that. Nobody asked."

"Just saying," he said, waving us through. Penelope and I exchanged glances then continued on our way.

"What was that all about?" she asked as we exited into the arrivals section. I could see the massive car park through huge plate glass across the vast tiled floor. I couldn't wait to get out of here, out into the glum weather, get home, and have a cuppa. Why does coffee in another country never taste as nice as from your own kitchen?

"Beats me. Must be having a bad day."

We squeezed through the throng of people, the noise intense. Everyone was arguing a lot, bickering about how each other looked, about the weather, about their holiday, about being late, early, whatever. Guess vacation stress was a real thing.

And then all the background noise faded away as I saw a vision in green. My beautiful daughter, flame-red hair in tight curls, shining like the sun, smiling at me with an angelic face that brightened the dullest of days. George wore a tight green dress with bare arms and legs, with high heels. She looked so damn smart. She was her own woman and never followed the trends of other teenagers, favoring instead pencil skirts, frilly blouses, or retro dresses. She ran over and hugged us both.

"Did you behave?" I asked.

"Of course. I always do."

"Hmm."

"How's it been having the house to yourself?" asked Penelope.

"Awesome! Um, but I missed you guys, obviously," said George with a huge grin.

"Obviously. I hope you haven't had any boys over," I warned.

"Arthur!"

"Dad!"

"What? Just saying. Come on, let's get out of here."

"You should say thank you, you know. I've come to pick you up," said George, frowning.

"Oh, um, sorry. Thank you, George."

She stormed off ahead, heels clattering on the tiles. Penelope and I both looked at each other as if the other had the answer. "That was strange," she said.

"Sure was. What's with everyone today? Everyone's being..."

"Blunt?"

"No. More than that. Everyone's being honest."

We followed George out of the building. As we caught her up, I heard her say to a man who smiled at her, "You may think that makes me feel better about myself, but it doesn't. It makes me think you're a creep and might attack me. You look smarmy."

"I... You... I was just..." The man hurried away, looking sad and confused.

"What did you say that for?" I asked. George never acted this way.

"He looked at me funny." George studied us both for a moment before saying, "I think I'd like you both to never go away again. I felt lonely and I missed you." She put a hand to her mouth in shock. She was going through a phase where she never said things like that, kept it to herself.

"But," she continued, "you both need to stop treating me like a kid. I'm an adult now. Oh, and I did have a boy over, and I liked it."

She marched off, leaving me speechless.

"Something is very wrong," I said, my speechless phase not lasting long. It never did.

My phone rang. It was Ivan.

"Hey."

"Arthur, get over here right now. We have a serious, and I mean very serious, problem."

"What is it? Is Vicky okay? Are you? Will there be coffee?"

"There will be coffee, it isn't Vicky, or me. It's something bad." Ivan hung up.

"Honeymoon is over, babe," I said.

"Don't call me babe, it makes you sound like you're trying to be twenty. You're in your forties, so act like it." Penelope's eyes widened in shock. "Sorry, sorry, don't know where that came from."

"What is wrong with everyone?" I muttered, feeling well and truly put out as I chased after the two women. The women I lived with and who were now causing me to consider moving into the barn. Them, not me. I liked my kitchen too much.

Why Me?

George refused to drive, even though she'd come to pick us up. She wouldn't let us drive either. I couldn't be bothered to continue arguing after an exasperating ten minutes of her going on about how it scared her. We got a taxi to take us to Ivan's smart and expensive house, a building identical to all others in the row. Three-story Georgian with huge windows, white facades, shining gloss doors with brass furniture and black railings fronting them. This was money, yet understated too. There was no litter here, anything that drifted from the poor areas was promptly swept up by cleaners paid by the council. Keep the nice places spotless, let the ghettos fester.

It was one of the strangest drives I have ever experienced. The taxi driver let forth with an endless tirade against anything and everything. From his home life and his kids, to the state of the roads, the price of fuel, even moaning about the trees and the fact he found them annoying—go figure. All of this was interspersed with both Penelope and George repeatedly telling the driver they did not like him in general, and then they got into specifics about his facial hair, his haircut, even the color of his eyes. Everyone had gone nuts.

I was left bewildered and confused as I got out of the car and handed the guy his money with a nice fat tip.

"Cheers, mate. Most people seem to think a pound or two is a nice tip, it ain't. This is what I'm talking about." He grinned at me, scrunched up his already scrunched face at the women, sighed, then said, "Feisty pair, eh?"

"Yeah, don't know what's got into them."

"Good luck, mate, you're gonna need it." He drove off and left me to it.

Wasting no time, I hurried to the door which George had already knocked.

"You know I don't like this man," said Penelope.

"I know, but hush, someone's coming."

The door was opened by his aide, a woman I'd never been introduced to.

"Hi, it's Arthur." I held out my hand, feeling like I needed moral support.

"You are a very stupid man," she said. "We have met many times, you have been given my name repeatedly, and yet for some strange reason, or maybe you think it is funny, you refuse to acknowledge that we have been properly introduced. This way please." She turned and walked down the hall.

I glanced at the others for backup, but they just tutted and marched inside, leaving me on the threshold wondering if I could still make a run for it.

"Her name's Kim," called Penelope over her shoulder. "The woman you always refer to as the tall skinny one with the blond bob."

"Kim, Kim, Kim," I repeated. "Damn, I just met a Kim, didn't I?" I recalled Jake's girlfriend. She was Kim, wasn't she? How come that name had stuck but this woman wouldn't?

I steeled my nerve and entered the vampire's lair.

In the drawing room—Ivan was old-fashioned like that—Penelope and George were already sitting, and looking somewhat dazed. Maybe everyone was just tired? Tired of the weather when it was summer, tired because of the trip maybe? I know I was, in that way you get when you've relaxed for too long and feel more exhausted than if you'd just kept busy. Or maybe they were tired of me? Was Penelope regretting getting married? Did she regret us going to a tropical paradise and being wed by a local without friends or family? She said that was what she wanted, but now maybe she'd changed her mind.

Maybe I was the weary one and reading too much into this. Sleep, that was what I needed. I hated flying, it exhausted me, my body hurt from being cramped up, and the recycled air dried out my skin.

"Good, you're all here," said Ivan as he swept into the room looking like Death, meaning as bad as me, but that's a different story.

"What's this all about?" I asked, not in the mood for pleasantries.

"All in good time. Nice to see you, George, and you, Penelope. So, you're married?"

"Yes, we are. Look, Ivan, what do you want? I need to get home, I want to stare at my kitchen." I glanced around. "And you said there would be coffee."

"There is food in the kitchen, all prepared, drinks too. Maybe George and Penelope would like to help themselves?" Ivan stood aside and gestured to the door.

Penelope and George glared at him then George said, "That's not very polite. We came because I picked them up, so why should we leave?" I said nothing about us arriving by taxi because she'd gone mad in the head.

"It's business, dangerous business. I am thinking only of your welfare." Ivan ran a hand through slick short hair. If I didn't know him better, I'd say he was stressed and showing it. He never revealed his emotions, he was more like a preying mantis, all angles, bony, slender yet with poise that grew more powerful as his position rose in the vampire and criminal hierarchy.

"Fine," said Penelope in a huff. "But I don't like coming here, and I don't like what you do with the drugs."

"Penelope, there's no need for—"

"It's fine," said Ivan, interrupting me.

The girls left and we were alone.

"Are they acting strange?" asked Ivan. "No, don't answer, they obviously are."

"Just tired, a little grumpy I guess."

"We have a problem."

"Yeah, you said. Get on with it, I wanna go home."

"First, congratulations on the marriage."

"Thanks."

"Everyone is telling the truth."

"Honesty's the best policy," I said, grinning.

"You don't understand. Everyone, I mean everyone in the city, and it's spread somewhat, is telling the truth. Someone has done something. There is magic afoot."

"Magic afoot? What is this? Who speaks like that? Am I on TV?"

"I do. And no, you aren't. Somebody has done something to everyone, people are telling the truth about everything. Have you any idea how bad that is?"

"Um, very?" My mind went into overdrive thinking about the consequences, the white lies everyone told constantly to keep the world turning, to get along. Without that filter there would be chaos.

"We need to deal with it."

"Hey, cool it," I said, standing and holding out my hands. "Since when are we the magic police? You're a bloody gangster and a vampire, I'm a thief. I'm not the magic council, the authorities. Get someone else to deal with it if you think you need to get involved. Somebody will sort it soon enough, I'm sure. But count me out. I need to get back to some honest thieving. It's been bloody ages since I had a job that didn't result in everything getting way too complicated."

"There is nobody else. In case you haven't noticed, it is you, and often I, who are at the forefront of all magic incidents and large-scale events involving magic in the city. Like it or not, we are the focus, the ones who deal with things. You dealt with the Queen, you dealt with Cerberus countless times, you were there when foreign invaders came. When anything of significance happens you are involved, as am I. This is our role."

"What are you on about? I'm a thief, I nick stuff, and sure, stuff happens now and then, but it isn't like I always deal with major problems that would affect other adepts or the vamps or shifters and what have you."

"No?"

"No." I plonked back down and sank into the wingback chair. I thought over the last several years, back to when Ivan ascended and Cerberus became more active in defending what was theirs, trying to push things.

"Goddamn, I am always involved, aren't I? You too, usually."

"Exactly."

Guess I was truly back in the game now.

The Nitty Gritty

Seemed it had been going on for a week or so, the exact start impossible to pin down. Like creeping death, or a virulent plague, it became apparent people had taken their filter off and were saying exactly what they thought, nothing left unsaid. Lying vanished, and with it came a whole host of complications. The number of divorce applications had skyrocketed, crime both major and minor had doubled, and the growing incidence of hospital admissions led to the NHS becoming more overburdened than it already was, accident and emergency now having a ten hour wait time as people got into fights and demanded speedy attention which wasn't forthcoming which led to more fights.

The underground had it worse. Criminals were getting caught as they blurted out their crimes, unable to lie about their business, magic users caused untold damage when they ceased hiding their abilities and let loose with the wild powers in the most inappropriate of places. And the shifters were the biggest problem of all. They had remained utterly underground for as long as anyone could remember, never revealing themselves, never showing their true nature. But they had decided, or been compelled, to show what they were, to change and let others see. Of course, so far it was all seen as a series of isolated tricks, a city-wide stunt being pulled, but soon enough the truth would finally sink in.

It was a very dangerous situation. They would be rounded up, studied, experimented on, seen as freaks, outliers, and distrusted, feared, maybe even hunted down. People don't like things they can't understand. Vamps were also a real concern, and this was Ivan's main worry too. His kind were also proudly showing off their abilities, no longer hiding, and although not exactly flaunting it yet, they were being honest about what they were to anyone who asked. Ivan had his hands full dealing with the aftermath.

Yet still, I didn't see why I had to sort this out, or how I could. I was just an ace wizard thief who sometimes got embroiled in a lot of the nonsense the main players were involved in, but it wasn't through choice and it wasn't my bloody job.

How was I meant to stop this? How could I find out who was doing it? And more importantly, why were they doing it? And most importantly of all, would this mean Penelope would keep moaning about my choice of clothes?

Our conversation was rushed and Ivan talked fast and gave details without embellishment. Why? Because the women were shouting in the kitchen and it was clear we had little time before they returned. Plus, he was a man of few words, which suited me perfectly as you know me, don't like to talk much.

"So what's the plan?" I asked.

"That's your department," he snapped.

"It affecting you too, is it?"

"No, it isn't."

"Oh, okay, then you're just being rude. What's the deal though? I'm fine, so are you, it isn't hitting everyone."

"Seems the stronger you are, the less it can infiltrate your system. Obviously something to do with magic, either innate, through the blood, or learned."

"But it's affecting shifters, they have it built-in, they're the most magical of the lot."

"They may be the exception. But again, the stronger they are, meaning the more ferocious the animal, the more powerful, the less it affects them."

I had a thought, and it sent me cold and shivering, my stomach squirming. "Please, for the love of God, tell me Vicky hasn't been affected."

Ivan shuddered. I thought I was gonna puke.

"Haha, no, she's fine. At least," he said, his brow furrowing, "I don't think it has had any impact. It's hard to tell."

"Trust me, you'd know. If you think she has the filter off now, you have no idea how bad she'd be with no-holds-barred."

"You're right, of course."

"And the plan?"

"I told you, it's down to you. You know this world better than I, but we are relying on you."

"Who is?"

"Everyone. The magical community, all of us who aren't citizens. And for the first time, citizens are relying on you too, even though they don't know it."

"I think you'll find it's the second time. Why'd you think I buggered off so quickly to get married and have my honeymoon?"

"Ah, yes, the incident with Death. I still find that somewhat hard to believe."

"Me too, buddy, me too. But I solved that problem, helped the citizens out."

"My understanding was that you shirked your duty and made another poor man resume the role he detested."

"Er, well, it was for the best."

"I'm sure. Sort this, Arthur."

Minutes later, I found myself out on the street with the distinct impression that somewhere along the line, without me noticing, Ivan had become my boss. Screw him, screw this, I was going home and maybe I could find something to calm down the two women who had seemingly made it their purpose in life to insult me in ways that chipped away at my self-confidence at an alarming rate.

Aargh

After a nightmarish journey home with Ivan's driver giving everyone grief for having had a good time and moaning about never getting out in the daylight, which led to an argument because Penelope politely pointed out he was a vampire so to suck it up—haha—and him getting arsey about that, we finally arrived.

Ah, it was beautiful. Calm descended as we all felt the peace and order envelop us. George had kept the house spotless, the kitchen anyway, and it would only take me three to four hours to bring it up to standard.

I stood there on my imported tiles, surveying the old oak, the gleaming steel, the fancy-pants coffee machine, my lovely tap, and drooled thinking about arranging the cutlery drawer. This was what it was all about, not buggering off to get sand up your bottom and be bored senseless apart from when you were getting sweaty in the bedroom.

George had apparently got to grips with the coffee machine while we were away so made the brews.

We sat at the table while I explained what Ivan had wanted.

Neither seemed very surprised, more relieved than anything, as they knew they were blurting things out they wouldn't normally. It was a relief for me too. At least maybe they'd be mindful of their words.

"Do you know...?" began Penelope.

"Yes?" I asked innocently.

"No, never mind."

"Say it if you want, but try to beat this thing. Say what you want to because you want to."

"Do you know that I love it when you get naked and bend over and—"

"No, absolutely not," shouted George. She turned to Penelope and said, "What is wrong with you? Why are you thinking that now?"

"Because looking at your dad sitting there all sexy, I got to thinking about having a shower, and then our bed, and then... Oh, gosh, sorry, I can't stop it. Arthur, we need to go upstairs right now. I'm going to say it, I am, and then George will know and—"

I pushed my chair back, grabbed her, and ran her out of the room as words came spewing from between her fingers as she tried to cover her mouth.

I have to admit, I liked what I heard. A man enjoys being complimented as much as a woman, and boy did she say nice stuff.

Shame now wasn't the time to do anything about it, but with George knowing why we'd come up it would have been weird. Several minutes later it was safe to return, and George watched us warily.

"You need to fix this. Ivan was right. No way am I living with you two talking dirty. It's freaky, and gross. You're both in your forties. Ugh!"

"Oi, we're still young. We still got it." I winked at Penelope. She giggled.

Maybe this whole truth thing wasn't so bad after all.

It was.

Woo-Hoo

With little let-up after the initial compliments, my ego was well and truly bruised, along with my shins and ribs after being repeatedly jabbed or kicked for apparently saying something wrong when trying to defend myself. So I was mightily relieved when my phone rang and I said I'd take it in the den.

"Arthur, why haven't you called?" asked Vicky, sounding petulant.

"Because I just got home, I had to go see your brother, and now I'm busy being insulted and beaten up. There must be a law against treating wizards this way. If not, there should be."

"You heard about it then?"

"I'm hearing about it constantly. I can't stand it."

"Congratulations on the marriage."

"Thank you. So, what's up?"

"Steve has a job for us." To say Vicky sounded excited was like saying she sometimes pulled her hair back into her ponytail a little too tight.

"He does? You and him still an item then?"

"Of course we are! I'm gorgeous and so is he. It's going really well and the girls adore him."

"Oh, it's just you never said before I left."

"That's because we were being chased by bad guys and I'd not long shot myself in the head."

"Fair enough." For once, she had a point.

"So what's the job? No, never mind, don't tell me. Tell him we'll take it. And by we, I mean me, but you can tag along to screw things up."

"You are so mean. When will we start?"

"Stupid question. Now, we start now." I hung up then went into the kitchen to tell my new wife the great news.

I escaped ten minutes later after a tirade of abuse, a lecture on my wayward lifestyle, moans about promising to be there for dinner and breaking that promise already, and several pats on the bottom for being a sexy beast.

With joy in my heart, Wand in my pocket, and boots on my feet, I got in the car and drove the hell away before I became entirely emasculated.

Here We Go Again

I parked in the barn I'd been in an hour ago, soaked up the silence, then walked through the Gate of Bakaudif and arrived in the kitchen of my city house. It was nothing like the proper one, but it was mine, and it was quiet. It was also in a new house because I'd had to relocate the gate after my front wall and most of the upper story had got a little exploded. Hopefully, the insurance would pay out, but I could afford it so had rushed through the purchase and had it fitted out simply but nicely before we left for our honeymoon. I quite liked it. Basic, Shaker style, minimal technology.

Keen to get back into the swing of things, I left the house and tried to recall what car I was currently using, and where I'd parked it.

After searching the streets, I eventually found the vehicle, thinking not for the first time that it would be easier to keep hold of one car rather than all this swapping about, but that's how people can trace you, follow you, so I guess I'd have to live with the inconvenience. Yet again, and it always came as a surprise, the keys were still safely stashed under the wheel arch. In all the years I'd been wizarding, I hadn't had a vehicle stolen.

I drove to Vicky's, anticipation building for a job, curious what it could be if it involved the shifters, and also wondering what I could do about this latest weirdness that seemed to have taken over not only the magical community but citizens too.

It could wait; I needed some good old-fashioned danger. Nothing too violent though, as I could no longer risk death, otherwise I would be Death, and that sucked.

At Vicky's, I parked up and before I was even out of the car I was greeted by two blond bombshells, or bombs more like, currently in the middle of exploding. They dragged me out, tugged at my clothes, begged to play tennis, then dress-up, then dolls, but really they wanted to watch TV with me, then I was unceremoniously pulled reluctantly into the house and through the hall into the kitchen where a rather bedraggled looking Vicky was standing in the middle of the room staring blankly into space.

"What you doing?" I asked as I tried to shake one twin from my leg whilst the other rifled my pockets. I moved her away gently and reminded her, "Wizard's pockets are dangerous places. Don't go snooping or you might get turned into a frog."

Her eyes widened and she snatched her hand away. They knew about magic, thought it was awesome, but weren't quite of an age where they understood the consequences or dangers of it all. They'd learn.

Vicky turned as if in a trance and sighed deeply.

"Why are you standing there?" I asked, shaking a leg but the limpet with blond hair hung on tight. I prized her fingers apart and threw a handful of sweets I kept in a super-secret pocket for such occasions into the hall and they scampered after them. Hey, don't judge me.

"It's the school holidays," whispered Vicky as she ran a hand through hair that had come loose from her ponytail. Something was seriously wrong for her to let that happen.

"Yeah, so?"

"So, I was trying to remain sane by taking a few seconds to myself. They have been off for a week now and I think I'm down to three brain cells."

"That's all you started with anyway."

"Very funny. You don't understand what it's like, you missed this bit."

"Don't remind me," I said wistfully. George appeared as a fully-grown teenager on my doorstep when her mum died, I never even knew about her until then so missed out on all the rest.

"Sorry, I know I shouldn't complain. I'm just tired."

"Not sleeping?"

"Do I ever?"

"No. And you need to eat. You're losing weight again. Sorry." It was my turn to apologize. We'd been through this enough times for me to know it was pointless nagging. Vicky had her issues and telling her about them didn't help.

"It's okay, and you're right. I'm distracted. Harried, that's the word."

"So what's the job?" I asked, knowing that would snap her out of her funk.

"Oh, you'll love it," she said, smiling and jigging about a little.

"Will I now? Usually when you say that I end up hating it and there's no payout."

"This is for the shifters, you know what they're like. There's always a fat stack of cash."

"And I know they are flaky."

"But Steve is running this, and he's stoked. We have to do it."

"What about this thing, this truth thing? Has it affected him?"

"A bit. He's been acting odd, that's for sure, but—"

"Mummy, Mummy, can we have ice cream?"

"Can we have a lolly?"

"Can I have mine in front of the TV?"

"I want mine in the garden." Tweedledum turned to me and asked, "Will you sit in the garden with me?"

I shrugged my shoulders, turned to Vicky, and said, "I'll have a choc ice," then led the girls by the hand into the garden where we eagerly awaited our snack. I don't think Vicky even realized it was dinner time, or maybe they'd already eaten. She tended to lose her mind somewhat when the girls were home, so for all I knew they'd just had breakfast.

The Job

"Wotcha, mate," said Steve as he sauntered down the garden.

"Hey, Steve, been a while."

"Sure has. Where you been hiding?" Steve kissed Vicky and searched for the girls but noted the closed curtains at their bedroom. I saw the relief when he realized they were sleeping. He loved them, but they were a handful, and getting more so with each passing day. Plus, you couldn't talk business with them constantly asking questions and interrupting.

"You know how it is. Bad guys, getting married, the usual."

"Oh yeah, congratulations. Now we'll get even less chance to go for a pint." Steve ran a hand though annoyingly tidy hair, at odds with the hipster beard full of product that made it shine. No, I didn't feel challenged, I liked the scruffy, unkempt wizard look. Mainly because I had no choice.

"Thanks. So, a job?"

"Yes, a job. I'm getting a cut of twenty percent of the value of this thing, so don't screw it up." Steve's eyes widened and he put a hand to his mouth. Vicky and I laughed.

"That's good to know."

"Twenty percent for running a job? That's nuts."

"Damn, I hate this bloody thing, whatever it is. Forget you heard me say that. And twenty is fair, I'm running it. You guys will get paid, and plenty. This is a high value item, but my cut is twenty, it's arranged."

"Fair enough, don't stress about it," I said, still smiling. People in the game never admit how much they earn, it leads to all kinds of issues and arguments. Everyone thinks they should get paid the most, that their role is the most important one, when truth is it all comes down to how much you can swindle out of the next guy as your payout always means someone else is getting shafted. So, the less the other person knows, the better.

Steve certainly had my interest now though. If he was getting twenty percent of the list value of this, then it had to be worth a mint. Because we were getting paid too.

"Here's how much I had in mind." Steve slid a piece of paper across the table. I unfolded it and glanced casually at the number. I kept my smile in place, just to unnerve him.

Steve knew I had him over a barrel now, even though I didn't know what the job entailed yet.

"Come on, you know I don't even get out of bed for that. Let's hear about this job first, then we can negotiate."

"Fine, fine." Steve took the paper back and wiped at his forehead.

Over the next hour or so, Steve gave us the lowdown on the job, what it entailed, any difficulties he thought might arise, and sent Vicky encrypted files containing plans he'd been given, and plenty of other bits of intel. It was mostly garbage, nothing concrete at all. Speculation, various locations. They obviously had no real idea where the artifact they wanted was located.

"All of that sounds good," I said after he'd finished, just so he'd feel better, and knowing I could make my own inquiries and discover what I needed to. It also meant I could jack the price right up to something stupendously eye-watering, and that always brought a smile to my face. "You left one thing out. What are we taking?"

Steve glanced at us both then mumbled something.

"What?"

Again with the mumbling.

"Speak up, I can't hear you."

"Steve, why are you being so evasive?" asked Vicky, squeezing his knee.

"Fine. It's the Wild One. We aren't taking, we're rescuing."

"All shifters are Wild Ones, aren't they?" asked Vicky.

"Yeah, that's what people call us. What we call ourselves. This job is to get *The* Wild One. You know, her."

"Then you seriously need to reconsider your offer," I noted. "And how are you getting twenty percent of the value of the artifact? How is there even a price on her?"

"Because that's the ransom. She's been taken, kidnapped, and we need her back. She has to be returned, but the top guys won't pay. The Wild One herself wouldn't pay, wouldn't let anyone, not that she's old enough to make those decisions or anything. But it's how we roll. Never pay a ransom, that's why nobody ever gets kidnapped, because everyone knows we never pay."

"But she has been kidnapped," I said. "So what gives?"

"Honestly, man, I don't know. I told our people I knew you, that you were a close friend, and rather than get our own people, they suggested I hook up with you. As to why? I don't know. And that's all I know."

"You know what she is though, right?"

Steve scratched at his beard for a while, handsome as always even when frowning. I was used to the pheromones he gave off now, but damn he was a good-looking man. All Wild Ones were like this, an animal magnetism that drew you to them like a moth to a flame, but they were dangerous, and many were unstable, and yet loyal to the very end if you made a friend of them. Steve was a good guy, one of the best, and I liked him, but if this was business, and he was an intermediary for the higher-ups even though they didn't have bosses or anything as organized as that, then they had to pay. Plus, I was keen to find out what he knew about this almost mythical creature.

"I kinda know, but it's all rumor and third-hand info. You know how it goes."

"I know."

"What are you two talking about?" asked an exasperated Vicky. "Who's the Wild One? Is it a thing, or a person?"

"That's debatable," I said.

"It's a person, a girl to be exact. A young, supposedly very powerful girl. One of the most unusual shifters if the rumors are to be believed. Very rare, to be treasured and kept safe."

I turned to Steve. "How did she get taken?"

"Just nabbed, by all accounts. You know our kind, you can't keep us locked up. She had protection, but those guys got killed, a raid, and now her kidnappers want paying."

"It's an odd job to get me for," I said.

"Not really. You're good at the stealth side of things." I snorted and we both looked at Vicky. "Okay, usually," said Steve, knowing as well as I did that Vicky was prone to causing a scene on jobs and getting us both into trouble. "You can get her, get out, and not risk her being killed. If our guys go in, they'll shift, things will turn ultra-violent, and she'll be put at risk."

"Were you two laughing at me then? What do you mean about usually being stealthy?" Vicky gave us the hard mom-stare and we both cringed away.

"Nothing. It's cool, babe," said Steve, giving Vicky a reassuring smile.

"Hand me that paper," I said. Steve passed it over and I pulled out a pen and wrote my counter-offer. I pushed it across the table.

"Come on, it's a young girl. She'll be scared, this is a little mercenary."

"And there is more to this than you or I know, so that's my price. I don't see you skipping your fee. It doesn't wash that your people don't want to rescue her, there must be a reason and it will mean a load of crap for me. So that's the price."

"Fine." Steve nodded. And then he said, "I could have gone higher." He bit his lip and muttered, "And will you please sort out this damn truth thing, it's driving me nuts. How's an honest criminal meant to make any money when he keeps blurting out the truth?"

"You have my sympathies.

Game on.

The Wild One

Steve stayed for a beer then said he had to report back to those who'd put him onto this. We arranged to meet up later and I said I'd let him know when and where once Vicky and I had gone over the details and formulated a plan. Time was of the essence, so we had to get our skates on. The drop was meant to be the following day so this had to be accomplished well before then. The kidnappers would be on high-alert, so this wouldn't be easy, but we had magic on our side, and I knew we could pull it off.

Okay, white lie. I wanted to do something after being laid up for a fortnight, and this was all there was. I had no idea how to do this, and magic is not always the best policy.

I spent a while filling Vicky in on the details about the Wild One, although, just like Steve, what I knew was all second or third-hand knowledge, but there were tales about such shifters going back to the beginning, and they were all alike to some degree.

This particular Wild One was a young girl, prepubescent as far as I knew, about ten, maybe eleven years old. She had been different from birth, inherited her parent's abilities, able to change at will into her main creature, except soon after she was born it became apparent she could change into not one but two creatures. This by itself was unusual and certainly made her special and cherished by both her parents and the community, as it was a rare thing indeed, even when both parents were shifters.

By the time she was three her true nature became obvious. The more she learned, the more pictures of animals she saw in books or on TV, and the more she experienced, so the more animals she could shift into. She could turn into anything, any creature she had knowledge of. This was different to the innate ability shifters have where their main creature is theirs at birth whether they have a name for it or not. This was more like shape-shifting than true shifting, and yet it wasn't. She became the animal, had it's nature, it's abilities, and that's shifter gifts, not shape-shifting.

It made her dangerous. To herself, to others, and to the community. It also made her unstable in ways that made me shiver. Can you imagine a young child coming to terms with such abilities? Can you picture the things they would do just because they could, how they reacted when they didn't get their own way and had a tantrum? She couldn't master it at that age, couldn't be expected to, and it led to serious trouble, same as it had down the ages with every single true Wild One.

Children cannot suppress their emotions. They burst into tears, they have tantrums, they get angry, even violent, but they are children and can be controlled by adults.

Try calming down a three-year-old bear cub that's pissed it can't watch In the Night Garden, and begins to rip the sofa to shreds because it really, really wants to see Iggle Piggle fall over with his red blanket. Again. You kinda can't, because shifters become the animal and it is only through learning that they can retain their own self and keep the beast under control. So all shifters go through this to a degree when growing up, but it is only one animal. When nobody knows what the next shift might be, and that includes the child, it's impossible for the animal nature not to have free reign.

So Wild Ones are cherished and almost worshiped as the pinnacle of shifterdom, but they are also prisoners of a sort, kept away from everyday life much moreso than most young shifters for their own protection and that of citizens. This Wild One was captive in her own home, a compound somewhere outside the city at a location known only by those who needed to know. When she was old enough, she would take on a crew, be powerful, popular, and rich, but until then she was guarded, taught intensively because there was a helluva lot to learn, with numerous invited guests teaching her the ways of the many and varied animals she could shift into.

And now somebody had kidnapped her. A valuable, some would say priceless, artifact of the human variety who could become a very powerful weapon in the wrong hands. The downfall of the whole community too if she was ever captured by one of the many organizations who would use her to cause havoc, terrify society, or merely experiment on her, test her, force her to do things in the name of science.

She had to be returned safe and sound, and for some strange reason that was now my job.

"Wow, that poor child. I'd never really thought about what it's like growing up being able to shift. Poor Steve." Vicky cried a little.

"Yeah, it's tough all right. Imagine being a kid and doing that kind of thing. But Ivan had the same, turning into the wolf. You lucked out by not doing it until recently."

"I guess. What about the girls, do you think they have it?"

"Time will tell, but they haven't shown any signs, so maybe not."

"I hope not. I've thought about it so often, why I didn't change until recently, but I can't figure it out."

"It's different for everyone. Some shifters don't get the ability until grown, others when they're old. It can be a single event, like with you, that changes everything and the true nature emerges. So, fingers crossed for the girls."

Vicky got a faraway look in her eyes, thinking of her children and the horrors that undoubtedly awaited them no matter what I said to make her feel better.

"Read the files Steve sent you and find out where she is. I'm going for a walk."

As Vicky objected, I got up and left, then drove into the city.

Space to Breathe

I needed activity, noise, the hubbub of the city even though it was evening and the shops were closed. People were still about, going to pubs, restaurants, the small independent cinema in town, buying takeaway or rushing through the streets after staying late at work. I needed to be around people.

Don't get me wrong, I don't like people, most anyway, but I had to know they were still here, that things continued in my absence. I needed to see the grime, the graffiti, the sad faces and desperate smiles of people who know they have to be nice to get a tip. This was real, not some holiday in the middle of nowhere where everything was fake.

But it was more than this, and I was surprised I'd missed it to be honest, but I guess the city was as much in my blood as the country. There was another reason why I was sitting on a bench in the city center watching people go about their lives.

I wanted to witness firsthand this issue, this "truth infection" many had succumbed to.

Life continued as normal. The people I saw were doing what they'd always done, and whatever was happening in their lives, it was reassuring to see. Sure, people were bickering, and there was a vibe, an edge to things, but plenty were sitting outside the pubs, determined to wear shorts and vests and be outdoors because it was summer, no matter that it was England and had been raining and would again soon. Arguments were commonplace, hardly surprising, and yet there were also many people, couples especially, who seemed closer than ever, more in-tune.

Guess one, or both, of you telling the truth will lead to some very serious chats in a relationship. It would either make you or break you. You either got closer than ever when someone told you the truth about their lives, how they felt, what they thought, or you'd pack your bags, or pack theirs, and that would be that.

Same went for family.

Would mine hold together? Sure it would. After all, I was perfect, and so were George and Penelope. We'd get through this, even if I had to put up with jibes about my combats and them saying having so many pockets was stupid. What did they know? You can't have enough pockets, it isn't possible.

One thing that was certain, the truth infection was a real thing, and it was magical in nature. I felt it in the air, permeating the city like smog, creeping under doorways, stealing up people's nostrils and affecting their brains. That's how I imagined it anyway. As a mysterious smoke that everyone inhaled and became infected by. But it couldn't really be like that, it was a magical emanation, everywhere and nowhere, polluting the very air, the essence of things, and it wasn't anything anyone could even do.

How could you?

Sure, there were many adepts much more powerful than I when it came to niche arts within a broad spectrum, but I knew this wasn't possible, or hadn't been until now. If it was, then wizards or witches would have taken over the planet a long time ago. A few determined people with such mad skills would be world rulers, control everything, so this was something new, unique, and all the more worrying because of it.

I decided there and then that no way could I fix it. The magic council, that gabble of twats, would have to get the big guns out, the heavy-hitters, and negate it themselves. It must be done by someone they knew about, because this level of expertise never goes unnoticed.

Happier because I knew I was out of this, and had a job instead, I went to the chip shop and bought greasy food where nobody smiled and certainly didn't expect a tip.

Food in hand, grease soaking into my sleeve as it soaked through the paper it was wrapped in, I went to the park and sat on a different bench and thought about the Wild One and the terrible life she must have had and how scared the child must be right this minute. I shouldn't be sitting about, I should be off saving her.

So that's what I decided to do. After I'd finished eating.

Never Deal with Kidnappers

The shifters were right about one thing, you never dealt with kidnappers. They never let anyone hold people or things to ransom as that way lay no end of trouble. The minute anyone knew you would pay, it would be a field day for the magical underground. We were, I'm afraid to say, a rather untrustworthy bunch, which comes with the territory when most magic users or magically imbued entities were criminals because of what they could do.

You couldn't be expected to be a regular citizen when you had all these mad skills, that would be a waste. So most wizards, witches, shifters, and many vampires, along with endless oddballs, were outside of the system, always on the lookout for a caper, a job, a way to get the megabucks. I stole artifacts because people paid a fortune for them, but there were others who would steal people if they thought they could get a good payout. It was why the shifters, same as the rest of us, refused to deal with kidnappers. If you paid, your whole kind were open targets, and the more unscrupulous wouldn't hesitate to take advantage.

There simply weren't cases of shifters being ransomed, hadn't been for the longest time, because everyone knew there was no point. But someone had decided taking the Wild One was worth a punt, and to be honest it was. She was valuable if the shifters would pay for her return, but it went beyond that. She could be sold on, and there were many groups who would happily pay, either to turn her to their side and use her abilities, of which they had endless uses, or one of the covert organizations who knew about the magical communities would pay large sums for such a fine specimen to study.

Imagine how useful a shifter could be if you had crime in mind, or spying, or any manner of subterfuge. She could turn into a mouse and creep under doors, listen to secrets, or infiltrate security easily and help you nick a load of stuff that could set you up for life. Most shifters couldn't turn into tiny creatures, there seemed to be a limit, but this Wild One was unique, so was prized.

Who would take such a wondrous artifact of the human variety if their intent was to hold her for ransom, not use her, and where would they take her?

Buggered if I knew.

I finished my fish and chips, binned the greasy paper, licked my fingers, and smiled. I sure loved a mystery. Maybe I should buy a trench coat, I already had the hat.

Getting on With It

Feeling more myself again, meaning I was a bit smelly, annoyed with people just for being people, and with the cloying city air hard to breathe, I decided to return to Vicky's. The girls were asleep still, no funny business where they kept getting up and whining about the TV and why did adults get to stay up so late, so Vicky was relaxing with a glass of wine. I skipped it as I'd had enough booze to last me several years in the space of two weeks, so was on the wagon.

I joined Vicky on the sofa and watched as she expertly navigated between various tabs on her laptop, most of it gobbledygook to me. Code streamed down the screen in green, which I thought was only for in movies, not a part of normal computers. I relaxed and left her to it, the ferocious tapping of the keyboard—Vicky went through laptops like nobody's business—comforting after our lack of regular work lately. Every so often she'd grunt, bang extra hard on a key, then snicker as she clearly got what she wanted.

You wouldn't think it to look at her, but Vicky was an ace hacker and not afraid to tell you, whether you asked or not. She had mad skills and genuinely was an important part of the team until she knocked something over and got us both caught. But she always managed to disable alarms, find blueprints for properties, and uncover secret rooms, that kind of thing. She could also find things, people, places, all manner of stuff I wouldn't have a clue about, by navigating through the digital cesspit that was the web. Secret servers hidden away by corporations where they thought their dirty secrets were safe were anything but that when Vicky cracked her knuckles and got down to business.

Vicky could do some serious blackmailing of her own if she wished, knew a lot about a lot of people and businesses, but it was a no-go zone because you were asking for trouble, a bullet in the head or worse, if you messed with such institutions. So we nicked magical artifacts for collectors or adepts, got fat payouts, and hardly ever got into trouble, and most certainly never got caught. Ahem.

Vicky closed her laptop and twisted her neck side to side, a nasty click the result. She sighed, arched her back, then grabbed her wine and downed it in one.

"Ah, that's better."

"Well?"

"I have no clue where she is, what her name is, where she was taken from, or any idea where to look."

"What about all the stuff Steve gave you?" I asked, shocked.

"He just gave me a load of info about a ton of buildings spread around the city and further afield. I don't know what any of it means, but as far as I can tell she wasn't in any of them, and isn't in them now."

"How do you know"? I asked suspiciously.

"Because I checked records, cameras, routes in and out of the houses, farms, warehouses and what have you, and none of them looked dodgy, not in the way we want. Many are shifter places, and they should be more careful as I saw a lot of things they won't want getting out there, but there's no sign of a young girl like the one we're after."

"Ugh," was all I managed.

"Steve said she had long blond hair, very straight, and the face of an angel. Innocent, pale, rather skinny, lanky for her age, with no signs of womanhood yet. I saw nobody like that. And besides, I think he's clutching at straws, desperate."

"This doesn't seem legit, does it? Why would he give us a load of random places if he's got all the bigwigs behind this? Surely they'd have at least some idea where she is, and would certainly tell us where she'd been taken from."

"Something fishy is definitely going on," agreed Vicky. "He doesn't know a thing. Guess none of them do. Maybe nobody knew where she was. And what's her name? Do they know her name?"

"Steve didn't mention it, I think it's all hush-hush, need to know kinda thing." Vicky frowned, she knew as well as me that this was flaky bordering on insulting.

"So, either they know absolutely nothing at all about this girl, or they, or Steve, are hiding information from us, not telling us the whole truth or anything close to it?" I didn't want to say more, to insult Steve, as he was a great guy, but this was becoming annoying.

"Seems that way. Why so evasive if they want us to get her?"

"Because she's so special maybe," I mused. "But if we're gonna find her we need at least something to go on."

"I'll call Steve, get him back here."

"Wait, first we need to go on a little jaunt, see what we can uncover on our own."

"Arthur, he might have information he can give us to save us the trouble."

"If he did, he would have told us already. Why would he keep it back?"

"I don't know, maybe he was told to."

"Then he won't tell us now, will he?"

"Guess not. It seems wrong though, going behind his back. He's meant to be part of this, to tell us what we need and help out."

"And he will help, but we have to know what we're involved in first. And who the hell has her. Come on, grab your coat."

"I can't, what about the girls?"

"I thought you had a babysitter?"

"Do you see a babysitter? Do you?"

"Um, no."

"I didn't think we were going yet, thought I had time to arrange something."

"You mean you forgot because you got sucked into your computer stuff."

Vicky mumbled then went into the kitchen to get her phone and arrange things.

Steve was playing funny buggers. I didn't like this, not one bit.

But that's what made it so much fun.

A Strange Woman

No more than ten minutes later, the door was knocked gently and Vicky went to answer. She returned with a tall woman, skinny, with aquiline features, all sharp nose, high cheekbones, pale blue eyes like an Icelandic beauty, and a short blond bob haircut.

"Babysitter's here," said Vicky happily.

"Um, hello?" I said, rising from the sofa.

"Hi," said the woman.

"I'm Arthur, pleased to meet you." I held out my hand. Both women exchanged glances then frowned at me. I was left hanging so dropped my arm and said, "Suit yourself."

"Is he going to do this every single time?" asked the woman.

"I honestly don't know if he's winding you up or he genuinely can't remember," said Vicky.

"It's very insulting. He has seen me splattered in blood, I have told him who I am repeatedly, he has come to the house many times, and yet he treats me like this. I saw him today, earlier."

"Did not," I protested.

"He is a fool," said the woman, turning to Vicky.

"I am here you know, and what are you talking about?" If I focused on the babysitter I could maybe, vaguely, sort of a little bit, recall seeing someone a bit like her before, but I did not know this woman. She was vampire, that was obvious, but I was so attuned to their wavelength now that they weren't the faceless nobodies others saw them as. I saw them properly, just as I saw this woman. So who was this?

"I'll try one more time," said the woman. "I'm Kim," said Kim.

I smiled at Kim. "Nice to meet you. I met a Kim not long ago. She had blond hair too, but it was long, and she had a junkie boyfriend."

"That wasn't me," said Kim.

"Um, no." There was an awkward silence then Vicky said, "Okay, let's get going, Arthur. Thanks for babysitting, Kim, you're a lifesaver, again."

"It's never a problem, I adore the girls. It's just a shame I don't get to play with them. But they need their sleep."

"Yes, they do," said Vicky. "The more the better. And don't forget you can drop them at holiday club if playing with them gets a bit much."

I smiled at Kim then hightailed it after Vicky.

Outside the house I demanded, "Who is that woman?"

"It's Ivan's girlfriend, you muppet. They've been seeing each other for ages. What's with you and her?

You've met her loads, she always shows you in at Ivan's house. She's his aide, and his lady."

"Really? I think I'd remember that. Hmm." I really had no memory of her, but there were vague images of me being shown in to Ivan's house, of an incident at a warehouse where somebody was covered in gore splatter, but there was no memory of a face or person being attached. She was like a blank, a missing piece, and that went beyond even what citizens saw when they encountered vampires.

Just me getting old, I thought, my mind dismissing things of little or no import to ensure I had space for the important things like where I put Wand or how to drive. Speak of the devil. While Vicky dashed back in as she forgot her keys same as always, I released Wand and brought him up to eye-level. "How you doing, buddy?" I asked.

"All good here. What's not to like about being stuck in a stinking pocket for days at a time with a musty smell and right next to a pair of saggy, old hairy balls?"

"At least it's warm," I offered.

"I'm a stick, I don't feel warm, or cold."

"You also can't smell, or see without eyes, but you seem to manage that."

"It all depends on your perspective."

"What does that mean?"

"Um, not sure. It made sense in my head."

"But you don't have a... Ugh, forget it. Do you recall this Kim woman?" I asked.

"That nice woman you gave the money to so she could leave her druggie boyfriend?" asked Wand, squirming in my hand, a warm fuzzy feeling of his contentment washing over me for the good deed I did.

"No, Ivan's aide, his girlfriend?"

Wand paused to think, and it dragged out. "Nope, I got nothing. He's got a bird? Lucky sod. Wish I did."

"You can't have a girlfriend, what would you do?"

"We could rub together, really fast, that would be awesome."

"Ugh," I shivered at the thought. Weird mental images of sticks getting it on were confusing but somehow smutty at the same time.

"Hey, don't judge me," warned the stick.

"Wouldn't dream of it. Now, to business. What do you know about the Wild One?"

"Not much more than you. She's ten, almost eleven, I know that. She's meant to be the most powerful shifter for fifteen generations, has more abilities than she, or anyone else, knows what to do with, or how to cope with properly, and she's spent her whole life isolated from the regular world."

"A lot of shifters do though. Most of them are controlled until they're old enough to handle the change and it isn't like they go to school when they're young."

"I know, but she's different. It's a whole other level of paranoia and protection. She's dangerous, and she'll be powerful, already is, so she's always guarded, always protected."

"So what's her name?"

"No idea. And before you ask, no I don't know where she was being held, or where she is now, but I do know her location always changed, always moved, but nobody could keep track of her, pin it down."

"A right mystery. So nobody ever really knew where she was guarded, how she was kept protected so nobody could find her, and Vicky reckons there's no sign of her at the usual shifter places or anything remotely like a pattern of where people would be coming and going who looked after her."

"Correct," said Wand, just to make me feel like I wasn't telling him stuff he obviously already knew.

"So where could she have been held? How did they keep her protected and hidden for so long?"

"It's easy, this country has thousands of people in witness protection or given new identities."

"Ah, but they interact with the world."

"And if they didn't, if they stayed inside and nobody saw them, it would be even easier."

"I guess. Or, and I'm winging it here, they put her somewhere she couldn't escape because that's what kids would try to do, right? Escape."

"Exactly!" Wand grinned broadly as me, or gave the impression anyway.

"So, we know where she must have been?" I asked, confirming it with my smart familiar.

"We sure do. To the Wandmobile."

"Whoa, wait just a minute. It's the Wizardmobile, and don't you forget it. I'm the star, you're the occasional help."

"No way, dude, without me you'd be useless."

"I managed before," I grumbled.

"Did you, did you really?"

"Yeah."

Wand went silent so I pocketed him as Vicky returned with the keys, looking sheepish. I didn't have the heart to remind her I had my car so let her use hers.

"Where to?" she asked once we had our seatbelts on.

"To the port," I shouted, pointing forward. I hoped she hadn't drunk too much wine.

"Um, isn't it over there?" asked Vicky, pointing in the other direction.

"I have absolutely no idea. Do we even have a port?"

"No, we're not on the coast, you muppet. It's bloody miles away."

"Okay, fine, then I guess we better pick Steve up first."

So that's what we did.

A Long Drive

We swung by to collect Steve from his suitably bohemian home, a large loft, all brick and steel beams, and bloody expensive, then continued our journey.

Both asked why the port, but I said we'd speak later, when we were there. I needed to think this through, decide how to broach this subject with Steve without pissing him off or insulting him too badly, even though I felt insulted myself for being if not lied to then certainly left out of the loop.

This may have been the first time in my life that I considered what I was going to say before saying it. It felt weird, and I couldn't sit still until I decided to take the opportunity to top up the magic best I could under such circumstances.

Turns out that because I'd become an expert at zoning out when Vicky started banging on about something or other of no interest, I could enter the Quiet Place with ease and go deeper than I'd anticipated.

Many hours later, I was rudely shaken until I opened my eyes and Vicky said, "We're here."

"Sweet," I said, rubbing my hands together.

Port, Shmort

Topped up to the brim with the good stuff—it beats a beer any day—and keen for action, I restrained myself as we had a lot to talk about first. Rather than do it in the car, I figured it best to be outside where we had space to all see each other properly. And besides, the car was cloying, little room for air when Steve's aftershave and numerous grooming products fought a battle for dominance with Vicky's perfume and whatever it was she slathered on her face to make it look all plastic and shiny.

We exited a car park and wandered along a pristine promenade close to the vast port. Much of it had been renovated ten or more years ago, but they were always doing something to spruce it up and make it more enticing to potential homeowners and the many visitors who now came to spend time at a pleasant location. Like most ports in the country, it had fallen into decline as the ship building industry slowly collapsed in on itself like all other manufacturing industry. No coal, no steel, no nothing made here anymore. Mostly it was a port for expensive boats, and the real work went on a half mile away where vast ships carrying thousands of containers docked and were unloaded by robots. But this was the old port, where the front was lined with brick warehouses now converted into swanky apartments, with landscaping and sculptures and nice neat canals and all the usual stuff you see at these types of places.

People loved it. Cafes and restaurants did a brisk trade at all hours, pubs the same, and there were plenty of people just taking the sea air now the rain had stopped and the weather warmed up to a tolerable temperature. I liked it.

We walked in silence for a while then sat on a bench made from a piece of shipwreck, a gnarled old beam smoothed by sea, wind, and rain, the elements slowly turning it into something almost as beautiful as when it grew in rich loam. Almost, but not quite.

"What's with the weirdness?" asked Steve, rubbing at his chin and looking nervous even though trying to hide it. "And why are we here?"

"All in good time," I replied, thinking it best to let this play out a little longer. I sat, I hummed, I watched ships and boats glide past, the massive liners off down the coast strange ghostly apparitions, beasts of the sea lit up with a thousand lights yet still almost invisible.

Vicky got antsy, repeatedly standing then sitting, tapping her foot then walking in circles. Steve stood for most of the time, gazing off into the distance, his face turned away. He looked sad, almost broken but trying his best to keep himself together. Eventually Vicky stopped her pacing and put an arm around him. She glanced over his shoulder, a hard thing for my tiny sidekick to do, and shook her head about as if telling me to talk to Steve.

"Okay, let's get this over with," I said, standing and joining them both.

"Get what over with?" asked Steve.

"What was with all that stuff you gave to Vicky? It was meaningless, like you and your people had no clue where she might be, where she was taken from. Pure guessing."

"It was, nobody knows a thing."

"Is that right?"

"Yeah, it is. What's with you, Arthur? You're acting strange."

"No, you are."

"He's right, Steve," said Vicky. "There's something, or lots of things, you aren't telling us. What is this all about?"

"A little girl has been taken and we have to get her back. That's all we need to know. You'll get paid, you're the best person for the job. I know you, Arthur, you too, Vicky, you can do this. I wouldn't trust anyone else."

"That's so sweet," said Vicky, beaming at the praise.

"It's a nice compliment," I agreed, "but it doesn't excuse the fact you know more than us, are holding back. How are we meant to find her when you won't tell us anything? What's her name?"

"Sunshine, her name's Sunshine." The words caught in Steve's throat.

And then I got it, why he was being so strange, but not why he was holding back. I decided to save what I knew for a while, to see what he would tell us first. I wasn't playing games, I wanted the information, and the less emotional he got the better for us all.

"Great, that's a nice name. And what else aren't you telling us? Why all those odd locations?"

"Because nobody knows where she was being looked after or where she is. Nobody."

"What do you mean, nobody? Surely your people knew?"

"No, or not anyone who's talking. I told you, her protectors are dead, all of them. Anyone who went to teach her things was never shown where they went, it was all super hush-hush, nobody ever told, nobody ever knew where she was. Everyone figured it was for the best, a way to protect her, keep her safe. Fat lot of good that did," he muttered, turning away and looking out to sea.

"So how do you know she was taken? How do you know everyone protecting her is dead?"

"Because that's what the kidnappers said. They said they killed everyone apart from her, and she'd go the same way if the money wasn't paid. There, happy now? Any more to this interrogation?"

"Hey, buddy, listen." I took his shoulders and turned him to me gently. "We're gonna help, okay?" Steve nodded. "We'll get her back, we will, and I'm only asking you these things because it's important, understand?" Again, he nodded. "But you must be honest. This is us, your friends. Damn, your girlfriend and your best buddy, you can tell us anything, but we are here to help."

"She's my daughter, all right?" Steve blurted, and I'm not sure if it was the damn truth curse or he merely couldn't hold it in any longer, but either way his eyes widened and he put a hand to his mouth.

"Your daughter!?" shouted Vicky.

"It's okay, buddy, I know."

"You knew?" accused Vicky.

"It just slotted into place when he was talking," I explained. "This is why there's so little to go on. Nobody else knows she's been taken apart from Steve. Am I right?"

"Yeah, just me. They killed her mum, everyone looking after her. They sent a video, a link anyway. I checked it out. They showed everyone being killed then the link was dead. No way to retrieve it."

"We'll see about that," said Vicky. "Why didn't you say?"

"Because I wanted you to do a job, not get involved personally. I wanted it kept professional so you'd work your best. I know what it's like for you guys when it's family. You care, and I wanted you to just do it for the money and the thrill as I know how good you are at stuff like that."

"Thanks, I think," I said. "Why not tell your people? Nobody else knows at all?"

"Nobody else, just me. I told nobody because I know what my lot are like, plus I was warned not to. My lot would bash heads and cause trouble and find nothing out. Even if they somehow miraculously discovered where she was, they aren't exactly subtle. It would be all shifting into creatures and storming the place and that's a surefire way to get Sunshine killed. Them too. So I came to you, Arthur, hoping you would help."

"And I will."

"Me too," piped up Vicky, squeezing Steve's hand.

Steve smiled weakly and I patted him on the shoulder. "We'll find her. And don't worry, no fee. How were you gonna pay us anyway?"

"Haha, figured I'd work something out. I have money, quite a lot actually, and the rest, well, I would pay you back, promise."

"No, you're almost family, you get to keep your money. And your daughter."

I hoped I could make good on that promise. Kidnaps never went well. Usually everyone ended up dead.

An Emotional Time

"I should have told you guys, I'm sorry." Steve turned to Vicky. "Forgive me?"

"Of course, I understand." They had a nice big hug and smiled at each other. Steve broke down then, the release physical. He crumpled to his knees, bent his head, and sobbed. The poor guy had lost his daughter, taken in the worst possible way, and her mother was dead. Sunshine was with mean, violent men in a strange place, they wouldn't be treating her well, and she would be scared. And held in a less than savory way—she was a powerful shifter with insane skills, so these sick dudes wouldn't be taking any chances.

"I haven't seen her for a while," said Steve, standing and rubbing at red eyes. "Me and her mum, well, it didn't work out. I was kind of a player back in those days," he said sheepishly. "What can I say, the ladies love me."

"Idiot," laughed Vicky, digging him in the ribs.

"I know. Anyway, we were together for a while, then it went sour. This was when Sunshine was a baby.

We split up. I saw her most days though, my little girl is so beautiful. Then the problems started. Things became dicey when the news got out about there being a new Wild One, and Sue just buggered off with her, left and never told me where they were."

"That's cold," I said, knowing how that must have felt.

"Yeah, that's what I thought, but I guess she did it for Sunshine, to protect her. But I would have gone with them, to be close to my girl, but I wasn't the most reliable back then so I forgave Sue. Anyway, I saw them both regularly until recently. Sunshine had been playing up, and I mean big time, getting up to all sorts. Rebelling, wanted her freedom, not to be cooped-up away from real life. I don't know where it was, I was always blindfolded and drugged if you can believe it. Sue and her cronies took no chances."

"Who was with her?"

"People she trusted. Friends, and a few important members of the community who moved in with her and stayed put, never left apart from to take invited guests. That way, nobody ever knew where they were, it could have been anywhere. Man, what a fucking mess. Sorry, I have nothing to tell you. Sometimes the trip took two hours, sometimes two days. I got no ideas because I was out of it the whole time however long it took and I'd wake up in a room, and that was it. The location was always different anyway, a house somewhere, maybe by the ocean, maybe with a few acres around, but never a soul in sight and we never ventured away from the property. She wasn't allowed."

"How did they do that?" asked Vicky. "How could they move so much and nobody track them, find where they were going?"

"Someone did," I reminded them both.

"Yeah," Steve sighed, "someone did."

"And I know how they moved about. I know how they kept her safe."

"How?" they both asked.

"They used a boat."

"Damn, why didn't I think of that?" Steve slapped his head.

"That's why we're here?" asked Vicky.

"Sure is. They must have used a boat to travel about the country, maybe even Europe, stopping at different locations, keeping Sunshine away from people and with nowhere to go apart from on special occasions. It's what I'd do if I wanted to contain someone and ensure they never got away. You can't escape the sea."

"Unless you're a dolphin or a fish," said Vicky.

We both stared at her.

"What?" she asked.

"That's a good point," said Steve, as shocked as me.

"I have loads of good ideas," snapped Vicky, hands on hips in full angry-mom pose.

"Do you?" I asked.

"Yes."

"Can shifters turn into things like that?"

"Not usually. But Sunshine's not a normal shifter. I haven't heard of it. We're always oxygen breathing with lungs, not, er, how fish do it."

"You don't know how fish breathe, do you?"

"Do too! But I don't think she could do that, don't think anyone can."

"So they lived on a boat, ship, whatever. Hell, maybe even a submarine although that's pushing it, and traveled about. She couldn't turn into a fish, and hopefully not a dolphin, so the plan worked. But someone got to them and you want your daughter back."

"That about sums it up."

"You should have just told us, asked, saved the trouble."

"But you worked it out," said Steve, looking triumphant. "I was right. You worked it out without getting emotional and now we have a lead."

"Yeah, but it's a big coastline. A big port, and there are a lot of boats."

"But we have me," said Vicky. "Now I have something to go on I can check cameras, check boats coming and going. We'll find her."

"I hope so," said Steve. "We don't have long. Deadline is midday tomorrow, and then they want their money."

Getting Somewhere

We wandered about a bit, looking for clues, just checking the general vibe and seeing if anything untoward caught our eye. It didn't. But truth is we were all too tense, the immediacy of the problem exacerbated now we knew it was Steve's daughter. How could you slowly take in the sights, study boats and people, the comings and goings of the populace when you knew that at this very moment there was a frightened child somewhere? It was impossible to concentrate.

We headed back to the car so Vicky could grab her gear and then we went to a nice late night bar where there was plenty of room for us outside. Vicky got to work. For the next hour or so she sipped on a soda water and whacked the shit out of her keyboard while Steve and I held stilted conversation but mostly stared out to sea and imagined all kinds of horrors taking place. It wasn't a pleasant hour.

"It'll be okay," I said, my heart going out to him.

"Will it? I know you'll try your best, I have total confidence in you, but I'm not so sure. These people must be nuts to try something like this. They know nobody will pay, or they should, but they did it anyway."

"But you would pay, wouldn't you, if you had the money? I do."

"Do what?"

"Have the money. You can have it if you want, to pay them. I would, I'd pay and then I'd kill them. I'd spend the rest of my days if I had to, but I'd pay. I'd get her back, then hunt them down and kill every last one of them."

"I wouldn't ask you to pay them, but thanks for the offer. That means a lot, it really does. But it isn't our way, it's not what we do. I can't, I just can't. I've gone over this a million times, wondered if I could get the money and give them what they want, but I've decided I won't pay, not even if I could."

"She's your daughter, man," I said softly. "Is it worth the risk?"

"Come on, Arthur, you know as well as I do that there's no fucking way they'll let her go. They'll keep her alive until they get their money, just in case I insist on seeing her before the trade, then they'll kill her, or try. They won't risk anything going wrong, her identifying them, and apart from all that they know who she is, what she's capable of now, and what she'll be capable of in the future."

"You mean they don't want her coming after them?"

"Exactly. They are well aware of the insane power she'll accumulate over the years, and they know they'll always be looking over their shoulders, that when she's old enough and the time is right, she'll find and kill them. So, no, I won't pay, it isn't our way, and I can't let this become the norm. You don't deal with kidnappers. That's our policy, and it remains our policy."

"Fair enough. What about telling your people though? You sure they can't help? Maybe they can help track them down."

"None of us, including me, and trust me I've spent years trying to do it, have been able to even find where Sunshine was living, so there's no chance of us finding her now."

"Don't be so sure. These people have been stupid enough to take her in the first place, so they found her, and they have to be pretty dim to try this on, so maybe your people stand a chance."

"No, you're the best at this, so if you can't find them nobody can."

I didn't want to ask but I asked anyway. "Have you considered that this is one of your kind? Maybe someone you know? Could it have been someone on the inside, who was there already, supposedly to protect her but deciding they'd try for a windfall?"

"I've thought about it, and it could be. Hell, I don't know anything anymore. I can't think straight." Steve put his head in his hands and squeezed his eyes shut tight as if he could block out the pain he felt. It wouldn't work. Nothing would, apart from holding his daughter in his arms and knowing she was safe.

I gave Steve an awkward pat on the back and said, "We'll get her back, don't you worry," and arched an eyebrow at Vicky as she glanced up from her laptop. She shook her head; she had nothing.

The sadness I felt deepened, an ache in my heart I knew didn't even compare to how Steve felt, and then, just like that, as if a scalpel had been wielded by an experienced surgeon, I felt nothing.

My head cleared, my body felt weightless, thousands of thoughts, ideas, and tentative plans slammed into my mind, and I saw this for what it was without the emotional undercurrent. It was a simple theft, we had to go steal a precious artifact and the owners didn't want to relinquish their prize.

I smiled, I knew what to do. But where had the emotion gone? I didn't care one way or the other.

With a glance at Steve and Vicky, who both stared at me in confusion and if not concern, then wonder at the sudden change in mood, I knew they felt the same way.

We were all empty of heart.

Strange Feelings

"What just happened?" asked Vicky, shaking her head and rubbing her arms as if that would help.

"Beats me," said Steve, a deep frown on his face. He froze then, searched inside same as we did, and gasped when he understood what had been done to him.

"I can't feel it, the love, the connection. Everything's remote, like it isn't important, not really. Or not the same. I miss her, I want to get her back, but I've lost that deep bond, like I don't feel affection the same way."

"I'm the same. It's like my heart has been emptied. Emotion's been chopped off, or stunted, or something. Ugh, this is weird." I almost toppled off my chair as a wave of dizziness washed over me and threatened to rip me from my mooring.

My will surfaced to battle this intrusion, to ground me, bringing me back myself, and through wet eyes I saw the others fight the same inner battle. We raged against the emptiness that would consume us and leave us shells of human beings, lost to what made life worth living.

And then, just like that, the void vanished and I felt normal again. Sadness settled in for the long haul, my heart cried for Sunshine's safety, and I vowed to do all in my power to save this little girl.

"You feeling okay now?" I asked Vicky.

"Yeah, what was that? It was so strange. It was almost like I was a different person, like I didn't care.

"Same here. Scary stuff. But I feel okay now." Steve was visibly shaking, the thought of not caring about those you knew you loved more than life itself was a lot to take in and accept. It made you feel like the worst kind of person for being able to think that way, to not care.

I checked the other people at the tables around us. Several were still dazed, and a few were trembling like Steve, clearly having come out the other side of this. Maybe we'd recovered faster because the truth fog hadn't touched us fully, that we were magic by nature so could fight it easier. It wasn't like that for your average citizen, and a lot of them were already arguing, some storming off, others in each other's faces, shouting and screaming.

"Let's go somewhere quiet," I said as I got up and grabbed my things.

We left the clueless citizens to it; there was nothing we could do. We had our own set of problems to deal with and they took precedence.

Coincidence?

"This has to be related, right?" asked Vicky, trotting along beside us to keep up.

"Oh gosh, you should be on Mastermind with an intellect like that. You'll be champion for sure," I replied, maybe with a slight undertone of sarcasm.

"I was just saying. First the truth thing, then the emotional withdrawal, the empty heart, and now Sunshine being taken. You think they are connected?"

"I don't think, I know." I turned to Steve. "You ever heard of shifters who can control the emotions of others?"

"No way, not our thing at all. None of us could do it even if we wanted to. How could you?"

"I dunno, that's why I'm asking. You can't influence people's emotions?"

"Only through our innate animal magnetism."

"Then that's it then. Let's be honest here." I stopped and the others did too. "You're a good-looking guy, you have this thing about you, it draws people in, makes people fall for you. Female shifters are the same,"

I said, the mood suddenly dark as we all recalled how I'd fallen for a sexy shifter and what that led to.

"Yeah, we all have it," said Steve with a smug smile. Damn but he must have had a lot of action over the years. Lucky sod.

"You can kind of play with people's emotions then. You can make them do things because of your draw, almost like a vampire glamor, and it extends beyond the area you're in, to people all around you."

"I see where you're going with this," said Vicky, smiling.

"I don't". Steve frowned. Bless him, he never was the smartest.

"Your sphere of influence is tight, and it's mostly about sexual desire, the intense pheromones you give off, but there's something else about shifters too, they heighten senses in others, make people take notice whether they want to or not, and they don't always know it's because of you."

"I guess, still don't see what you're getting at."

"What I'm getting at," I explained patiently, wondering not for the first time if Steve was secretly smart and this was all a front, "is shifters can influence emotions in the simplest of ways through pheromones, sheer presence, but it goes beyond that. What if a very powerful shifter, say one who didn't have all this figured out yet, was in distress? Maybe the signals she sent out would be all messed up. Maybe she's fighting for her life and trying to force her captors to tell her the truth about what's happening. Maybe she's trying to not feel scared, to empty her heart of all emotion so she can focus on her escape. Maybe."

"Maybe it's Sunshine!" said Steve, his face lighting up with hope.

"Yes, you could be onto something there," I said, now in no doubt Steve had definitely bumped his head a few times when he fell out of the smart tree. Plummeted, more like.

A Break

While I patiently, meaning I only shouted a little because he was sad, explained to Steve what I thought was happening, Vicky stumbled about with her face stuck in some small digital device. Apparently, it was just as good as a laptop. She alternated between tapping, squinting, cursing, and apologizing to the people she bumped into because she wasn't looking where she was going.

"Yes!" she shouted, making us turn and hurry back as passersby glanced at her before hustling past, scared she too had gone nuts and would start criticizing their clothes or punching them just because she felt like it.

"What is it? Have you found something?" asked Steve, hope there despite the lack of progress so far.

"I have." Vicky grinned, looking mad, and when she had that look on her face, a mixture of smug and happy, you knew she'd done her job well and wouldn't be afraid to explain in detail how she did it.

"I managed to bypass the doobie and blast past the dongle and then sandwich a bison between the onion network and the server wedgie then insert myself right up into its..."

It went silent, and after several seconds I realized this and emerged from the zone I always entered when Vicky explained things in technical talk.

"Were you listening to me then?" Vicky stood on tiptoe and gave me a hard stare.

I gulped.

"Sure was. Something about a sandwich and an onion and doing stuff with code. Maybe a bison as well?" I ventured. "Although I don't know what that is."

"You always do this," she complained. "You zone out and make up words in your head."

"Do not," I protested. The nerve of the woman!

"What did I say then?"

"You said you were going to bypass the technical jargon and tell us what you found because we don't have much time and neither of us understand a word you're saying when you bang on about networks and servers and code and jackknifed security systems and firewalls or any of that stuff."

Vicky glanced from me to Steve and when she saw the state of her boyfriend she relented. "Fine. Thought you'd appreciate all the hard work I do."

"We do, honey, but you're too good at this stuff, leaves us shaking our heads in wonder," said Steve. Damn, but he was smooth. Maybe he wasn't so dim after all.

Vicky fawned over him then smiled sweetly and gave us the lowdown without preamble. A first.

She'd hacked into the cameras that were all over the port, every movement recorded as you entered or exited. The same firm also had cameras all along the waterfront to keep an eye on the expensive boats moored up in the harbor directly across the quay from the cafes, bars, and restaurants. There was no way to avoid them. If that wasn't enough, most of the businesses were also hooked up with the same company, guess they got a discount, and the company also had uniformed security people who patrolled day and night and were always on hand for any emergency or crime committed.

All of that is to say that Vicky may not have had such a hard time as she tried to make out, but she had hacked into their archives and retrieved the data, run it through esoteric software that could trace patterns of repetition. When that failed, she'd simply checked out the timeline around when Steve got the call, which had been early afternoon, and worked her way backwards.

"There they are," she said triumphantly.

"I can't see a bloody thing." I squinted at the tiny screen but it was all blurry.

"You've got old man eyes," said Vicky.

"Have not, you have. They're fine, the screen's too small."

"It is a little hard to see much," said Steve.

"Fine, let's sit down." Vicky huffed, then moved over to the harbor wall where she sat then fished out her laptop. In a few minutes she had the same video playing on the larger screen.

"How do you know it's them?" asked Steve.

"Watch." Vicky adjusted the angle so the overhead lights gave off less glare, and we all studied the screen.

"It's just two guys and a woman," said Steve.

"Yeah, but look how they're acting, and watch for the fuzziness," I said, wondering how Steve had managed to stay alive so long.

We focused, and as Vicky switched between cameras you could clearly see the shape of the men and woman. They were dressed in tight clothing, typical hipster style, casual but less conspicuous than normal. They all wore hats, the men in baseball caps, the woman with a wide-brimmed straw hat. Long brown hair tumbled down past her shoulders in loose curls.

Each carried a long canvas bag that was heavy although they tried to hold them casually like they weighed little. They knew where the cameras were, avoided putting their heads up or turning so you could see their faces, and they were walking too fast to be off on a nice jaunt.

Every so often, one would turn sharply away from the camera to talk to one of the others. The cameras would go fuzzy, the screen flickering, and I knew from experience this was when a slight shift in appearance would have happened. Shifters often showed a hint of the animal side when in each other's company, especially when emotions flared, and it played havoc with technical equipment like cameras. There was something built in to them that messed with it, and it was just as well as it kept them secret, never filmed, never outed.

They hurried down the jetty and got onto a large boat, something that must have cost a fortune, a huge thing with wide decks and a towering cabin.

Within minutes they were gone, ropes coiled professionally, unhitched and they were away.

"Now all we have to do is find them and we have our guys."

"And woman," said Vicky.

"Yeah. And woman." I didn't like this one bit. And it hadn't even started yet.

Go, Go, Go

"Come on," I said, marching along the water's edge, heading for the boats.

Steve and Vicky came chasing after me, whispering questions I didn't feel inclined to answer with people constantly walking past.

When we reached the moorings, I pulled Wand out of his cosy resting place and as the sigils sparked to life, I asked, "Which one?"

"I can't see," he complained.

"Muppet," I muttered, then spun him in my hand so he was "facing" a different way.

"That one," he said, tilting forward and aiming straight at a monster of a boat, almost a ship. It was a large, swanky vessel with a streamlined front like the wedge of a lemon and a fat midsection. Steel rails gleamed, the deck was huge, the cabin monstrous, and it was as clean as my kitchen, sparkling under the hardcore lights that lit up the quay and the water like it was daytime.

"Good choice." I turned to the others and said, "Get on, quick, and act like it's ours." The pair of numpties glanced around looking about as casual as a camel in a pet store and then checked out the other boats for anyone watching.

"Just get on," I hissed, despairing. Had Vicky learned nothing after all these years? How did Steve get bodyguard work when he couldn't even step onto a boat without looking dodgy as fuck?

I led the way, moved aside the rope across the gangplank and strode onto the boat like I owned it, which I most certainly did not. I let Wand work his magic on the cabin door lock then entered a cool interior like something out of a spaceship. In fact, it was exactly how I'd imagined the command deck of a spaceship to be. Swivel chairs upholstered in white leather, dark wood paneling where hi-tech gadgetry and plenty of buttons had been expertly crafted into the curved, warm mahogany.

Wand angled down sharply and dragged me over to what looked like a push start button. He jabbed forward and the engine came to life, a low rumble beneath my feet like I was standing atop a snoring dragon.

Vicky and Steve came in behind.

"Wow, this is awesome," noted Steve.

"Look at all the buttons," shrieked Vicky with utter glee, then she dumped her bags to study them with unbridled curiosity.

"They've got everything. Satellite tracking, maps, all the routes to anywhere of interest for the whole of

Europe. The thing even drives itself. Um, do you drive a boat?"

"Steer, I think you steer a boat," I said, unsure if that's what you called the, er, driving.

"There's satellite internet, same for phones if we need it, for if we lose our signal, and there's radar and there's—"

"So it's a nice boat," I said, cutting her off. "Get ready, because we're going right now."

"But we can't go now," protested Vicky. "We aren't ready."

"What do you mean?" I snapped, keen to get going.

"We haven't got stuff, you know, to take down the bad guys."

"And what would you like to have?"

"Guns, big ones."

"No, guns are bad. We have all we need right here. We need to get a move on and get these bastards as soon as we can. So let's go."

"Yeah, let's go get them," said Steve. "I can't believe we've found them. Um, but we haven't, have we?"

"No, we haven't. We know they went in a boat but we don't know where they went. So, Vicky, while we sail out of here, I want you to see if you can track them."

"Will do." Vicky pulled out her laptop, took the bench seat that ran along the wall, and Steve sat in the captain's chair which I thought was rather cheeky, and I went to unhitch the moorings.

With the ropes wound up tightly then secured on the boat, I checked the perimeter to see if there was anything else I needed to do. Would the anchor be down? I had no idea. I couldn't see anything, so with a shrug of the shoulders I returned inside, told Steve to move aside while I got us out of here, and got funny looks from the pair of them.

"What?"

"Do you know how to handle one of these things?" asked Steve.

"Arthur, you don't even know how to drive a car properly."

"I do. But no, never driven a boat. It's just forward or backward, and, um, sideways, right?" I said, affronted.

"Mate, there's a lot more to it than that. It's tough, you need to be very precise and know exactly what you're doing."

"And you know, do you?"

"Yeah, I do. Been on loads of them. Worked on one for a year, sailed all over the place. To South Africa, all around the Med. I was a deckhand, ended up steering for months, controlling something even bigger than this. Man, you wouldn't believe how much these things cost, and then you have to pay staff, never mind the fuel, and the mooring charges are astronomical.

"Okay, okay, you drive, steer, whatever."

Steve grinned at me then resumed his seat. He spun in the chair then pulled back on a large handle. The motor roared as we eased back out of the harbor. He performed flawlessly, and it was clear he did know what he was doing. Maybe sometimes I take too much for granted, that I'm the only one who can handle situations, when truth is, others are more capable than me at certain things. I know, hard to imagine, right?

Within minutes, we were clear of the harbor, the other vessels were left undisturbed thanks to Steve's expert boatmanship, Vicky's head remained deep in her laptop as she searched for the other boat, and I felt like a third spoke, unsure what to do to help. I did not like that feeling.

Yay

While Steve took us out to sea with no destination in mind—it's always better to keep moving than sit around procrastinating—I explored.

Damn but this was one hell of a vehicle. The deck was large but it still felt a little cramped with only a few feet between me and the sea. So I went below to see what I could see. Oh, how the other half live. I always thought I had plenty of money, but this was on a whole other level. Or maybe the owner was ostentatious, whereas I was rather conservative in my spending habits, born of many years of deprivation, and the understanding it could be taken away from you at any time, which it had been on many an occasion.

That isn't to say it wasn't bloody lovely, because it was. The lounge area was white leather seating built into the walls, with a large table fixed to the floor made of the same dark mahogany as the rest of the interior trim. It was carpeted in a thick cream pile, all edges were rounded, many sheathed in brushed steel, and the kitchen was like my idea of paradise but in miniature.

Expensive taps, full-sized cooker, the shelves neat and orderly with bars running across the front to stop anything falling out. Even the fridge was stocked with expensive food; the owners were clearly planning on taking a trip the following day.

And there was a coffee machine, hip, hip, hooray, so I wasted no time making a delicious brew for us all while we headed out into the unknown.

Once ready, I returned reluctantly to the pair of degenerates I had been lumbered with, only to find them silent, and hugging. Vicky was facing me and she shook her head; Steve wasn't doing too well. Poor guy, he knew the score, knew the chances were high Sunshine would be killed if she wasn't dead already, and that the people who took her would be on their guard, expecting the unexpected. He shook, sobbing quietly while Vicky held him and whispered soothing words in his ear.

I put the drinks down on coasters and left them to it.

I returned to the lounge and relaxed for a while, centering myself, steeling my nerve for the ordeal sure to come. It wasn't just that we would be fighting bad guys, if we found them, it was that it may well all be for naught and Sunshine would be a lost cause, dead when we finally found her.

If we tried anything too confrontational with her kidnappers they could use her as a shield, threaten to harm her if we didn't leave or pay up, so this would be tricky and then some.

How did you go about rescuing someone from a situation like this? Not that I even knew what the situation was. They could be anywhere, they could have sailed to Europe by now, or merely nabbed her then set ashore and had a hideout all lined up. Guess we'd find out soon enough. Maybe.

After finishing my coffee, I headed back up onto the deck and peered through the window to see if the coast was clear. It was. Steve was back at the controls, Vicky was on her laptop.

Closing the door behind me as the wind was chilly, I entered the warm interior. Wow, they even had heating on these things. Awesome.

I began to ask where we were at, but Vicky held up a hand. Steve winked at me—men in this together. Minutes later, and it must have been a record for Vicky, she sighed, then closed the laptop.

"We know where they went," she said. "All the large vessels, and the small ones, um, all vessels, have to have trackers, and they have to check in with the authorities. Not that these idiots did, but I found their boat, found out what system they had, and I traced their route via their signals from their um, whatever you call it, the map thing on the screen."

"Whatever," I said, waving away unimportant details. "You know where they went? They didn't tell anyone?"

"Yes, and yes."

"And we're heading there now?" I asked.

"Yes."

"Do you know where they are now? Shouldn't we go get 'em?"

"I lost track of them, something changed, but at least we know where they went. Maybe they're still there."

"It's a good start. But look, guys, we have to prepare ourselves. Steve, when we get to where they headed, you stay behind at first, you too, Vicky."

"No way," they both protested.

"If they stopped for hours somewhere in the middle of nowhere that means it was to nab Sunshine from a boat, and that means if the boat's still there it will be very, and I mean very, unpleasant. So you both stay behind."

"I've seen plenty of dead bodies," protested Steve.

"Me too," said Vicky.

"I know, but this is different. So you wait."

Nobody argued, but I knew this pair. They would ignore my wishes, and I didn't blame them. For better or worse, we were in this together. I just hoped Steve could handle what we found. "Wake me when we're close. How long do you think?"

"A few hours," said Vicky.

"You said this thing can drive itself?"

"Sure can," said Steve.

"Then set that up and go get some rest. Once we find the boat, there won't be much time for resting after that." I left out the bit about the reason, mainly because it was sure to be so horrific none of us would want to close our eyes.

I went below decks and took one of the small bedrooms. I flopped onto the bed and lay there with my hands behind my head. Plotting the downfall of those who would steal little girls.

Ghost Ship

I knew before Vicky knocked on the bedroom door that we'd arrived. The slow rumble of the engine, the tense atmosphere, and the magical emanations growing stronger by the minute told me all I needed to know.

But when Vicky came in and said, "We're here," her face grim, I gave her my thanks and got off the bed, my bones creaking more than the frame.

I followed her up the narrow stairs and into the control room where Steve was pacing and looking all kinds of rough. I think it was the first time I'd ever seen him with his hair looking mussed. When he saw me, he went to the controls and maneuvered the boat a little so we were facing the other vessel side on. He flicked a switch and strong searchlights lit up the boat still a distance away but close enough for it to be unmistakable as a veritable fortress on water.

"Guess that's it," I said.

"Sure is," agreed Vicky.

"Let's go." Steve rubbed at his face like he was crawling with ants.

"Remember what I said. You two wait here. I'm not going to argue about it, I want you to wait. If I need your help, I'll call. Okay?" I stared hard at each of them until they relented, nodding their acquiescence.

With a grunt, I grabbed my jacket and got ready for the horror.

Steve remained at the controls and slowly pulled up alongside a vessel the antithesis of the usual pleasure boats. This was a squat oblong box more than anything else. Gunmetal gray, no easy sign of access, and the sides were high with slits for the occupiers to see out of, and no doubt shoot the shit out of anyone trying to get aboard.

The cabin loomed large, and appeared just as secure as everything else. There was little in the way of glass, just beefed-up security consisting of a lot of welding and other modifications done by skilled people but not professionals or anyone who cared about the finish. No way would this ever moor where it could be seen, it would have been used in secret locations and the work carried out away from prying eyes.

It was like a ghost ship with the dark panels and the air of abandonment, but we all knew this wasn't the case. Inside, bodies were only now cooling, rigor mortis setting in. And there would be blood. Lots and lots of blood.

Nothing new for The Hat, but it still made me balk because seeing dead bodies, especially when you weren't there when they died, is always an experience verging on surreal. It doesn't quite compute, and however many times it happens you never really get to grips with it. Were these lumps of eviscerated meat really once people with hopes and dreams, with lives lived and a future lost? Too much for the brain to process, to accept that it could be you next.

There were several small boats high on the sides in cradles, probably used to go ashore and not arouse suspicion, decent-sized vessels in their own right, only seeming small because of the monstrous size of the main boat. The true scale became apparent as we bumped gently against the hull and Steve cut the engine.

"It's bloody massive," noted Vicky.

"Sure is," I agreed. "Like something from Mad Max."

"This must definitely be where Sunshine spent a lot of time. It's big enough to have everything you'd need." Steve cupped his hands and squinted through the glass, as if mesmerized by the sight because it brought us one step closer to finding his little girl.

"I'll be back soon. Steve, come out and help me hitch us up so you don't drift away. And, er, how am I going to get across?"

"I have the perfect thing for that." Steve smiled wickedly. I got the impression I wouldn't like this.

Eek

I was right. In short order, I found myself clipped onto a length of rope tied to our boat and hooked over the steel sides of the other one by means of a grappling hook. I was now sliding through space with only a flimsy piece of metal stopping me falling into the freezing water. It wasn't merely plummeting that had me concerned, I'd certainly taken a dive from higher, it was that I'd be in the water and it wouldn't be easy to get out again.

So I may have squeaked a little as I jerkily slid down the rope and then came to rest with my feet on the sides of the boat. I grabbed hold of the sides, eventually managed to release the carabiners with fingers numb from fear rather than cold, although it was bloody freezing, and I dropped onto the deck with relief. The Hat was still alive.

Everything was cast in deep shadow as our lights couldn't reach down over the high walls, so I did as instructed and went straight to the cabin. The door was ajar and blocked by a large lump I knew was a body. I fumbled my way to the control panel and searched for the switches Steve told me to find, then flicked them on.

The room lit up in all its stark, uncompromising glory, and so did the rest of the boat once I finished with the switches. There was no key to start the engine but the backup generator seemed to be working fine, more's the pity.

Blood was everywhere, on a staggering scale, although, again, you'd think I was used to it by now. But the five liters or so inside every adult human is a vast quantity of liquid to be sprayed over walls and floors, and it had certainly been spread creatively inside the cabin. A large, once strong man was lying on the floor, still clutching a heavy duty assault weapon.

He'd been ripped to shreds. Not only were his carotid arteries exposed, there were numerous wounds all over the corpse. Combat gear was in tatters, and by the look on his face, he hadn't enjoyed his death one bit. He'd definitely come up against a shifter or two who wasn't impressed by the unwanted entrance and had gone to town. The blood spray from his neck had decorated the walls and glass, covering everything in a dark reddish brown coating now it was drying. There was no sign of the people who made this fortress a home.

I returned to the deck and hoisted myself up to peer over the metal walls. I gave a thumbs up to Steve and Vicky to tell them I was okay then dropped back down and continued exploring.

On several of the upper levels, of which there seemed to be many, I found more bodies, but these weren't of attackers, they were of the defenders. I recognized two of them, older shifters who'd been around since forever, with reputations for being tough, traditional, and uncompromising in their loyalty. The perfect people to protect the Wild One. They'd had their throats cut cleanly then left where they fell.

Down in the bowels of the boat, I found several more men and women, each death a little more grisly than the last, the struggle evident. It was chaos. Furniture, weapons, and a young girl's belongings were in disarray. Bloody handprints smeared the walls and strange animal prints marked the ceiling and floor. Two shifters were naked, their clothes in rags beside them. They'd put up a good fight but had succumbed to the simple power of a bullet once the kidnappers got off shots in the cramped space.

There were large dining and living rooms, very cosy and comfortable with lots of soft furnishings, and everything was well lived in, making it clear the place had been occupied for years. There were several bedrooms for couples, a few singles, and one that was clearly Sunshine's.

Was this where she was taken from? Doubtful, as there was no evidence of a struggle. Everything was neat and orderly, a normal girl's bedroom with posters and books, movies, TV, heavy on the pastel colors, and a wardrobe full of the average kid's clothes. If it wasn't for the fact I was on a ship it would have seemed utterly incongruous.

Eventually, I came to the scene from the movie Steve had been shown. The kidnappers had tracked

Sunshine and her mum to a panic room where they'd locked themselves away. Peeking inside, I found supplies to last a week, bunk beds, a small bathroom, entertainment for the girl, and one very dead mother.

Sunshine's mum was splayed out on the bed. Long blond hair hid her face, but not enough to hide the bullet hole in her forehead. How long had it taken them to get inside? The door was solid but they'd cut through it eventually, using a heavy duty piece of equipment left beside the door, and probably found on the ship. That was a silly oversight, to leave your welding equipment so your attackers could get you no matter how well you hid.

I hurried into open air so I could breathe easier and get rid of the metallic taste of blood in my mouth.

So, we had one dead kidnapper, lots of murdered shifters, and no girl.

I returned to the cabin to check the corpse of the guy but knew I'd find nothing but weapons and blood, plus cold squishy bits I'd have to move aside to check his pockets, which was always utterly gross.

And then he grabbed my arm in a grip that could break bone.

Devious

"What the fu..."

"Where are they?" grunted the man who moments ago was ripped to shreds and now seemed if not fine, then was certainly breathing and didn't have his guts hanging out or his carotid sliced clean through.

"Who? And ow, that hurts." I scowled at the man, not letting my surprise continue to show, confident as I felt Wand's power warming my leg and other bits, which was odd. I wished he'd stop doing it.

"Tell me or I'll rip you to pieces." He stared hard, was still for a moment, then said, "Ah, wizard is it?"

"Yeah, wizard. Pretty good fucking wizard too." Wand tore through my pocket—we really had to come up with a new design—and slammed into my free hand. Without preamble, I whacked him down on the top of the man's head with a mighty thwack that dazed him and allowed me to scramble back as his hold relinquished.

Catlike, or maybe creakylike, I jumped to my feet and grinned as Wand powered up to eleven and the sigils flared bright and joyous in anticipation of battle.

This was no ordinary criminal, he was a wizard like me, the illusion enough to confirm that. Guess I'd caught him unawares and he'd fallen back on one of the oldest tricks in the book. Play dead. Damn, I always seemed to fall for such simple tactics. This time I had an excuse. The magic in the air from Sunshine's heightened emotions was playing havoc with my magical sense and I was amazed I could do anything at all the way my thoughts were so fuzzy and my awareness so stunted.

Then I realized quite how subdued they were. I didn't care about this guy, I wasn't that bothered about Sunshine either, not on an emotional level. It was more a sense of pride in my work that made me continue this. I wasn't so far gone that I didn't understand that wasn't right though, I knew I shouldn't be feeling this so that was something. What it did confirm was that Sunshine was one hell of a powerful girl and the cause of the emotional turmoil.

And there was one more thing. Something I'd overlooked and should have made a priority. If the emotional shockwaves were centered around the city, then chances were high that was exactly where she was. She wasn't out at sea, she was back in the heart of the madness.

Time to go.

There was just one problem.

I ducked as a stream of purple energy shot over my head. "Hey, watch it, you could damage Grace."

"Grace?" asked the numnuts, pausing before he tried again.

"The hat, you dickhead. And I'm The Hat."

"That makes no sense. Are you on medication?"

"No, but you soon will be." I snapped Wand to attention and with a joyful "Whee," he let forth with a torrent of angry energy of his own, far superior to this guy's. The focused beam of pure magic infused with my annoyance—I wasn't emotional enough to feel true anger—and pride in my wizardly wildness, hit with precision right on his upper arm. He dropped his own wand, just a stick with nice carvings on, and yelped.

"You're an amateur," I said, hardly believing it.

"I'm learning," he huffed, affronted. "Pretty good, eh?" He grinned at me then glanced at the ground and went for the large machine gun.

"Yeah, but not good enough." Wand blasted the weapon away into a corner and the man stopped short. He looked at me, then the gun, then back again, trying to gauge my levels and his chances.

"You can try if you want. Well, what's it gonna be, punk? Make my day, why don't you?"

"Huh? What you on about?"

I sighed. "Never mind. Why are you here? What's the deal? Where's the girl?"

"Gone, they took her. And the bastards left me behind. No power to get out of here, just had to wait for someone to show up. I'm gonna kill them. They double-crossed me. Me! This was my bloody idea."

"Was it now," I snarled, raising Wand.

"Hey, hey, come on, man. I didn't want anyone to get hurt. It was them, they got carried away, cheated me and took the girl."

"Why'd you pick her? Why take someone like that?"

"Because she's..." He broke off mid-sentence and his eyes widened in shock and surprise. He stared down at a spreading stain through his military shirt and then the tip of a blade poked through his abdomen. He fell forward, revealing his murderer behind him.

Somewhat Miffed

"Steve, you utter plank," I shouted, my anger boiling over, my emotionless state having seemingly vanished.

"He helped take my girl. He planned it."

"Yeah, and he was about to tell me why, and a lot more besides. Hell, what is wrong with you?" I bent to check, but the man was definitely dead.

"What's wrong with me," Steve hollered, spittle flying, his face puce, "is that my daughter who I love more than life itself, who I haven't watched grow up because of who she is and because I'm an utter fuck-up, has been taken away and is most likely already dead. So, sorry, but this bastard had it coming and I will not apologize for killing him. I'd do it again if he wasn't dead." Steve kicked him and carried on kicking him. I let him, he needed an outlet and it wasn't as if the guy could feel it.

Eventually, he calmed down, the kicks became weaker, the tears became heavier, and the sheer overwhelming realization of what was happening gripped Steve tight and dragged him to his knees. He bent his head and sobbed his heart out, not for the first time, but this brought it all home in a way he hadn't accepted yet, clinging as he was to hope against all the odds.

Now he knew, or at least acknowledged truly and deeply, that she'd been taken and it was unlikely he would ever see her again.

"Come on, let's go," I said, putting out my hands and helping him to his feet.

"Sorry, it's just..."

"I know, buddy, I know. Don't worry, we will not let them get away with this. I promise."

We left, both knowing that if they did this to one of their own, they weren't averse to hurting the girl.

Outside, Steve stopped. "Wait, what about Sue?"

"Her mum? She's dead, Steve, nothing to see. They holed up in a panic room but got taken anyway. You don't need to see that." I had an idea, unsure if it would help or not. "Come on, I have something to show you."

Steve walked into his daughter's bedroom like he was entering a shrine, full of respect and awe. Guess he'd never been in a bedroom of hers that was permanent, just transient places with little real sign of occupancy. This was where she'd grown up though, with a hundred telltale signs of her changing from a young girl to the one she was now. Stuffed animals and ancient picture books sat alongside video games and gossip magazines, things picked up from trips to the mainland. She had posters on the walls, even several photographs stuck to a small dressing-table mirror.

Steve plucked one such small photo from the mirror and showed it to me.

"One of the happiest days of my life." He showed me the photo. It was of him and a pretty young girl, maybe seven or eight, smiling, their faces up close to the lens.

"We snuck off for the whole day, just me and her, walked about in fields, got insanely muddy, found a little cafe and had tea and cream cakes. Just us, together. Her mum went spare but I didn't care. By this time I was hardly allowed to see her, so it made little difference. I knew it might have been the last time I saw her. We had a few more visits after that, but this was the only time since she was tiny that we were on our own."

Steve pocketed the picture and we left the boat.

As we sailed away, so Sunshine's influence faded too. We'd succeeded yet failed utterly too. All we knew was that they'd lived out at sea, had been taken from their home on water, and that Sunshine was very powerful, enough to make me scared of what she might be capable of.

And wizards were involved. That's never a good sign. You can't trust them.

Back in the Thick of It

By the time Steve parked—do you park boats?—and we'd wiped it down then reached the car, it was into the early hours.

We were all exhausted. Stress is the true killer, it gnaws at your bones, eats through your energy reserves more than running away from bad guys or blasting the magic in a carefree manner.

As cortisone levels rise, so your body consumes energy at an astonishing rate. Add to that the mental focus it takes, the worry, your mind whirling, and it leaves you in a sunken, depressed state, everything verging on closing down. We all felt it, we all fought it, yet there was no time to rest. There was only panic and that awful, gut-churning sense of impending doom you only get when your loved ones are in peril.

I hadn't felt like this for some time, not concerned like this for friends or family, and it was eating me up inside. Not only was I worried deeply for the little girl, but I knew what it was doing to Steve. You couldn't avoid it.

He was visibly shrinking before our eyes. His hair was disheveled, his face was gaunt, deep dark bags hung low under usually clear blue eyes, now rheumy and constantly close to tears. His actions were erratic and jittery, he was either manic or lethargic, and if I hadn't known better I'd assume he was high, or coming down from seriously hardcore drugs. He was on the verge of a breakdown, unable to relax for a moment, stressed out of his mind, and trying to stop the nightmares from invading his thoughts.

"Come on, let's get out of here," I said, then started the car and began driving back to the city.

After a few minutes, Steve said, "I shouldn't have killed that guy. He was our only lead and I blew it."

"Don't worry about it, we'll find her. We'll find them."

"How?"

"Vicky, you found them at the harbor, so where did they go once they got Sunshine?"

"I'm working on it," she said, not looking up from her laptop. "They could have come ashore at any number of places. They definitely didn't return to the port."

"Doesn't the tracking thing you used show where they went next? Why did it stop working?"

"I don't know. It just stops. No sign of them. Nothing."

"Maybe they got wise and ripped out the electrics?" said Steve.

"The boat wouldn't work then, would it?"

"No, it wouldn't," said a distracted Vicky. "And they would have disabled it earlier. Something else happened."

"Maybe they only just realized so did it once they had Sunshine," mused Steve.

"Whatever the reason, we can't track them that way, correct?" I asked.

"Yes."

"So what's the alternative? You can check other ports, other places they could have moored, right? How many can there be?"

"Arthur, this is the bloody United Kingdom. It's a small island surrounded by water, they could have landed and come ashore absolutely anywhere."

"No, you're wrong. If we're feeling the influence of Sunshine, if she's making everyone go funny in the head, then she isn't up in bloody Scotland or down in Cornwall, she's close. They took her and then they brought her back to the city. They must have. Or somewhere close anyway. That means they had a tight schedule. Think how long we took to drive to the port, and how long we'll take to get back. They'd have to do the same so check out the nearest places and see if there was any sign of them. When did it all start with people going funky?"

"Um, it was this morning, wasn't it? Just started this morning. I mean yesterday morning. Damn, I can't keep things straight in my head." Steve shook his head like that would make it better.

I glanced over at Vicky and she pulled a face-Steve wasn't doing well at all.

"But they didn't have her then, did they?" I was getting mixed up too now. When had I come home? Yesterday evening, and it had been happening for longer than that morning, hadn't it? That's what Ivan said. What the hell was going on? Was I wrong about all this? Were we going in completely the wrong direction? No, something told me this was right, I was right, so how had Sunshine been making people feel like this if she hadn't even been taken then?

When situations like this become complicated and you can't find the answer, you have to take a step back and come to the logical conclusion.

"They took her earlier than we thought. You got the call yesterday afternoon that they had her, and the truth thing had been going on for a while then, maybe even a week, so that's when they took her."

"Arthur, that makes no sense. We saw the kidnappers go to the port yesterday," said Vicky.

"Yeah, but maybe they were going for another reason."

"No, because I traced them to the boat. They went and got her yesterday."

"Damn, you're right. Okay, so this telling the truth thing happened before then. How?" Seems like the simple explanation isn't always right.

"Because she was already influencing everyone, before they took her?" ventured Steve.

"Yeah, must be."

"Why? How? She wasn't stressed out then."

"Maybe she was. Maybe something happened on the boat and she was worried, wanted everyone to tell her the truth and it spread to the city, to other areas. Maybe she was trying to focus on you, Steve. Maybe she was reaching out, telling you to get to the truth, that something bad would happen."

"And I did nothing."

"Dude, how were you to know?" I asked. "Nobody knew who was doing this. We're onto something. She was worried, she reached out, wanted you to ask questions, find out the truth, and then she was nabbed. That means one thing."

There was silence, they hadn't caught up yet.

I sighed. "It means this was done by someone on the boat, someone who was there. Something happened so they left and then they returned and took her. Bet she overheard a conversation and panicked, thought something bad would happen. Maybe she'd even shifted and listened in secret, and reached out to you."

"What about her mum? She'd tell her, wouldn't she?"

"Maybe she did, maybe she didn't. She's a kid, she could have done anything. Maybe her mum didn't believe her, or maybe they were all ready and confident they could protect her. Or maybe she said nothing. I don't know, this is all conjecture, but my guess is that she knew it was gonna happen so freaked out and the shockwaves hit the magical community."

"This is nuts," said Vicky. "You can't do things like this, can you? Get panicked and force everyone to tell the truth, make everyone lose their emotions?"

"Obviously you can. She's an outlier, different, and young. Many gifted people were more powerful as children before they put the filters on, learned how to control things. She's scared, reached out to her dad, and hoped he'd come find her. Why her mum didn't get in touch, or believe her, maybe we'll never know. But that's what happened."

I wasn't convinced, but we had to remain confident. If we thought we were heading back to the city for no reason, Steve would be a gibbering wreck by the time we arrived. So, unsure as I was, I tried to convince them this was what had occurred as we made our way back into the heart of darkness.

I prayed I was right, otherwise I'd have the death of a young girl on my hands.

A Pause

"What do we do now?" asked Steve. He leaned forward from the back and stared first at me then Vicky.

I gulped, then whispered, "I don't know."

"Haha, come on, mate, seriously. Don't screw around. You're The Hat, the great Hat, you always have a plan. What do we do? Where we going?"

"I don't know. Goddammit, I don't know what to do, where to go, who to talk to. How to find her."

I slammed my hand on the steering wheel, beyond frustrated, and then the tears fell. I felt like an abject failure. I'd let Steve down, I'd let Sunshine down. For the first time in a long while, I felt absolutely helpless.

The momentum had ceased, there was no build-up from one event to another. We'd hit a dead end and I had nothing.

"It's okay. At least you tried." Steve slumped back into the seat and I drove to my new house in silence.

We entered without a word, what was there to say? I left Vicky and Steve in the living room and went into the kitchen to be alone for a few minutes. I filled the kettle then flicked the switch and busied myself preparing for coffee. The Gate of Bakaudif loomed at the fake door to the garden, already housed behind a professional coat of plaster. It flowed seamlessly into the space but I knew it was there, knew its power, and was tempted to run through screaming and sprint all the way home to have a cuddle from Penelope.

What should I do? Who should I talk to? Where was she?

It was too stressful, I didn't like the pressure. This was why I stuck to nicking artifacts—I either got it or I didn't. Nobody would die if I failed to complete the job. At least nobody I cared about.

Exhausted beyond my usual semi-comatose state of being, I rested my hands on the Formica tabletop and let the guilt and shame wash over me. I let it all out, didn't hold back, allowed this human body and mind to experience what it wanted to the fullest, no holds barred.

Tears fell for all the scared children in the world, adults too. My body shook, but I continued, allowed all the emotion to surface, to peak, and slowly, over several minutes, it eased. You have to detach from it all, allow yourself to be what it wants to be, and then you can take back control and focus, get shit done.

That's what I intended to do. We'd get things done.

Sunshine needed us.

"I won't let you down," I whispered.

The kettle had clicked off minutes earlier, so I switched it back on and poured in the milk while I waited. Then I made the drinks and took them into the living room, wishing with all my heart I had something to say, a plan that had suddenly formed, but all I had were three mugs of flavored water.

Vicky and Steve were sitting silently on the new Scandinavian beech sofa, their red faces in stark contrast to the pale green cotton of the covers. They held hands so tightly their knuckles were white, and neither spoke. The smell of fresh paint made my head spin. I felt sick. I was useless.

I carefully placed the drinks on three new coasters I already hated because they showed heat rings and who needs that in their life, and then I sat opposite them.

With a deep breath, I said words I never thought I'd have to say. "You guys have to come up with a plan. I don't know what to do next. Sure, we can go around the usual dodgy suspects and bash a few heads, but I can't see that working. We can put out feelers and I have no doubt that given time word will come back and we'll know who did this, but we haven't got time and we haven't got their location even if we knew who did this. So, you'll have to help. Vicky, you find anything with your snooping?"

"It isn't snooping, it's research. Work."

"Whatever. You got anything?"

"No. All we have is the people going to the port, the boat drops off the radar, and I can't find them after that. But you said they must have come back to the city.

I tried looking at road cameras, but I don't even know what I'm searching for. There's too much to sift through. I never even saw their faces."

"Okay, Steve, who could it have been that took her? Who looked after her on the boat?" I realized then that I should have made Steve check out all the bodies so we'd know who was dead and who wasn't. But then, he didn't recognize anyone from the footage Vicky found, and if he'd known them he should've been able to pick them out even without seeing their face. This wouldn't help, but it was worth a shot.

"A few I knew, the old-timers, the ones who were always around, but some of the others changed every year or two."

"And you know where to find the old dudes?"

"I guess." Steve shrugged.

"Would they tell you who the others were, because of what's happened?"

"No, they won't know. It was all super-secret. Nobody ever knew what was happening apart from the ones in charge and her mum. They switched things up, kept everyone in the dark. We can go ask though. It's a start. They might know who was there and who should have been."

"Good, let's go over the ones you knew were always there and I'll describe who I found on board."

For the next half hour we sifted through the details and came up with a depressing realization. Everyone who Steve knew was always around was dead. As for the rest, as best I could describe them, Steve was at a loss.

"And we have no idea who anyone is who's alive?" I said, just to be clear and maybe to make us all even more depressed.

"None."

"In that case, it's plan B."

"Which is?" asked Vicky.

"Magic. If in doubt, it's always magic."

Inspiration Hits

I almost fell off my chair as the mention of magic jolted something inside, releasing a sliver of hope clinging to my heart like snot on a pane of glass.

"Change of plan," I stammered. Heat rose from my stomach, all warm and fuzzy-like, and I knew I was onto something.

"I thought there was no plan?" asked Vicky, squinting at me.

"There wasn't, now there is. Forget plan B, this is plan fucking A!"

"What are you on about, mate?" asked Steve as he edged forward on the sofa.

"I'm talking about the blindingly obvious that we haven't bothered to even think about."

"Which is?"

"Wait here. I'll be back in a few minutes if my hunch is right."

They both protested, thinking I was gonna go off on a mad one and leave them alone for the night, but I wouldn't do that to Steve. Vicky, yes. Steve, no.

I went into the kitchen and exited through the door into the back garden. I promptly returned inside and grabbed my boots, carried them through the house, grinning foolishly at the others as I passed back and forth, then put them on and tried again.

Cat-like, I hopped the new fence and crept across the neighbor's lawn, then repeated the actions until I came to the end house. Peering over their hedge to ensure the coast was clear, I scrambled over then squatted down and snooped around the corner into my street. I had a good vantage point, merged with the shadows, and I waited.

Nothing moved, and then I nearly jumped out of my skin when a cat sidled up and began rubbing against my leg.

"Shoo, I'm busy."

The beast glared at me then shrugged and wandered off down the street, acting like it owned the place. Bloody cats.

I focused on the individual cars, but there was nothing to see, nobody coming or going. Knowing I was right, or praying I was, I waited, unmoving, as still as Vicky's eyebrows after she tied her hair back.

There it was! A faint glow coming from inside a car. No sooner was it there than it was gone. Bloody amateurs. Probably checking in with the others, or social media or something, but looking at their phone had given them away.

Wasting no time, and with my ace ninja-wizard skills, I dashed low across the road and hugged the hedge on the opposite side. I waited a moment then hopped the front fence, not risking the gate squeaking, and made my way to the rear garden. Then it was more hedge-hopping until I figured I was one house behind the car. I stepped carefully around the side path and crawled along the wet lawn then peered over the hedge.

There was a guy inside, face turned away from me, looking directly at my house.

All this running around when I should have known better, thought about it logically and recalled what I knew about how kidnappers acted.

They were nervous, jittery, and they wanted their money. What they did not want was you telling the police, or anyone else, and they certainly didn't want you taking it upon yourself to find them. They expected you to try, but they kept eyes on you if they could so warnings could be issued if you got too close.

As far as they were concerned, it was best if you did look for them. It kept you busy, stopped you doing anything too stupid, and that way they knew you hadn't called in the big guns.

We were obviously living up to expectations and they were happy to keep an eye on Steve and make sure he did nothing rash.

I'd show them rash.

Kerpow!

I hunched down behind the nondescript Ford and released Wand. He was already burning bright, so I covered him up quick before he gave us away.

"Tone it down," I whispered.

"Oops. Hehe. We gonna blast the hell out of him? We are, aren't we? Shall I make his head pop? Like a melon? That would be cool."

"You need therapy. What is wrong with you?"

"It's been ages since I got to go wild. We don't get any action at the moment. Well, you do, but I don't."

"Look, I know it was a quiet few weeks, but you've been in action since we got back. And anyway, no, you can't explode his head. We need him. We have zero leads apart from this guy, so we need him alive and we need him to talk. Do not kill him," I warned.

"Fine. You are such an old man. Can I at least blow some of him up?"

I thought for a moment. "Okay. Just a bit. Nothing on the head," I said hurriedly, knowing what he was like.

"How about an arm? Arms are always good. All gristly and bony and it freaks them right out."

"Of course it freaks people out if they get their arm blown off. You need arms, they have fingers on the end and that's super important."

"Don't see what the big fuss is. They're just like crappy sticks all bunched together tight. You humans are such babies even when all grown up."

"Wand, have you ever been in pain? Have you ever felt agony, the feeling like you'd rather die than put up with the hurt for a moment longer?"

"Huh? No, I'm a stick."

"Exactly. So you don't get to judge. You're an extension of me so you know how much I hurt at times. Don't dismiss pain and the right to bang on about it for ages as inconsequential, it's what makes us human."

"Whatever. We gonna blast or we gonna bicker?"

"We usually do both," I noted.

"True."

I stood rapidly, lowered Wand, grinned as he flared to life and the guy in the car turned his head, then I released him as my will shunted down my arm with as much force as I could muster. To keep the noise to a minimum, I focused the energy as tightly as possible, and thankfully Wand did as I intended.

He shot through the rear window, making a perfect hole, so fast and accurate that I heard nothing more than a whisper. For a moment I panicked, worrying he'd shoot straight through the guy's head and out the front of the car, but he behaved and swerved at the last moment, darted across to the passenger side, readjusted, then sprang forward and curved around to come to a stop a fraction of an inch from the man's eye.

The mark stayed very, very still.

Whistling, I sauntered around to the side and opened the door.

"Hello," I said genially. "Nice evening for it."

"What do you want?" he asked with a sigh, knowing he was well and truly busted.

"I merely wondered if you would like to come in for a nice cuppa? There's biscuits. With chocolate on." I wiggled my eyebrows; who could resist such an offer?

"If I say no?"

"Then Wand here will pull back a little, and then he will slam as hard as he can right into your eyeball. It will pop, making one hell of a mess, and you will scream. And then he'll do the other one. And then you'll come in for a cuppa, but I won't let you have any biscuits for being a naughty boy."

"Fuck you."

"Hey, Wand, remember that thing you wanted to do?" Wand lowered his tip. "You have my permission to do it."

"Whoa! Wait. What? What's he gonna do?"

"Too late, buddy. The Hat never asks twice."

Wand spiraled around and around the man's head at a dizzying speed, and I shut the car door quickly to muffle the sound as he dived down hard and true. A series of sigils flared along his length, lighting up the interior like an eighties disco. I hummed 99 Red

Balloons by Nena, man what a song. The German original's better though.

The screams were muted, but still loud enough, prompting me to check around to ensure nobody was woken. All good.

I watched as Wand burrowed his bottom deeper into the guy's arm. As the last sigil lit up in the correct sequence, so magic that was mine and his and yet neither of ours erupted in all its magnificent glory. The man's arm burst apart from the elbow down in a shower of gore that coated the glass and made it impossible to see through

I gave it a few moments while he screamed, and until the built-in painkiller in the spell took effect, utterly numbing the arm and stopping my victim going into shock so I could do more nasty stuff if required, then opened the door.

The man whimpered and stared in horror at his missing arm. I picked a finger off the dash and handed it to him. "Is this yours? Very careless of you. Now, about that coffee?"

The guy nodded. Wand shot back into my hand and I pocketed him like a gunslinger happy with his death count.

"That's more like it. Out you get." The man took a while to emerge, understandable, and I said, "Lead the way. After all, you know where we are, right?"

He snarled, then stumbled across the street.

Oops

"Shit, shit, shit."

The man dropped to all fours without warning, make that all threes, and his clothes shed from his back like autumn leaves in a strong gale. His stocky frame rippled, and his already hairy back sprouted as though fertilized. Thick tufts of hair grew rapidly, covering the broad expanse of muscle that bunched tight beneath. His shoes split and the heels extended until I wondered if he'd been considering joining the circus, but this was no laughing matter, especially when I saw what his arms were doing.

A quick glance to check everyone remained tucked up in bed, oblivious to the nighttime terrors going on below them, then I said, "Go on then," and Wand yipped as he blasted up from my pocket and shot forward then did a sharp turn and halted right in front of his eye.

The beast ceased all movement, froze like a rabbit in the headlights as Wand vibrated merrily in front of him.

The impasse lasted only a second, and then the man decided to risk it. As he grabbed for Wand, my faithful familiar decided enough was enough and snapped forward like an elastic band released at full stretch.

The pop was audible, the scream not so much as Wand extricated himself from the idiot's eyeball and wedged himself between the man's teeth.

"Get him off, he'll leave teeth marks," moaned Wand as I hurried to collect the shredded clothes then grabbed an arm, already back to normal human size, if rather hairy and thick around the wrist. Fast as I could, I dragged the protesting lookout up the front path and knocked on the door.

Vicky peered around the door, and I hissed, "Open up, hurry," then pulled the dead weight inside and dropped him in the hallway. Vicky slammed the door shut and I said, "Help me get him into the living room."

She took a leg and I pulled on his arm as Steve appeared.

"Clear a space. No, actually, we'll dump him on the couch. No, wait, he'll get blood on it. Go into the kitchen and look under the sink. There's a canvas bag in there, bring it in. Um, please. Thanks, Steve."

Steve nodded and skirted around us then hurried off.

Vicky and I continued moving the huge guy inside and eventually got him into the front room.

Panting, I took the bag off Steve when he returned and pulled out a large folded sheet of plastic, a roll of tape, and a hammer.

"Prepared for a spot of blood spraying, were you?"

"You never know," I grunted.

"What's the hammer for?" asked Vicky.

"Whacking them over the head or breaking their fingers." I glared at the man as he eyed the hammer warily.

"Get him on the couch please," I asked as I laid out the plastic over the new sofa and taped it at the back so it wouldn't slip off.

Vicky and Steve manhandled him but he was too heavy so I helped. When he was in place, I punched him in the stomach. With an "Oompf," he opened wide and Wand tore away, spun around the room, then stopped in front of the mirror over the fireplace.

"Am I damaged? Has he ruined any of the sigils?"

"No, you're fine. You're made of bloody unicorn wood, a set of teeth won't hurt you."

"Is he talking to Wand?" asked Steve.

"Yeah. Annoying, isn't it?" Vicky replied.

Wand spun several times to check himself out, he of zero eyes, then sped for my pocket where he nestled deeply like a puppy wanting the comfort of its mother. It's nice to feel loved.

We turned our attention to our captive. He didn't look that great.

A Warning

"Do not say a word until I tell you to," I warned. "Do not move, do not moan, and do not bleed on my soft furnishings."

"What's going on?" asked Steve, glaring at the guy because obviously he was no friend of ours.

"Where's his arm?" asked Vicky, mesmerized by the oozing stump and the jagged bone sticking out.

"He lost it. And this is someone who is involved in the kidnap of Sunshine. I realized they probably had people keeping an eye on you to make sure you tried nothing that would risk them being paid. It's how they work, and I was right. He was in a car. Now he's here. Wand wanted to pop both his eyes, but I only let him do one."

"My bloody eye. You bastard. And my arm, it's all numb."

"I said no talking," I hissed, slapping the hammer head into my palm. He shut up.

We stood staring at him, none of us saying a word. This was it, crunch time. We knew it, he knew it.

But what now? Torture wasn't my thing, I couldn't do nasty stuff to somebody to get them to tell me things. Or I could, but I wouldn't, because it leaves such a terrible stain on your soul. It would eat away at me, at all of us, and we would be despicable human beings.

Good thing was, the dude with the missing arm and eyeball didn't know that. Vicky wouldn't do it either, but Steve was another thing altogether. This man knew where his daughter was, had taken her, terrified her, maybe done awful things to her. Maybe hurt her. If it was your child, what would you do to get her back? Would you torture the person who could help you get her?

"Now, I do believe I offered you a cup of coffee," I said amiably. "But no biscuits," I warned.

Steve frowned. "You're gonna give this scum a drink?"

"Yes, I am. He'll have his cuppa and then he'll tell us everything we need to know."

"I won't," he gasped.

"You bloody well will. You know Steve here is her father, right?" The man nodded. "So what do you think he'll do to you to get information? I haven't got the stomach for it, and look what I've done just to get you inside. You think it'll go any better for you? You want me to remove the spell of numbness?" I asked, glancing at his arm. I pointed at his eye. "I wonder which one will hurt more?"

I left them to it and went to make the drinks.

Strangely Agreeable

I half expected to find the man with his head caved in, or at least in a worse condition than I'd left him, which wouldn't have been easy as I'd maybe overreached a little. Poor guy had no arm, no eye, and no hope of a future unless he was very lucky.

But when I returned with the drinks, it was to discover all was quiet. Vicky and Steve hadn't moved, they merely stood and stared at the man who was trying to remain dignified and acting hardcore, but it was clear the numbing agent was wearing off and he was in for one hell of a world of hurt pretty soon. His face was slick with sweat, skin ashen, and his head kept drooping as his body threatened to shut down as he went into shock.

"You okay, Steve?" I asked.

"Yeah, but I don't see why we're being nice."

"Because I've already been nasty, and now we have him. If you want to kill him go ahead, but—"

"You better bloody not kill me," interrupted the guy.

"And what will you do if we decide to end your sorry life?" I snapped, my eyes as hard as Steve's. "Do not interrupt me again," I warned. "Now, where was I?" I turned back to Steve. "We need him to talk, and he will, so let's be nice. If he cooperates, we don't need to sully ourselves by hurting him."

I handed the drinks out, not too worried about the man trying anything as he was in no fit state and he knew that as well as us. For several minutes we all focused on our drinks, us to freak him out, him to fight off the encroaching shock. The sugar-laden strong coffee seemed to do the trick and I upped the power of the spell still swimming through his system although it wasn't very effective. I was never very good at controlling spells after the initial blasting ceased.

With a nod to Steve and Vicky, the three of us placed our cups down and stepped closer to our captive.

"So, talk," I said, giving him my loveliest of smiles.

"Nothing to say," he croaked, hiding his fear behind sipping his coffee.

"Okay, Steve, this is my house, and my soft furnishings, but you have my permission to kill him slowly and messily. Vicky, let's go. I will not be a party to torture, and I'm sorry about that Steve, but this isn't my daughter. If it was, then I'd do whatever it took. So let's go." I retrieved our empty cups and made to leave.

We got further than I'd expected, two whole paces, before the man said, "Wait, wait, okay, you win."

With our backs to him, Vicky and I exchanged smiles then turned around.

"Who are you?" I asked.

"Scum, that's who he is," said Steve.

I tried not to roll my eyes. I knew he was having a hard time, but this wasn't helping.

"I'm Paul. Paul Simmons."

"Okay, Paul, why were you watching us? Why are you following Steve?" He glared at me, defiant. "Fine, and this is getting very old. If I have to ask you a single question more than once, then I will leave this room and you will never see me again. You will be left with Steve until you give him the answers he wants. And trust me, he will keep on asking. He'll keep asking until you tell him. Understand?"

For a moment I thought Paul would spit or say something that would end his chances of ever leaving here alive, but he obviously thought better of it. "Okay, I'll talk. On one condition."

"You do not get to make the rules, buddy. There is a small chance of you staying alive, that's it. Talk, and make it easy on yourself, and maybe we'll let you live, or let Steve deal with you and then you die at the end. That's the deal. No discussion." Again, he considered it, but not for long.

"Fine." He sank back, deflated, knowing he was beaten.

"Why were you watching Steve?"

"To make sure he didn't get other shifters involved or call the police or anything stupid."

"Did you tell the others about me and Vicky? About what we were up to?"

"Course I did. That's the whole point."

"And did you take Sunshine?"

"Me? Haha, no, mate. That was the others. Can't set foot on a boat, makes me puke my guts up."

"But these others, they took her and you're a part of it?"

"Yeah."

I put a hand to Steve's shoulder as the man answered, talking like it wasn't the life of a little girl we were discussing.

"Why?"

"Why what?"

"Do not fuck with me. You know what the question means."

"Money, always money. She's important, powerful, and nobody knew where she was apart from us. So we nabbed her, figured it would be good money with minimal hassle. Your man here, no offense, isn't known for being the sharpest, and we figured he'd do as he was told, get us our money. Plus, we knew he was your mate, and that he was with Vicky. You both have plenty of cash so we figured you'd give him what he needed."

"You didn't think maybe I'd decide to hunt you down and kill you all?"

"Yeah, we thought you might, that's why I'm watching. If you got anywhere near us, Steve would get a call and be told to back off. Simple, but effective." Paul smiled, I was nearly as compelled as Steve to punch him in the face. Somehow we both restrained ourselves.

"Bit risky, isn't it? Taking Sunshine just to force Steve to get money? What if we didn't have it, or didn't give it to him? You know shifters never deal with kidnappers, right?"

"We know, but it's bollocks. Been loads of cases, done a few myself. Nobody talks about it, they don't want to be seen as weak, but it happens a lot. Everyone says they won't pay at first, that they don't deal, but they always come around. Especially once they get one of their loved one's ears sent by special delivery. Haha."

Before the smug smile was gone from his face, Wand was out, and I was lunging forward. With a silent force of my will, Wand cut clean and true with a sliver of magic as sharp as Death's infinite scythe. The man screamed, I stepped back, and waved an ear in front of his face. "What, one like this, you mean?"

"I thought you said no torture," said Vicky.

"That wasn't torture, that was to show this fuckwit we don't find his jokes amusing."

"My ear!"

"You got any more jokes to tell?" I growled. Paul shook his head. "Good. Now, where were we?"

A Moment

Paul took several deep, raggedy breaths. He wasn't faring too well, and unless he spilled everything and fast, we'd get no sense from him for a while. His ear would be throbbing, or the gap where it used to be, as there was no saving him from the pain any more. I allowed the rest of the numbing spell to dissipate.

"It's gonna hurt real bad, real soon," I warned. "I've been keeping it all numb, but that's wearing off, so unless you wanna be in utter agony I suggest you keep talking."

"I will, I will," he gasped. He stared at his stump and his remaining eye began to roll up in his head. He was losing it.

I stepped forward and slapped him gently on his cheek. "Stay with us, Paul, almost over."

"What will you do with me?"

"Just keep talking, or you will be killed," I warned.

"Why me? Why her?" asked Steve.

"It was Duncan's idea. He was a bit dim, but this sounded perfect, so we went for it."

"Duncan's the guy your lot left to die on the boat, right?"

Paul's eye opened wide. "He wasn't dead?"

"He is now," I said.

"So it's just for a payout, that's it?"

"What can I tell you? We score big with these ransoms, one a year and we live the good life."

"Bastard," shouted Steve.

"Here's the big question, Paul, and think very carefully before you answer. I will ask you once, and if you don't tell us then it will go badly for you." I eyed his injuries. "Worse than it already has. Understand?"

"Yeah." Paul was sweating profusely and almost green, shock truly gripping him tight.

"Where is she?"

"Private place, so we can contain her. Locked in a room."

"Where, you fucking idiot?" I shouted.

"Bushy Heights, that new housing project just outside the city, all those fancy homes still being built. Workers are off on vacation, nothing happening for two weeks. We got her in one of the almost-completed houses. Nice and quiet. Big house for us all, perfect."

"How many of you?"

"How many?"

"People? How many people guarding her?" I hissed, exasperated, knowing he would be unconscious soon.

"Just the others," he whispered, and then his hand went limp and his face fell slack.

I stormed over to him, shook and slapped him until he woke up. "There's one more thing," I said. I turned to Steve; he knew what I meant.

Steve walked forward, face grim, and he bent so Paul could watch as he pulled his stubby, well-worn knife from his jeans pocket. He eased the blade from the polished wood slowly and carefully, and then said, "This is for Sunshine, and for all the others." Steve slid the knife into Paul's other eye until fluid trickled down his cheek, then thrust deep, killing him.

"I thought you were gonna let him go," shrieked Vicky.

We both turned to her. "Why?"

"Um, it sounded like that's what you were telling him."

"Nope," I said, standing.

Steve grunted as he pulled his knife out, wiped it on Paul's trousers where they weren't soaked with urine or blood, then got up. "He's a murdering kidnapper of little girls, what did you think would happen?"

"I don't know. He deserved it, but..."

"But it's nasty, horrible, cruel, and gross?" I asked.

"Well, yeah."

"Good, because that's exactly what it is. Some people don't deserve to live, Vicky, you know that."

We were all silent for a while. None of us felt uplifted, but we sure felt no worse either. The world was a better place, but it left three people one step closer to losing their humanity.

Tidying Up

I stepped out of the room and trudged into the back garden for some air. My head was fuzzy, my emotions blunted, everything surreal, like I was there doing these things but one step removed, present but not connecting.

"Goddamn," I muttered. "It's the girl." Call me daft, call all of us daft, but I hadn't realized quite how cold and callous we'd been when dealing with this Paul character. It was Sunshine's influence, numbing our hearts, our emotions, emptying us out so we could get one step closer to finding her.

At least, I hoped it was. Otherwise, it meant I really was a stone-cold son-of-a-bitch. Guess there was a little of that too.

I made a quick call to the Cleaner and wasn't surprised to hear the front door minutes later. I didn't want to see her, there was no point. I didn't want to see anyone. A while later, Vicky and Steve came out into the garden to join me.

"The living room's clean," whispered Vicky, not wanting to wake the neighbors, although how they'd slept through all the crap with Paul must have been testament to the amount of wine they drank to unwind from the stress of the day.

"Great," I said, feeling deflated and utterly drained of energy.

"It's Sunshine, right?" asked Steve. "She made us lose it, made us not care even a little about that guy. Not that I would anyway, but I just realized I felt different, that I was colder, harder, didn't feel a thing."

"Yeah, it's her. She's upping the game, becoming something else, something very different. This goes way beyond anything I've experienced. It would take a proficient and experienced adept to do a fraction of what she's doing. But let's not forget, it's partly because she's young and doesn't know what she's doing that this is possible. She certainly isn't to blame. She's scared and her emotions are seeping out and affecting everyone. Even those that were immune before. My guess is that the closer we get to her, the more intense it will become. We have to remain alert as I honestly didn't give it a thought when we captured Paul. I thought it was just me, how I am now, and I hope to God it wasn't."

"Me too," said Steve. "I did what I thought was right, but now it seems like a dream. That guy on the boat, now this, I did it without thinking, without caring at all. That ain't right."

"No, it isn't."

"It's okay," said Vicky, hugging Steve. "He deserved it."

"Yeah, I guess."

We stayed for another five minutes, just taking the air, trying to get a handle on this, each of us lost in our own thoughts, knowing there was more to come and trying to ready for it in our own unique ways. Some calm before the storm.

I searched my soul for my true identity, unable to ascertain if I would have done things differently or not, knowing only that I should have felt more than I had. Was that Sunshine or just me being older and more jaded? My best guess? A bit of both.

Sometimes I wished I could just go into a corner and cry, be left alone with my fears and insecurities, never have to speak to another soul. Run away, roam the world, never return. Lose myself to the wonders of planet earth and be done with all the heartache, the responsibility, family, friends, obligations, regrets, even love. To be a nomad, no strings, no ties, caring for no one and no one caring in return.

Sometimes I felt like that was what I needed. Or maybe what I deserved.

Obligations

Life isn't like that though, and for good reason.

It's testament to your inner fortitude that you don't go running and screaming into the hills never to return. Staying the course is what makes you a good human being, someone who cares and can be cared for in return.

Life is a series of challenges, of facing adversity. Be that demons and dark wizards, caring for family members, raising children, or the act of struggling to survive. Each is a battle, a challenge, and yet with it comes a sense of purpose, a reason for getting up in the morning. The trials of life mold us, make us who we are. How we handle them defines us and makes us well-rounded human beings or not. It is our choice. We choose the path, or at least how we walk it.

So I would not run away, I would help a friend, save a little girl, and not cave under the pressure of it all, under the sadness and horror of what people could do. This would not crush me.

We snapped from our reveries simultaneously. Without a word, we turned and strode with renewed purpose back into the house to ready for what was to come.

The Hunt is On

Citywide construction was on an endless loop of building, demolishing, rebuilding. Houses went up, houses went down. Ghettos were gutted, fancy homes erected, the residents moved to worse ghettos and the city split ever wider down the middle, the gap growing exponentially between the haves and the have-nots.

But the majority of construction was somewhere in the middle, neither exorbitant, nor cheap enough to be classed as social housing. Middle-class homes for middle-class folks, those with steady jobs, two cars, two point four children, and enough income to wrangle a mortgage from the banks to cover the cost of buying into the dream. Albeit temporarily, until the rot set in.

The houses went up fast, sealed boxes where you could lock the doors, close the curtains, and shut out the world for a while. Who could blame anyone for wanting that? To feel safe and secure, confident that just for a while your children were protected and nobody would harm them? That's what everyone wanted, and if you could afford it, you could play such games.

We headed to one such development a few miles out of town down the motorway, coming close to completion. Half the properties were already sold, and soon people would move in, even while construction continued on the others. But for now, before the roads were graded and the infrastructure signed off, the development was deserted. No residents, an abandoned construction site while the crews took vacations and readied for the final push.

The streets felt wrong, eerily silent, but it was just me being sensitive to the tension that hung like a physical weight in the car. Steve was understandably jittery, Vicky was holding his hand, being quiet, which was always unsettling, and I had nothing to say.

We were as ready as we'd ever be.

Sure, we could have prepared, spent time getting all manner of gear, things we may or may not need, but that would cost us time and time was in short supply. Better to have surprise on our side. Paul had been tasked with watching us, so fingers crossed the kidnappers were feeling complacent as he'd given them no warning. The only problem being that we didn't know when he should have checked in, or even if they had such a system in place, which they would have if they were halfway competent.

These guys weren't amateurs, so chances were good that Paul was meant to call or text regularly and if he missed it they'd know something was up. Meaning, it was now or never, crunch time. We might already be too late, so that meant we were silent, low in spirits, and scared as hell.

Finally we arrived. I parked up a short distance away and killed the engine and headlights.

"Wait here, please." I was working on my people skills, so had been making an effort to stop being so bossy. "I'm gonna check out the perimeter. If they're holed up here, they must have put their own people on patrol. There would have been guards as these places are ripe for the picking when the crews are away, so they've either killed them or they were their people to begin with. Either way, we need to get rid of them. I'll handle it alone, then come get you both."

"Then we go in," said Steve.

"Yes, then we go in. Please do not get out of the car and risk anything going wrong. You know me, I can handle this." I gave Steve, and especially Vicky, a hard look; they nodded. We were on the same page here, neither would do anything that risked Sunshine's life.

I gave Vicky the keys, just in case, and headed for the new houses.

Across a wasteland of scrub and gravel, where another development would probably be built right after this one, I moved as fast as possible under the cover of darkness. At the fence line, I squatted beneath a tree and waited for a minute, listening, getting used to the different lighting. It was low-level, just a few streetlights already wired in and giving the night-patrolmen something to see by. Once this place was finished, the streets would remain lit up at all hours, safety for the residents, but for now it was full of shadow and strange, looming structures.

Once I was confident I hadn't been seen, I moved along the perimeter slowly, listening and watching for the patrols. I could see no sign of movement, no houses with lights on. I didn't expect to.

But I knew people, and I knew gangsters, and I knew cocky gangsters. They always screw up. Situations like this were always the same. They'd have one, maybe two people patrolling, the rest would be inside, thinking it best to watch the girl. Truth is, you're best having as many bodies as you can outside, there to stop anyone getting close enough to the house to be a problem. Another thing in our favor was there wouldn't be many of them anyway. If only three had gone to get the girl, and Paul was an extra person, that would be about it. Maybe there were only two or three, maybe several more, but we weren't looking at a large operation. These type of gangs were small, close-knit, but utterly without loyalty when it came down to it. Hence the dead dude on the boat. No honor amongst thieves, not most anyway.

I continued making my way around the perimeter, stopping frequently in the shadows of trees or hunkering down in the long grass. Soon enough my investigation paid dividends and I watched as two men came from different directions and met up mere feet from my station. One came from the perimeter, the other from a street still waiting for asphalt to be laid. So, one walked the fence, the other roamed about just to be sure there were no infiltrators.

Amateurs, that was obvious. The building site was huge, there were endless places to hide if someone made it through the fence, so what good was wandering about aimlessly?

I watched as they talked quietly for a few seconds, then they continued on their way. One walked right past me, never even glanced my way. Unfortunately, and it only got worse with age, a curled-up Hat looked remarkably like a gnarled boulder.

Once the other man had returned to sweep the streets, I withdrew Wand and without a word let joyous energy flow down my arm. Boy was I tired, but adrenaline and the need to succeed with this job buoyed my magic and powered up my mojo. The light was dull, and discreet, and he cut through the chain-link better than any snips ever could. With the gap wide enough, I eased the wire back, squeezed through, pulled it tight behind me, and ran silently after the perimeter guard.

As I spotted him, I slowed, then walked at a sedate pace just fast enough to catch him up but slow enough to remain silent, like a ninja. I smiled at the thought, and wished I was a young boy so I could buy myself a cool ninja costume and have swords and nunchucks and stars and a mask and everything. Maybe even those cool slipper things too. I'd never had any of that stuff, never had anything cool, just an emptiness in my belly and a constant state of unease. All in the past, all gone. I had more than I could have ever imagined now, and I would not lose it, would not die, would not fail on this, what felt like the most important mission of my life because it was for a little girl, an innocent.

I crept up behind the man and tapped him on the shoulder with Wand.

Fair play to the guy, rather than turning in shock to see what it was, he elbowed backward and caught me right in the side of the head. Smart move, no wasted opportunity, no doing the obvious. He had training, street smarts born of living the life of a shifter no doubt.

As he whirled while I was disorientated, he was already shifting, his clothes shedding as his frame shrank and he began to morph into something I couldn't discern.

He shouldn't have bothered, as he was already dead.

"Look at your shoulder, fucker," I said casually.

He glanced at the exposed bone and writhing muscle that tried to continue the change, but it was being eaten away at a rapid pace. I shot my hand out, smothered his mouth, and locked an arm around his neck. I yanked hard to the side, and broke his neck. Feeling empty inside, like I'd turned the cap on a stubborn milk bottle, I dropped him where he lay and ran after the other guard even as the magic dissipated and the hole in his shoulder stopped devouring his flesh.

One down, one to go, then the real fun starts.

I dashed through the empty streets, the dark silhouettes of people's hopes and dreams for the future loomed over me with their exposed studwork, looking like grinning monsters observing The Hat at play.

All Sneaky Like

The one drawback to hunting men in urban environments is that they have just as many places to hide as you do. Sure, there are plenty of opportunities for surprise attacks, but you have to find them first, and that means you can run right into your enemy as you turn a corner if you aren't careful. So I crept, catlike, flowing across shadows. The exterior paper wrap on the houses flapping where it had come loose made me edgy, constantly alert and expecting an attack.

He could be anywhere, taking any number of routes, and the only way to find him was to keep moving and hope I spotted him before he spotted me. It was slow going, and the longer it took the more anxious I became. Would they be on high alert now Paul hadn't checked in? Would the man be waiting for me? Had he seen me? Nothing for it but to continue and remain vigilant.

Stress levels rose, my heart hammered in my chest, and I got cramp in my stomach. What was going on? Normally I was cool, calm, and collected in situations much worse than this.

Because it was important, for Sunshine. Not just about me or some stupid artifact, but genuinely important stuff. She needed me, needed her dad, needed us. The vibe was also increasingly tense, the air fragmented with whispers of strange emotions drifting lazily by, affecting my mood, my thoughts, how I acted. I had to nail this down, control it, not let it influence me or I'd do something rash and it would be game over. A dead Hat was no use to anyone.

Aha, that was it. I was actually a touch scared because I had no lives left to waste, would be trapped in a special kind of hell if I died this time. Taking up the mantle from a very pissed off Death who would have a thing or two to say about being tricked into holding down the worst job in existence.

I was frightened because I didn't want to die.

That too passed, and I understood it was Sunshine's influence yet again, morphing from making me unafraid of anything, uncaring even about her, to being swarmed with heightened emotion and hardly able to move under the crushing weight of responsibility and fear of the afterlife. The truth was somewhere in the middle, as so much always is.

I continued, checking the streets as I went, making my body as small a target as possible. Hunched, I crossed between buildings packed tight together, detached houses only in name, so close to their neighbors they may as well have been joined, but then status was lost, so everyone got what they wanted.

There he was, at the end of the street. He checked both ways, looked toward me and I flattened against the side of a finished house, and waited for him to continue his sweep.

Wasting no time, I dashed across the road, took a path between two buildings, and then watched as he walked just ahead in the middle of the gravel road, head constantly turning left then right.

He was smoking a cigarette. Oh, what I wouldn't give for a smoke right about now. Ah well, no point stressing about it, time for action.

A Bit of a Cock-Up

While he was blinded by the flare of the cigarette as he blew on the tip, I sprinted forward with Wand already out and glowing brighter than Vicky's forehead after she had a workout.

And then I tripped on a loose chunk of gravel and splayed forward, scraping my knees against the rough surface. My palms dug into the jagged road surface, leaving tiny stones under the skin, and I even cut my chin.

I came to a stop in front of the startled man and looked up to say, "Hello."

Game On

"Motherfuck—"

With limited options, I punched out and up with as much force as my position would allow. With maximum magical assistance, I landed a perfectly clean shot right in the knackers, like being hit with a baseball traveling at a hundred miles per hour.

The man doubled over instantly, as we all do when assaults on our manhood are directed with such intensity, and as our eyes met I head-butted him so hard I got concussion and his nose split wide open.

Dazed, but not as confused as the new eunuch, I scrambled up and tried not to let the shame of my ineptitude show. The man lifted his gun with a shaky hand as he tried to stand erect, but I knew how hard I'd punched him and that he couldn't see because of the broken nose, so I dodged to his side and slammed a punch right into the already ripped cartilage.

He screamed, I danced like a butterfly, and then got behind and stung like a bee on steroids. Wand shot forward so powerfully in my hand I thought I would dislocate my shoulder, but he was looking after me, so all was good, at least for me. My magical partner in crime whacked across the dude's ear with a nasty slap that would smart like slamming into a sheet of ice. His head whipped sideways.

I continued to jig around until I faced him, then sneered as Wand whipped out again and slapped him across the other ear.

"Haha," I taunted, enjoying myself, then I kicked his gun hand and the weapon went flying off into the dark.

As the guy tried to clear his vision and recover enough to fight, I ducked down then uppercut to his chin. He crashed backwards and I landed knee first on his stomach, knocking all the air out of him. I sat there on his ribs, bouncing like a kid having a ride on a donkey, and then poked Wand right up to his eyeball and said, "The last guy, Paul, who saw Wand this close, he lost his eye. He also had his arm blown off, then he was killed by having a knife poked through his other eye. How does that sound? You want some of that action?"

The man shook his head carefully, eyes locked on mine.

"Good, that's good. Which house?"

"One street behind us, take a left, third house on the right," he croaked hurriedly, clearly valuing his life over payday.

"How many inside?"

"Three."

"Men? Women?"

"Two men, one woman."

"Plus the girl?"

"Of course plus the girl," he sneered.

Wand darted forward, punched through his eye, his skull, his brain, out the other side, and deep into the road surface until my fist bumped against the eye socket.

"Don't be cheeky." With a grunt, I yanked Wand out, cleaned him up, and with a nod of approval I let him rest up in the warmth of my pocket.

With my palms hurting, my knees feeling like glass was under the skin, and my heart weary from the killing, I stood and went to get Steve and Vicky.

Now we could begin.

Suddenly Cautious

Knowing from experience that it was easy to screw up once you thought you were winning, I was as careful returning to the hole in the fence as I had been going in. The guard could have been lying, although I doubted it, or someone could have come out for a wander and I'd trigger the alarm. So although I ached to run back and get this going, I remained stealthy and vigilant. Every action was annoyingly slow, but I remained a consummate professional, although I did consider running back and nicking the dead dude's smokes. Ah well, another opportunity lost.

With my body screaming to run, to get this thing underway quick-smart, I fought back the urgency and eventually made it to the fence. Once through, I reached the car in seconds and was pleased to find Steve and Vicky emerge from the scrub like professionals. I'd never have known they were there.

"You good?" asked Steve.

"All good. There were two on guard, both taken care of. There's two men and a woman in the house.

Sunshine is in a room somewhere inside, we'll have to find her once we get that far."

"Let's go," said Vicky.

"Wait," I said, trying to be gentle but knowing I had to make things very clear. "Do not go in all manic and rushing about like this will be easy. If we do anything stupid, they can hurt Sunshine. What will we do then?"

"I'll rip their fucking heads off," growled Steve.

"And risk them killing her? A simple gun pointed at her head and we're useless."

Both paused to think, something they hadn't considered, assuming once we knew where she was this would be easy. The tough stuff hadn't even begun yet.

"So what's the plan?" asked Steve.

"The plan is we need to know where she is, what the set-up is like, and then decide how to extract her before they get to her. We need to draw them away so one of us can get Sunshine while the others deal with the kidnappers. So go slow, stay quiet, and find out what you can without them seeing or hearing us. Understood?" Both nodded. "This is it, guys. We cannot mess up. We have to get this right or they'll kill her. No screw-ups," I warned.

"Why are you looking at me?" asked a petulant Vicky, hands on hips, eyebrows raised.

"No reason. I have to look somewhere."

"Good. So let's do this thing." Vicky marched off.

"Um, Vicky," I said, rolling my eyes, "it's this way." I pointed to the fence.

"I know that," she snapped, turning around then storming forward, arms swinging, arse wobbling.

"That's my girl," said Steve proudly.

I groaned inwardly. It would be a bloody miracle if anyone came out of this alive.

Three Little Pigs

Much as we wanted to run there and huff and puff and blow the house down, I gave the team a another pep talk before we went through the fence, warning them once more about the issues we faced and the danger Sunshine was in. One thing went wrong, she was either dead or we were. We had one shot at this and one shot only.

"So do not screw it up," I warned.

They both looked at me like I was an idiot.

"You remember she's my daughter, right?" asked Steve.

"I remember. But I know you, and I certainly know Vicky. You are impulsive." Again with the funny looks. "What?"

"Arthur, you're the most impulsive person I know," said Vicky.

"Apart from you and Steve, you mean?"

"Um, maybe."

"Exactly. So if I'm suggesting caution, then you two better believe we need it. When we get there, take it slow and easy. We have the rest of the night. They might be onto us by now, chances are that's likely, but we have them. They don't know what's happening, so we still have the element of surprise on our side. I check the front, you two go around the sides, meet up at the rear, then I'll come get you. Do not try anything on your own."

"Roger that," said Vicky, saluting.

"You got it, boss," said Steve.

I studied them both for a moment, trying to figure out why they were following my lead and doing as they were told. They were being responsible as they wanted me to lead them, to take control. Steve knew his limitations. Only problem being, he didn't know mine. And I was out of my depth here and totally winging it.

We ducked through the broken fence and I led the way, conscious of everything, unnerved by the timber skeletons, the ghost town vibe of unfinished roads and pavements that had yet to see foot traffic. These places gave me the creeps at the best of times. Disposable houses for disposable people, here to boost the coffers of those already rich, cheap construction disguised as something it wasn't. It'd be gone before the Victorian terraces that were still standing strong, it just didn't have the same curb appeal.

No cats, no rats, no nothing. Dead inside, just like me.

The air was humid, no breeze here, everything weighted and still, the only sound our breathing. Even that was muted, all of us trying not to make a sound. We took a circuitous route, just in case, and not because

I got lost and couldn't remember what the dead dude had said, until eventually we came to the correct street.

How did I know? Not because of the directions given, but because it was a veritable battleground of emotions vying for dominance. I could only imagine what it was like inside the house, and wondered how her captors hadn't killed each other by now or merely wandered off, forgetting why they were even here.

One moment I was ready to run right in, Wand blazing, the next I felt meek and unsure of myself. Then I became angry, but soon that too faded and I was left empty of heart, uncaring one way or another, just another job. Only my pride kept me from going home and to bed.

Steve and Vicky fared much the same judging by their expressions, but we fought it, and we won through, slowly attuning to the changes, letting them wash over but leave us unaffected. It was the knowing, that's what saved us. We knew we were being messed with, and once we acknowledged it and made peace with the vying emotions, the need to blurt out truths about one another, we could master it, lock this thing down. It was all a matter of awareness, about being strong, knowing our abilities gave us permission to be our true selves.

Or maybe Sunshine sensed our presence and let us off the hook, or her vibrations didn't resonate with us as we were finally here. Her saviors, or her executioners. Only time would tell.

Recon Time

There was zero sign of life. If you walked by, you would never know there was anyone inside. No light, no noise, no nothing. We crept closer until we split up, and I moved beside the building, a mock-Tudor construction with cheap brick, and wood stuck on to make it look "olde worlde." It did not work.

The windows were shut, covered with heavy black material of some sort on the inside, same upstairs by the looks of it. The door was solid wood, or fake solid wood anyway, and there wasn't even a letterbox to peek through, rather, there was a mailbox at the end of the short garden-to-be, currently little but building junk and clay—good luck growing much in that.

There were no exterior lights either, so next to nothing to see. Was this the right house? Yes, it was, I could feel it, sense the fear, the confusion, the inexplicable strangeness in the air.

Right up at the window, I cupped my hands and tried to get a glimpse inside but got nothing, just blackness. No crack, no hint of light or activity. How was I supposed to know who was where if I couldn't see anything?

With nothing else to do, I wandered around to the rear, checking for windows and a break in the blackout, but it was the same.

I found Vicky and Steve at the end of the garden, crouched against a new fence, staring up at the house.

"You get anything?" I asked.

"Nothing," said Steve. "It's locked down tight. What now?"

"What now?" I mused, then inspiration hit. I pulled out Wand and grinned at them both.

"I thought you said no going in blasting?" asked Vicky, her eyes sparkling at the thought.

"I did, oh tiny little troublemaker, but Wand isn't just good for blasting, are you?"

"No, although it is my favorite bit," he replied.

"Mine too."

"Is he doing it now?" asked Steve to Vicky. "Is he talking to Wand?"

"Of course. Who else would he be talking to while staring at a stick?" asked Vicky.

"Just asking."

I raised my hand, felt the transference of power from me to him, then relaxed my grip. For a moment, Wand rested there, then he lifted and darted forward out of sight as he shot up then disappeared down a stove pipe.

"Damn, we should have thought of that," said Steve.

"Going down a pipe?" I asked.

"Yeah, why not?"

"Because they aren't big enough for grown men. Now, maybe a woman in miniature could manage it," I mused, staring at Vicky and smiling.

She punched me in the side of my head.

"Ow!" I rubbed at my temple then said, "Wait, incoming transmission." I lay down on the dirt and closed my eyes, let Wand's sight become my sight, his experience become mine.

Trust me, it sucks being a stick.

Familiar Sight

My sight turned inward and the strangest feeling crept over me, like I was being watched. But I was the watcher, a voyeur, linked to my familiar, to Wand, until the boundaries became so blurred that holding on to a sense of self became a battle only a mighty wizard like me could maintain for any length of time.

With a sudden stabbing pain, my eyes rolled up in my head and I felt stiff, wooden, very stick-like. But free. Ah, such freedom. Whizzing through the air, feeling the wind against my skin, or my wood, anyway, it tingled in the most enjoyable of ways. I could smell the smoke of fire, and I panicked. I would burn, but I had to remember I was not made of wood and there was no smoke coming from the pipe, so this was just from a fire built many days earlier, the cloying smell lingering. And anyway, I had no nose, so how was I smelling anything at all? Wand sure was a funny creature, and no mistake.

All was blackness, with a hint of light at the end of what felt like a very long tunnel. I whizzed down, or we did, or he did, I was already lost to this strange conjoining, my familiar becoming as much me as I he.

I saw through eyes that were not eyes, but rather a magical sense of everything all around me, seeing in all directions yet in no direction at all. It was dizzying, it made me feel sick, and it confused the hell out of me as who can see everywhere at once? How does that even work? The human mind is not meant to experience such things, however, and if I tried to figure it out I would get nothing but a headache, so I relaxed best I could, went with it, and let the sense of seeing all wash over me until it became a knowing, a feeling, an experience as much as anything visible.

What I saw was rather unexpected.

Confusion

Wand hovered in the shadows of the wood burner, having squeezed through a vent, scoping out the room without having to move. The vantage point was low, and I saw the entire room as though through a fisheye lens.

It was well-furnished in a generic style, all plastic lamps and plastic looking furniture. Boring pictures hung perfectly straight on perfectly flat, magnolia walls, the show home doing a great job of featuring how boring it would be to live in a house devoid of any character, zero redeeming features. But hey, it was brand spanking new, would give its owners a sense of safety, keeping the nasty people out, and that's how citizens slept at night—by refusing to believe in all the bad stuff that lurked, like Wand, in the shadows.

Sitting on a plush sofa were a man and woman, seemingly watching something entertaining on a laptop perched on several books on a long coffee table. They chuckled every so often, nudged each other, and appeared relaxed, lost to their show. On the table were several guns, two walkie-talkies, and a veritable mountain of snacks, many demolished. They clearly weren't too concerned about anyone coming, assumed the scouts were doing their job, and by the looks of it there was no arrangement for those outside to report in regularly, at least that was my hope.

Where was the girl, and the other kidnapper? Why were they so chilled? Weren't they meant to be on edge, alert for Steve trying to get his daughter back? No, they believed he was with me and Vicky, far away, grubbing about for cash to pay them off. Ha, we'd show them.

Wand edged out from his hiding place, slid along the chemical-laden carpet, and made it to the door. He checked the hallway, or we did, as I felt like I was there, like the rough carpet was rubbing against my belly, and I gave in and scratched at my stomach even as I took in the rest of the house. The hall matched the living room, decorated simply, but well presented to show the kind of life you too could have for an astronomical amount of money.

Wand checked the dining room, the kitchen, and a downstairs cloakroom. All were empty, just a few telltale signs of temporary habitation, nothing more.

He went upstairs.

The landing was much like the hall, the bathroom the same.

The first bedroom was empty apart from a single bed and a chest of drawers and more pictures. Bedroom two was next. Wand paused outside the door and we listened with non ears to the sounds emanating from within. An argument? A man, and was that a girl? It was hard to tell as the voices were muffled and low, as if angry but whispered at the same time. Was there someone else here? Was this Sunshine and the other kidnapper? Was he doing something despicable to her? Wand pushed gently against the door but it wouldn't budge.

If he opened it, he'd give the game away, so he retreated silently, hovering at waist height as he headed to bedroom number three. Inside was a large bed with crumpled sheets, clothes strewn over another chest of drawers, a wardrobe with floor-to-ceiling mirrors partially open revealing nothing but dead space and coat hangers like insects waiting to crawl out and make a mockery of the suburban dream.

I felt Wand's intent, had the same urge myself. To barge into the room, blast the bad guy, and free the girl. But we didn't know exactly what was happening in there, or what would be done to her if he made such a move, so I sent my will through the ether. Wand acknowledged my message with a dip of his tip and zoomed down the stairs, shot across the living room carpet, and up the stove pipe so fast I almost blacked out.

I felt the familiar warm wood slam into my hand, let my eyes roll down, and stared at my friend with a grin.

Turning to Steve and Vicky, I said, "Let's go get the girl."

We Make Our Move

I must have zoned out, and I really couldn't be fucked with this any longer. Some little brat got herself kidnapped because she wouldn't behave, why should that concern me?

Of all the things I could be doing, like admiring my kitchen or cuddling up next to my new wife, here I was at the arse end of the world, risking everything, my future, my eternity, for a child that didn't deserve it.

I chuckled as I snapped out of it, and slapped Vicky and Steve on the back to return them to reality.

"Whoa, that was nasty. I was all ready to jack this in and go to the pub or summit," said Steve, shaking his head and grinning nervously.

"I was thinking really bad things, Steve, about Sunshine." A tear fell from Vicky's puffy eyes.

"It's okay, hun, just her messing with us all."

"How's she doing this?" I asked, wondering how she could possibly change people's emotions like this, and astounded that her kidnappers still had hold of her when she could clearly bend them to her will by affecting how they felt about the whole sorry charade.

"Told you, she's special." Steve rubbed at his perfect beard, looking uncomfortable, like there was something he wasn't telling us.

"Dude, if you have anything to say, then now is certainly the time to say it. We're going into that house to get her, but it could get ugly, you know that, so anything you can say to make this go more smoothly, to minimize the risk to Sunshine, then I think we have the right to know." My eyes narrowed as I studied this handsome man, so close in age to me I wondered how he looked so young and full of vitality, and then I understood something for the first time. Shifters really were very different to us. They manipulated their entire body chemistry, their actual DNA, so what's eradicating a few wrinkles when you can do that?

But there was something missing from this puzzle, from this whole toying with everyone's emotions. It boiled down to one thing. You couldn't bloody do it.

Something else was going on, and I got the impression Steve either knew, or was holding back on certain information.

"There's nothing," said Steve, rubbing at his jaw like that was how he got it so square. "Can we please just go get my daughter? I know it's hard, that what she's doing is freaking you out, me too, haha, but once we get her, save her, everything will return to normal."

I shrugged. "If you say so, buddy. If you say so."

And with that, we marched toward certain death. Only time would tell who's death that happened to be.

Time for Wizarding

Being a wizard is awesome. You get to fool around with cool stuff, you get to if not understand then at least experience the most wondrous energy in the entire universe, and you get to blast the bad guys, which always rocks.

Plus, now and then, you get to be a little dramatic.

And so it was, after some nifty lock picking, that I stood in the living room in front of two rather surprised kidnappers and glowered at them. Wand was clutched tight in my right hand, glowing with all the menace he could muster. My other hand shone bright and deadly as I stood with arms spread, my will flooding my system with magic of the most deadly variety.

They lunged for the guns on the table but I cast them aside with a glance, sending them clattering into the fireplace. Was it really going to be this easy?

"You kidnapped a little girl," I growled.

The couple exchanged confused looks, then nodded at each other as if coming to an agreement. "No, you've got it all wrong, it isn't like that," the man said, eyeing up the weapons.

"That's right. You don't understand. Now you're here I guess it doesn't matter. I'm glad, actually. This isn't what I signed up for, not at all."

The woman went to move but I wagged my finger and said, "No you don't. You stay right there. You people make me sick. What, thought it would be easy, did you? Take a little girl from her mother, kill her mother, and then what? Rough her up, terrify her?" I fought for control, but the thought of them scaring Sunshine was too much.

"You don't understand," yelled the man. "You've got it all wrong," he blurted, nervous as he saw how pissed I was.

"I think it's you who doesn't understand, buddy. You know how this goes?" I asked.

"We know," he said with a sigh.

"Good."

And with that I let loose, gave them exactly what they deserved.

Wand spat out lumpy magic so dark and despicable I almost vomited. Great gobbets of fat, misshapen, primal nothingness, each more deadly than the last. It wasn't showy, there were no bright colors, the time for drama was gone.

As the absence of all matter, a true nothingness, hit the still-seated couple, I watched for a moment as the emptiness devoured them. Cavities appeared in their chests, parts of their heads were chewed away, dissolved, taken like they'd never been there, and they screamed the most pitiful screams as I walked past them and out into the hallway, not even giving them the satisfaction of an audience to watch them die.

I spun as the front door slammed open. Steve and Vicky ran in, eyes wide, hyped on adrenaline, and I muttered to myself about their ineptitude before saying, "I thought I told you I'd handle this?"

"We heard screams," said Vicky, like that was a good excuse.

"Yes, you did. Well, come on, let's go get her."

We ran up the stairs as fast as possible. I hoped it wasn't too late.

Um...

With little choice, and knowing time was of the essence and that there was still a good chance Sunshine could be dead, I burst through the bedroom door, steeling myself for what we'd encounter. Steve and Vicky pushed in right behind me, putting me off-balance, and interfering with my moves, which was exactly why I didn't want them here. I got it though, this was his little girl.

We stopped just inside the room and I stared around in confusion. There was a dead man on the bed, a knife in his hand, his throat slit. Blood oozed from the wound, thick and jelly-like; the sheets were soaked through with his life-force.

Sat next to him, hands in lap, covered in the blood that had sprayed from the man's throat, was a blond child, pale of features beneath the gore, utterly serene, and not at all what I'd expected.

"You're a..." I turned to Steve, confused. "It's a..."

Steve frowned, as confused as me, and Vicky shoved her way between us and said, "What, what is it?"

"See for yourself," I said.

"It's a boy," she blurted.

We stood there, staring at a boy of about twelve, flummoxed by the turn of events.

"Hello, Daddy," said the child.

"Sunshine?" asked Steve as he stepped forward and went to the boy still sitting calmly.

"I prefer Sonny now, if that's okay with you?" The boy smiled, and what a smile it was. It lit up the room, made me feel all warm and fuzzy inside, like everything would be all right in the world.

"You're a boy?" asked Steve, his brow furrowed as he tried to get his head around things.

"For a little bit. And you ruined everything."

With that, Sonny leapt to his feet, screamed like a banshee, and sped from the room with his arms flailing about. Within moments, an almighty clattering could be heard from downstairs as it sounded like he was ripping the kitchen apart with his bare hands.

"What's going on?" asked Vicky, staring from Steve to me like I had any idea.

"I think he shifted into being a boy. Um, she shifted, now she's a boy. I've got a son." Steve smiled, then walked out to go find out what was happening.

"Arthur?"

"Yes, my tiny sidekick?"

"Does this seem right to you? What's happening here?"

"I have no bloody idea, but it's not good, I can tell that much."

"Sunshine is a boy now. He made that man kill himself. What did he mean we'd spoiled it?"

"I don't know. Why don't we go ask?"

Vicky got close then looked up at me and whispered, "He scares me. A young child scares me. All the things he can do, it isn't right."

"I know, I feel the same. No way is this a simple kidnapping. I think maybe he did it to himself." I tried to figure it all out, but knew I couldn't. Sunshine, or Sonny, had done something, and I got the impression it was something truly awful that would scar the child for ever. I hoped it wouldn't do the same to Steve.

"Come on, let's go see what all the noise is about." I took Vicky's hand, she was shaking, and led her out of the room.

The corpse stank. There is never dignity in death, just bodily fluids and an urge to look away.

Calm Down

"Everything's ruined. All of it," shouted Sonny as he rampaged around the kitchen, yanking open cupboard doors before slamming them shut again. He moved on to drawers, pulled out the few bits and pieces in them and threw them around the room mindless of who they hit.

"Calm down. What happened?" asked a flustered Steve. He chased after Sonny, tried to ease the boy's edginess, but the child was wild, had a faraway look in his eyes like he wasn't really here with us.

Emotions built, or rather they ceased to exist, and as he got more angry so I became increasingly dismissive of the whole thing. I wanted to blurt out exactly what I thought of him, tell the truth. That he was being a brat and didn't he know we'd risked everything to rescue him? I slapped my hand over my mouth before I said a word though, as the last thing I wanted was a battle with a kid. You don't hurt children, no matter what, but I was not myself, he was affecting us all, and I didn't trust myself to remain in control.

"You spoiled it all, that's what happened," screamed Sonny as he turned on Steve and got right up in his face. Spittle flew as he snarled, "I had a plan, it was working. Then you spoiled it. Why are you here?"

Steve looked at his son, daughter, whatever, in confusion. "You were kidnapped. I got a call for a ransom so we came to rescue you. What do you think has been happening? You're upset, confused, come and sit down." Steve put an arm gently on the boy's shoulder, and at the touch he seemed to relax.

"It all went wrong. Why did they do this? We had an agreement. I didn't know they'd asked you for money. I'm sorry." Sonny broke down, huge fat tears fell from oversized eyes as his shoulders sagged and he stood in the middle of the kitchen looking small and afraid and very confused.

"Come on," said Vicky as she moved closer to them, "tell us all about it. I'm your Aunty Vicky by the way."

"Hi," sniffled Sonny.

"And I'm Arthur," I shouted from across the room, keeping well clear in case the child did anything daft.

As if he could read my thoughts, he suddenly became animated and began to shake his limbs like he had to expend the energy. His body cracked and his muscles spasmed as he changed form rapidly, morphing from one creature to another, back and forth between a human child and a dog, a cat, a badger like his father, and on and on it went, faster than I could keep up with. The child screamed, a piercing wail that tore at my heart until it felt like it would remain broken, never repair. A deep, terrible anguish, telling of the pain endured, the sorrow of it all.

And then it stopped, the child snapped to attention, and there was an angelic girl with beautiful blond hair ruined somewhat by the red taint of blood and her own sweat and tears. Her arms hung limp by her sides and her head was bowed, but when she lifted her eyes to look at us we all gasped. Such a beautiful child. It was impossible not to stare, to be moved by her beauty. Was this her true self, or had she changed her features?

"Daddy?"

"Hey, honey, it's okay. Daddy's here now."

Sunshine launched at Steve and he hoisted her off the ground and hugged her tight, never wanting to let her go.

"Being a boy felt horrible," said Sunshine with a weak smile. I knew exactly how she felt.

"What do we do now?" whispered Vicky.

I shrugged. I had no idea.

Munchies

Steve ushered Sunshine over to the breakfast bar and hoisted her up onto a stool. She looked so small, all gangly and out-of-proportion after a growth spurt where her limbs had grown faster than the rest of her. Steve moved to the kitchen nook and leaned on the counter to look at his daughter.

"Hey," he said brightly, the love clear.

"Hey yourself," she chuckled, her eyes sparkling.

Vicky reappeared with an armful of snacks from the living room, a look of distaste on her face. She glared at me. Maybe even glowered.

"What?"

"Did you have to do that to them?"

"Yes," I said, defiant.

She dumped the snacks on the counter and for a while everything felt almost normal as we dove in and stuffed our faces. I was famished, and clearly not the only one. We munched through the food in record time and nobody said a word, just eyed each other and wondered where to start in discovering what this sorry mess was all about.

Sunshine seemed content now. She was relaxed, a hint of a smile on plump pink lips. Her aquiline nose twitched as she opened a new pack and sniffed. With a look of delight, she stuffed the Bourbons into her mouth and kept on going until the bag was empty. Then she tilted her head back and upended the crumbs into her open mouth.

Everyone laughed, we couldn't help it. It was such an innocent act, how children should be, and I guess we'd all assumed such behavior was beyond her. We had to remember, this was a child. Inexperienced in the ways of the world, with an awful lot to learn.

"Now, I think you owe me an explanation, don't you?" said Steve, his voice stern, at odds with his usual breezy way of talking.

"S'pose." Sunshine pouted and rummaged through the empty packets.

"All gone. Time to tell us what happened."

"Oh, it's such a mess," moaned Sunshine, putting her head in her hands. I was certain she was being dramatic on purpose, and when I caught the hint of a sly smile through her hands, I knew she was one to watch, that she could tie Steve around her little finger with a flutter of her eyelids.

"Just tell us. We've all been through a lot to get you. We saw the boat, we saw your mum."

"It wasn't meant to happen like that, it all went wrong." Sunshine broke down, huge sobs wracked her body as she crumpled from the stool.

I lunged forward and caught her before she hit the floor. She hung on tight, her thin arms wrapped around my neck. Her tears were warm. They were not the tears of an innocent.

I looked to Steve and Vicky for help, but they held their hands up as if to say I'd have to hold on until Sunshine decided unkempt old wizards weren't the best for cuddles.

Sunshine continued to cry, and I did my utmost to comfort her, but I felt uneasy, awkward, and God help me, a little scared of this frail girl clinging to me for comfort in her hour of need.

An Explanation

Several minutes later, and with Sunshine still holding on, I knew she was avoiding having to explain. So I whispered to her, I felt her body stiffen, and then she let go and dropped down to the floor. Her bare feet slapped on the cheap tiles.

Without looking at anyone, she moved over to the dining table and sat on a chair covered in striped purple material of some sort. It was truly awful.

"Well, come and sit down if you want to hear about it," she snapped.

"What did you say to her?" asked Steve.

"Just said I'd break her neck if she didn't tell us. That I'd use Wand and blast her to goo. That kind of thing."

"Dude, not cool!"

"I'm joking. Come on, let's hear this."

With much trepidation, we each took a chair and sat, waiting to hear exactly what this young girl had done, what trouble she had caused, what lives she had made forfeit.

"I just wanted to be normal, to be left alone," Sunshine said softly.

"Course you did, love," said Steve the doting father whose daughter could do no wrong.

"So I made a deal with some people who looked after me. Mum refused to ever let me do anything at all cool, we were always on that stupid boat or some stupid place out in the middle of nowhere. I never got to see anyone, play with anyone my age. It sucked."

"I know it did. Your mum thought it was for the best."

"And now she's dead." Sunshine broke down again, the tears flowed fast and free, and I knew this would take a while.

"So what did you do?" asked Steve.

"I arranged to get the hell out of there!"

"Sunshine, you watch your language."

"Sorry, Dad. Anyway, I'd had a guts full."

"Sunshine, I'm warning you."

"What, I am twelve, you know? You wanna hear this or not?"

"Just keep it clean," Steve sighed, rubbing at his face repeatedly until the skin became blotchy. Poor guy, this was a lot to handle.

"Some of the people on the boat were as fed up as me. They'd been around for years, supported Mum, you know that, Dad, but she went weird, really bossy, and even more secretive. Wouldn't let anyone do anything. So I made a deal. They'd help me escape if I promised to keep a low profile and not get into trouble."

"And where were you going to do that?" asked Steve.

"I was gonna come and live with you, of course." Sunshine beamed at her father; she clearly adored him.

"Really? Oh, wow, that would be so cool."

I think they were perfect for each other, one little kid, one big one.

"Yeah, and when Mum turned up we could tell her to shove it."

"Watch your... Ah, forget it. So you made a deal, what then?"

"It was going perfectly, we were all set, we were gonna put everyone on one of the small boats and then simply let them make their way back to shore. But they got wind of it, everyone freaked out a little, and then Mum went and took the keys and locked herself away."

"Let me guess," I said. "One of your people lost the plot and shifted, right?"

"Yeah, idiot. He shifted and he was always a dolt, couldn't control himself when changed, and he got in to Mum, they had a big fight, and by the time I arrived she was dead. The others went nuts at him, and were acting all strange, all secretive like, then they fought and then the boat came and we left."

"So you had another boat?" asked Steve.

"Just in case. A couple of others were in on it too. Um, they're outside actually, keeping watch."

"Not any more, they aren't," I mumbled.

"I'm sorry, I really am, but what's going on? We were waiting for it to be safe to come find you. The others said you were being watched and it was hard to get you away, that it all had to be timed just right. They said we couldn't just turn up as about a million shifters would try to get me, but once things settled down, once I was with you and just living with you, then it would be okay? It will be, won't it? Tell me it will all be okay?"

Steve plastered a smile on his face to hide his worry and moved to cuddle Sunshine. "Everything will be fine, honey, you'll see. Everything will be just fine."

We all knew it wouldn't. Sunshine had done a foolish thing, but was unaware of what her supposed rescuers had done, used her to make some quick cash, or at least try, but even with that problem solved there was sure to be plenty more to take its place.

The shifter community would be out in force, and after one thing. The most powerful shifter there had ever been. A girl of twelve who just wanted to go to school and hang out with her dad, watch TV, meet boys, and be moody. Just like all the other kids.

We had our work cut out, that was for sure.

And Now?

Steve and Sunshine went upstairs to pack up the few things she'd brought. Seemingly, she was unperturbed by the guy in the bedroom she'd manipulated so he would kill himself. Why had she made him do that if she was unaware of the fake kidnapping? One question amongst many others, another one I assumed I wouldn't get the answer to. She was a law unto herself, different to others, and dangerous because of it. But just a child.

Vicky and I sat at the table and stared at each other.

"Well?" she said with a pout.

"Well what? He's your boyfriend, what do you want to do?"

"They can't come home with me, not with the girls, not with people looking for her. You heard her, they put people on one of the small boats, they'll be out looking for her and won't know what happened, that her mum is dead." Vicky checked the room, as if speaking about it could make Sunshine go off the deep end.

"You're right. Man, I can't believe Steve kept this quiet. You okay about that?"

"Not sure. I understand his reasons, but I thought we were close, that he trusted me. He should have told me."

"Guess he was being sensible, keeping her secret, keeping it secret who he really was. Kept him and her safer. Maybe. Dunno. They do like to play their games."

"But I can keep a secret," moaned Vicky, getting up and pacing the room.

I raised an eyebrow when she wasn't looking. Vicky was the worst person ever at keeping a secret. It's like it burned a hole in her head until she blurted it out to someone.

This was a major mess, and I truly didn't know what was for the best. Who would be after her? Were there shifter communities who wanted her for themselves? Would they hurt her? Would they take her? Would others come for her? Did they even know? The shifters, unlike Vicky, were good at keeping their secrets. I'd never heard specifics about Sunshine, just hints and rumors that there was a powerful child shifter somewhere out there. Nobody would be able to connect such vagaries to Sunshine if she kept a low profile.

What about Cerberus? They'd kept awfully quiet lately and I didn't like that. They'd left me alone, I had no idea who was running things now, and wondered if they would try to take Sunshine. They wanted all the artifacts, didn't trust the magic users with them, what would they think of a young girl with seemingly limitless powers? How would that be classed? What would they do with her if they got her? I needed to find out such things, needed to be sure she could try to make a go of it.

The more I thought about it, the more I realized I had plenty of detective work to do before she could come back to the normal world. Ha, the normal world, like there's any such thing.

Off We Go

It wasn't long before the newly reunited father and daughter came crashing down the stairs making such a racket Vicky and I dashed out into the hall ready to blast and glower only to find they were grinning and laughing. Guess dead dudes in your bedroom are less distressing for shifters than other prepubescents.

Still, they were in good spirits, so what's an aging wizard and his equally aging sidekick to do but join in the jollies and up their game?

And so it was, without further ado, apart from a call to the Cleaner and a begrudging yes to an increased bill because of the distance and mess involved, that the four musketeers got the hell out of dodge. Actually, it was worse than dodge, it was the new burbs, where souls died, kids became trapped in their houses because the gardens seemed to shrink year after year, and adults slowly lost the ability to do anything but drive cars and sit on their bums. The art of walking soon became lost in these places, they weren't near anything to walk to, so why bother?

Speaking of cars, we soon made it to ours, and Vicky got in the front with me riding shotgun while the other two got in back.

We didn't discuss a thing, didn't sit down and talk about what we were going to do. With a nod from me, Vicky drove us away from what must have been the strangest kidnapping I'd ever heard about, let alone been involved in.

I'd have liked a little more action.

Making Plans

Vicky headed back to the city. It would take a while, so I had plenty of time to think. We all needed to talk about this, but I had to remind myself that Steve, bless his heart, may have been a tough guy when it came to fighting and stuff, unafraid of anything or anyone, anyone other than Vicky, but then she scared everyone a little, but he wasn't the deepest of thinkers. He'd be content he had Sunshine, even though she'd got her mum killed, and would accept he'd have to face trouble once word got out.

He didn't go in for thinking ahead, planning, or considering what might happen, which I guess was why Sunshine was kept with her mother, but this was serious and if he was willing to risk everything by just winging it then I'd have to do the thinking for him.

So while Vicky squinted at the bleak road, and Steve and Sunshine gabbled non-stop in the back like excited kids, I rested my head and I thought.

What was the truth about all of this? How had Sunshine convinced them to go along with her plan to make a break for it? They were people supposedly dedicated to protecting her, weren't they? Thoroughly vetted by her mother. Guess they got bored, could be convinced otherwise for a payout, even if they'd planned on getting the cash from Steve. Sunshine had made the suggestion to them to get her out of there, they'd gone along with it as they'd agreed between them to offer her for ransom. Okay, makes sense, so far so good.

Had Sunshine manipulated them into helping her, affected their emotions to help her out? Maybe, maybe not. Either way, they were still on the ball enough to ask for money, so it wasn't like she had them constantly under her influence.

What next?

This whole messing with people's emotions thing. It was scary verging on terrifying. She could do it to me, someone wise to the ways of magical influence, and she could seemingly affect people all over the city. It was something that truly made her a liability, that made her need to be kept safe, protected, and more importantly happy.

But how many twelve-year-olds are always happy? So that would be a major issue however you looked at it, and was clearly why she'd mostly been kept out at sea. Maybe until now the distance from land and people kept her influence to a minimum, or maybe she'd simply never been in such a heightened emotional state before so hadn't affected others not very close? I didn't have all the answers to that, didn't even know where to start asking Sunshine as my guess was she wouldn't know.

And who would be after her? Everyone? Sure, anyone with dubious intent, anyone who wanted power, anyone who liked the exotic, they'd all want such a child, a creature unlike any other. Hopefully few people knew about her, and most were dead, but there would be some that would find out soon enough and might decide to make a play for the girl.

And I still had Cerberus playing on my mind. What would their role be in all this?

I yawned, closed my eyes, and prepared for a doze.

"Oh no you don't," said Vicky just as I began to drift off. "We have things to talk about."

"Really, like what?" I asked as I lifted a heavy eyelid.

"Don't get smart with me, mister." Vicky glanced in the rearview and I realized all was quiet. "They're asleep so we can talk. What are we going to do, Arthur? Who will be after her? Where can she go? What if she makes everyone do what she wants? Can she do that?"

"All in good time. Don't get your knickers in a twist. I've just been thinking about it all and I think I have the solution, at least for now."

"You do? Awesome." Vicky grinned at me. "You always have the best plans."

"I sure do."

"Is it cunning?" she asked.

"Is my hat nice."

"Yes!"

"Then let me rest, we'll talk later."

"Roger that."

I sighed at Vicky's nonsense, but couldn't help smiling. She was starting to grow on me. Like mold.

More Questions

"Something isn't right," I grumbled as I opened my eyes only to find the dawn sky unusually clear, the motorway busy, and I wasn't dead, which is always the best way to wake up in the morning.

"Just worked that out, did you?" Vicky grinned, probably because she thought she was being funny, but she wasn't, because I was the funny one, she just looked funny.

"I don't mean Sunshine. Okay, I do, but there's something else, there has to be. Something else is happening that we aren't aware of. I can feel it in my bones. My wizard senses are tingling, trying to tell me something, but I don't know what. We need to pull over, all have a chat."

"Are you sure that's a good idea?"

"Unless you want wee in the car it is." I clenched my bony buttocks, maybe that would stop my bladder bursting for a few seconds.

"I meant having a chat. She's been through a lot, has been taken advantage of, poor child, maybe we should leave it, not force the issue."

"Vicky, stop it. When you act sensible it freaks me out."

"I am a mother. I know children, and I know sometimes it's best to let them dictate the pace, that way they tell you things properly, because they actually want to. They don't like being made to do things that are uncomfortable for them."

"I know, and I get that, but if Sunshine is to stand even a remote chance of getting through this without something monumentally terrible happening, or happening again, as her mum getting killed is one hell of a burden to bear, then we need to talk, and we need to do it now."

"I guess."

The car remained silent, apart from the sounds of snoring from the back seat until we found a service station and Vicky slowed then wiggled around the bendy roads that led to the parking area.

"That way, go that way," I shouted.

"Where, where?" Vicky screamed, panicked, as she continued to head into the parking area for buses and trucks.

"Over there, through that tiny gap." I pointed at the narrow road that led to the main car park close to the service station. Vicky swerved, a car honked behind us, and she shot forward, changed up a gear, then slammed on the brakes and skidded to a stop between two cars, lining up perfectly.

"Smooth," I congratulated.

"Ta." Vicky beamed.

"Don't know why every service station in the country makes it so hard to find the right way to get into the damn place. It's like they want to confuse sleepy drivers." I pondered this mystery for a moment, then turned to the back and asked, "Everyone awake?"

"How could we not be?" asked Steve, rubbing at his head where he'd slammed into the window.

"You are so cool, Vicky," said Sunshine, staring in awe.

"Aw, thanks, sweetie." Vicky turned to me and said, "See?"

"See what?"

"That I'm cool."

"She's twelve, she doesn't know what cool is."

"What, and old men are a better judge of what's cool?" asked Sunshine with a giggle.

"Let's just get out, I need a bathroom break, and fast."

"He's always grumpy when he wakes up. And the rest of the time too," whispered Vicky as she winked at Sunshine. The girl giggled, then I ran for the bathroom.

I don't know what it was about getting older and how water ran through my system. It's like I didn't absorb any liquids inside my body or something, and that I actually produced more than went in. Such are the problems of downtrodden wizards throughout the ages, but I seemed to be singled out for punishment in every way imaginable.

After I took care of business and had a good wash then had my hands half blown off by a new hand dryer capable of flaying skin, I sauntered out into the main area where people milled about looking dazed, unkempt, or stressed. Everyone was drinking coffee, munching on fast food, or playing on the gambling machines. Why do people feel the sudden urge to waste their money on these machines when they never play them anywhere else? It's weird. I also really wanted to have a go, but resisted as I had an addictive personality and my one overriding addiction was enough to handle as it was. Yeah, addicted to being awesome. That, and magic.

"Right, let's get something overpriced and utterly devoid of nutritional value to eat, then we can have a chat," I said brightly. "My treat."

"What is this place?" asked Sunshine, staring around in utter wonder, eyes wide, smiling brightly, trying to take everything in. Her nose twitched, her eyes darted this way and that, and she looked either ready to burst into tears or song.

We stared at each other, realizing how out of our depth we were. This was not a normal child, she wasn't from this world, she knew next to nothing about it. We had to tread carefully, be mindful, or it would definitely go horribly wrong in the most spectacular of ways.

"Remember what I said," warned Vicky.

"Yeah, I will," I replied, for once admitting that Vicky was right. Hey, everyone has to be at least once in their life.

Dirty Tables

Disgruntled, I handed over more money than was possibly fair to a dude as enthusiastic about serving as I was about paying. The food looked even less keen, so limp because it was embarrassed by the label "consumable."

"Apparently," I said in a conspiratorial tone to Sunshine, "some people actually go to these places on purpose, and enjoy the food."

"I know. Awesome, right?"

"Um, you do know I was being sarcastic, don't you?" I asked, dejected.

"Haha, got you, Uncle Arthur."

"Damn, you sure did, kid. And I'm Uncle already? That's neat."

"Neat? Haha, who says neat?"

"Why, you cheeky little... For someone who doesn't know much about the world, you seem to know a lot about how kids talk."

"Duh, there is the internet. Just because I don't go places, doesn't mean I don't talk to loads of other kids."

"You should watch out," I warned. "I bet ninety percent of the young people you think you're talking to are actually perverted men sitting in their mum's basement holding on to their, um, ah..."

"Their willies? Oh, I know all about that. Mum warned me about men, so did Dad, and I know what they do. But don't worry, I never did anything rude, and anyway, I couldn't exactly go meet them, could I?"

"No, guess not. I wonder if it's too late to send George to a boat for a few years?"

"Who's George?"

"Oh, she's my daughter. You'll love her, she's totally awesome, just like me. She's got crazy red hair, never lets anyone tell her what to do, say, or think, and always wears really nice clothes. She's perfect, as is to be expected, because I'm her dad."

"Can I meet her then?" asked Sunshine, turning serious. She held my gaze and I saw the hope, that I would give her an honest answer, not fob her off.

"I promise you will meet her, that you can settle in the snug and play video games, all night if you want, and you can meet my wife, Penelope, and see my awesome kitchen. It's got a drawer just for tea towels, and I've got this special cutlery tray that lets you—"

"Who cares about kitchens?"

"What!? Such sacrilege. Wait until you see mine, then you'll understand. The tap is a thing of beauty. Mine's on this long hose that means you can pull it out and er, um, spray water about in the sink and over the dishes and stuff. Um, you have to see it to truly appreciate it. Trust me, it's great."

"Okay, Uncle Arthur, if you say so."

Vicky and Steve smiled at me, nodded their approval at my interactions with Sunshine. Perhaps my earlier judgment had been too harsh. She seemed like a nice kid, had a good head on her shoulders, and might possibly even make it in this crazy world. I hoped so. She deserved the chance more than most, after the life she'd led. I just hoped that Steve was up to the task and we could protect her until we figured out what to do.

We sat at a dirty table, just like all the rest, so I went up to the serving counter and asked for a damp cloth to wipe it down. The kid stared at me like I hadn't spoken.

"You do know what a cloth is, don't you?"

"Yeah, sure."

"And you understand the concept of damp, as in moist, not dripping with water? Damp."

"Yeah, man, I get it."

"But you haven't."

"What?"

"Got it."

He stared at me blankly.

"Let's try this again," I said. "Can I have a damp cloth please, to wipe down the dirty table so I can eat without being even more grossed out than I am already?"

"That's our job, to clean the tables."

"Oh, okay," I beamed. "Be my guest. It's that one over there." I pointed at the table.

"Um, but I'm busy here."

I leaned forward until I could see the whites of his pimples. Quietly, I said, "Give me a fucking cloth in the next three seconds or I will—"

He dashed off then returned with a cloth. It was dry. "Try again."

He yelped a little as I leaned further forward then returned again with a cloth and waited as I took it.

"Thank you."

I didn't blame him, he was young, didn't want to be here, but it was his job and he was getting paid. Either do it properly so you have the right to moan, or let someone else earn the money.

I wiped the table then returned the cloth to the counter. He took it from me with a smile and a, "Thank you, Sir."

"You are most welcome."

Back at the table, I unwrapped my food and ate in silence like the others. It was all gone in a few minutes and we were good to go. Except we weren't. As Steve made to stand I said, "Wait, we need to talk."

"Now?" he asked.

"Steve, I love you, and you're a great friend, but you have a habit of not looking ahead. Yes, now. This is important. What are you planning to do?"

Steve sat, and looked dejected. "Not sure. Go home I guess. Make up a room for you, eh, kiddo?" Steve winked at Sunshine and nudged her in the ribs.

"Yeah, great."

"No, not great," said Vicky. "You can't do that. Is it safe? If anyone comes looking, any shifters, those who know you're her father, that's the first place they'll look."

"Yeah, guess so. What then?"

"I have a plan, a very temporary one," I warned. "But it doesn't solve the problem. Sunshine, is it okay if we ask you a few questions about your abilities? Just us, nobody else needs to know. Okay, maybe the wife and daughter, but nobody else. And let's do this outside, just to be safe."

"Sure, you can ask. But no funny business," she warned.

"Um, sure. I don't know what you mean, but no funny business."

"Cool."

We headed outside but I had to run back in for a pee. Curse this strange affliction. Maybe I needed to see a doctor.

Unexpected Answers

With the weather still freakily mild, I nonetheless put my battered leather jacket back on and checked I looked as awesome as usual. Not too bad, apart from the hair. I splashed more water on my face then left the bathroom and met the others outside.

They were sitting at a picnic bench on a lawned area; nobody else was around.

"Okay, where to start?" I mused. "Sunshine, do you know that you can affect the emotions of others?"

"Sure."

"And can you do it on purpose, or does it just happen when you are feeling extra emotional yourself?"

"If someone is very close, like next to me, then I can pretty much make them feel any way I want. But mostly it's just if I get upset, or angry, or want everyone to start telling the truth, that kind of thing. It sort of spreads, I guess. Dunno. Mum always tried to make me control myself, not get upset or cross, said I had to learn to think about other people. But it was usually just the people on the boat, or some stupid farm somewhere, not like I could do it to people miles away or anything."

We all exchanged a look. "You sure, honey?" asked Steve.

"Course. Mum would have said."

"Maybe," I mused. "If she even knew. Or maybe there's something else going on too."

"Like what?" asked Vicky.

"No idea."

"So you've never been told about your influence spreading very far?" I asked, trying not to make it sound like an interrogation.

"Nope."

"Do you know how it works?"

"Something to do with being a shifter." Sunshine shrugged her shoulders. "Dad has it too, Mum did, everyone does. Everyone who can shift, anyway."

"But that's pheromones, isn't it?" asked Vicky. "Shifters and their animal magnetism. It's the smell, the musk, they use it to draw people in, but they can't control it, and it certainly doesn't make people change their emotions. At least, er," Vicky blushed but continued, "not in the ways we're talking about."

"Mum did explain it, and she told me not to tell you, sorry Dad, but she said it went beyond the usual shifter scent. It's the same but different. I think it was down to mine being more concentrated, that I... er... well, I guess it's in the sweat, the molecules that escape into the air. She said mine were so concentrated, because everything about me is so heightened, that it doesn't take much for it to have an effect."

"I bet that's it," I said, nodding sagely as it began to make sense. "Sunshine feels something, wants something, and she lets that emotion out in numerous subtle ways. Those magical molecules get spread about, taken by the wind, distributed all over, and if they're powerful enough emotions, and maybe if the wind is blowing in the right direction, they stay grouped together, travel far and wide, and can hit even remote locations and affect people there."

"That's pretty cool," said Steve, smiling at Sunshine.

"It is," I agreed.

"No, it isn't," wailed Sunshine, face contorted, cheeks red, tears falling. "I'm a freak! I don't want to do all this weird stuff. I want to be normal. I want to go to school and not stress out that if I feel anything, get upset or angry, or anything, that I'll make everyone hate me."

Vicky scowled at me and Steve and shifted close to hug the child. Sunshine snuggled in tight and buried her head in Vicky's jumper as her body shook while she cried for a life she could never live.

The waves of her emotion hit, as I guess they had been all along, but this time there was nothing subtle about any of it. I jumped to my feet, Steve too, and we ran off with our hands over our mouths before we told Sunshine the truth about everything we were thinking. Guess Steve had plenty on his mind he'd rather she not hear, same as me, because boy was he running fast.

The power faded as we turned the corner around the side of the building, until I could force it down, control myself. Steve was waiting for me, looking worried.

"I was about to ruin our relationship for good," he said. "I love her but I was gonna tell her some truths that would make her hate me for always."

"No, she wouldn't. Poor kid must be used to it from her mum. I bet she's heard all sorts of horrible things. Everyone thinks badly of everyone now and then, it's human nature, so I'm sure she'd forgive you."

"Not nice for a kid to hear nasty things from their parents though, is it?"

"No, it isn't. Sometimes the truth is the last thing you should tell a child that's getting on your nerves. They're young, they can't help what they do. They're wired different."

We turned at the commotion and realized that several customers had congregated around the side of the building where the sun was coming up in the east. Men were throwing punches, women were pulling hair, everyone was shouting, name-calling was disturbing with its viciousness, and the language was blue.

"Damn but this is gonna be complicated. How do we get her to control this?" asked Steve.

"She needs a specialist. Someone who can teach her how to control not how she feels but what she emanates. It's all about getting a handle on your body, telling it who's boss and making it do what you want. It's a mental thing, believe it or not. Mind over body."

"And you know someone?" Steve had hope in his eyes. Poor guy was out of his league by a long way.

"Sure I do. I'm a wizard, I know a guy for everything that ails you."

"Awesome. Then let's go tell her, that'll put a smile on her face and maybe stop this lot tearing each other to bits."

We took another look at the fighting strangers then I said, "Good idea."

We headed back to the girls, hoping Vicky had managed to calm Sunshine down already, as tears and me, and Steve too, made it hard to think straight.

As the picnic bench came into view, Vicky screamed before someone dragged a hood over each girl's head. Then they were hoisted over two burly guys' shoulders before being dumped in a van angled across the cut grass. The side doors slammed shut, the men jumped in the back and closed the rear doors from the inside as the van chewed up the manicured lawn and bumped down onto the road and sped away with tires squealing.

"They found us," I said as we ran for our car.

"Who?"

"No idea, but I'm guessing it's the shifters from the boat."

"Yeah, you're right. I think I recognized one of them actually."

I rolled my eyes; Steve really was a simple kind of guy. I liked him a lot, but he was slow bordering on glacial at times.

The chase was on. I was amazed it had taken so long.

That Itchy Feeling

There are times when magic almost overtakes me, when my body trembles, my insides churn, my muscles spasm, and my will gathers focus to direct the inner turmoil whether I like it or not.

As I sped down the motorway with the sun glowing orange and proud behind me, washing out the road in fiery glory, I was all a quiver with pent-up frustration, rising anger, juices flowing from the strange manipulations forced upon me by Sunshine. It was all I could do to stop myself whipping out Wand who was babbling excitedly in my pocket and start blasting out the window like I was in a movie and shooting the bad guys in the most inappropriate of places.

But I didn't, because it would have been stupid, as what's the point trying to blast, shoot, or disrupt in any way the momentum of several tons of metal hurtling down a road with other vehicles when half the people inside said vehicle are the ones you want to protect? Not a lot.

Instead, I put my foot down and kept pace with them, wondering what to do, only knowing that for now we couldn't lose them or we might never get them back.

"Those motherfuckers," growled Steve, looking ready to shift.

"Stay with me, buddy. Last thing I need is you going wild in the car with me."

"Don't worry, I got it under control." Steve grunted, clenched his teeth as he forced his body to remain human. "It's the others from the boat, the ones they set adrift. I know it is. They've come to get Sunshine and lock her up again. I won't have it, I will not let that happen again."

"Yeah, I guess it's them. But listen," I said, unsure how best to put this, "are you certain this is for the best? You looking after her? You saw what she did to that guy in her room, and look what happened to her mum. Can you handle her?"

"That was an accident. She didn't do it, didn't want her hurt."

"I know, but she's young, wild, and very dangerous. She isn't like us, Steve, she's unique and it's going to always be dangerous, people wanting what she has, wanting her. Can you protect her, ensure she's safe?"

"Course I can! I'm her dad."

I nodded, left it at that. There was nothing more to say. What could I say? That even citizens with none of our skills often managed to safeguard their children better than our kind did? That everyone thinks they can keep their kids safe but bad stuff happens and when you lived how we did then they get exposed to all kinds of nasties as it's part of the life?

Secretly, we all know we're kidding ourselves thinking we will always be safe and our loved ones likewise. That life is a gamble, much of it outside our control, and all we can do is our best. So why shouldn't Steve do just that? Try his hardest? Was it better to lock Sunshine away and never give her the chance to become a rounded human being? Wasn't that asking for even more trouble down the line?

I didn't have the answers, all I knew was that I had Steve's back because if I was in his shoes then no way would I let my daughter be refused her basic human rights, no matter the gifts, some would say curses, she possessed, or was possessed by.

So I drove, and I drove hard and fast, and the longer we were on the road the more time I had to formulate a plan. Rule number one when it comes to wizards is don't give them time to plot, they are experts at being devious fucks. Never forget it. We really are awful at times.

A smile spread over my face as the minutes ticked by and the sun rose higher into a huge, washed-out sky.

"What you grinning for?" asked Steve.

"You'll see."

Old Friends

I knew many people from many places. In fact, over the years, I'd met most of the players in the world I inhabited. Many were scum, some were hard men and women, the majority were to be avoided, and a small group were genuinely nice folk. Odd, but nice.

With my ear always keen to hear news from the magical grapevine, I knew a lot about a lot of them. Some of it was ancient history, some was very recent. I knew the good and the bad they did, and I can tell you now that most of the magical criminal underground were not the kind of folks you would ever want to invite around for a cuppa, or even let know where you lived.

My mind raced through anyone I could think of who lived in the vicinity. Closing in as we were on the city, the number was surprisingly high, but I either dismissed them outright as utterly untrustworthy or failed to recall how to contact them in a meaningful time period.

Then I recalled that one of my very good friends, somebody Vicky already knew so might not freak her out too much, was right about now on his yearly vacation. No matter that his vacation consisted of emerging from his underground lair and hiking around this area of the countryside with as much food as he could carry, which was about enough to last him a few days despite his strength and size. He liked to feel the rain on his face, the wind raging against his dark skin, even the sunshine when it appeared, as he traipsed around the middle of nowhere in the nude if he thought nobody was about.

There were always strange stories about sightings, people reporting seeing wild animals off in the distance, huge bears and the like, when truth be told, it was just good old Beast.

And now here he was, right on cue.

"What the fuck is that?" asked an incredulous Steve as he leaned forward in his seat and stared at the man mountain right now rampaging down the bank at the side of the road and storming towards the van crawling along in the contraflow.

"That, my hairy friend, is Beast. You met him, remember? He's on vacation, getting some air as he spends the rest of the year working out in the sewers."

"He works in the sewers?"

"No, he lives there. He exercises, a lot. Okay, all the time. This is his week off, his down time."

"He's fucking massive."

"I know. And he hates people that would dare harm children. He had a hard time growing up, went through the mill worse than most, worse than me, so I knew he'd help."

"But you haven't called anyone."

I pulled my phone from my pocket and said, "Been practicing typing without looking. That's why I still use old phones. No touch screens for me. George said I should learn, that it would come in handy. I didn't want you to get your hopes up in case he didn't answer or wasn't near enough. He was, he is, and look, he's ripping the bloody doors off. Awesome."

We inched forward in the car but needn't have bothered as we stopped almost immediately because the vehicle in front was trying to reverse the hell out of there. Everyone began beeping their horns so me and Steve jumped out in time to see Beast simply tear away the rear doors like they were made of cardboard.

The two men jumped at Beast but he flung them aside like rag dolls before clambering into the back, making the van rock from side to side and the tires bulge.

"Good old Beast," I said with a smile as we sauntered forward past the gawping citizens.

"Yeah, good old Beast," said a confused Steve as we got close enough to see him pull the hoods from the girls' heads and snap the bonds at their hands and feet.

Vicky grinned up at Beast then leaped up to hug him before he grabbed Sunshine with a free arm and stormed off towards us with both of them grinning and chatting, Vicky presumably telling Sunshine he was a buddy.

Careful!

"Look out!" I shouted as something moved from the front of the van.

Beast smiled a knowing smile then nodded at me before carefully lowering the girls to the ground and turning, all with a fluid grace that defied his lumbering, troll-like appearance.

Something darted along the side of the vehicle and launched at Beast, gray fur streaked long and razor-sharp teeth and claws glinted with menace.

People screamed, Beast greeted his attacker with open arms, his huge back spread-eagled like the wings of a mighty eagle, as he leaned into the attack.

More furry danger sped in from both sides where Beast had thrown the kidnappers, large dogs all the size of wolfhounds. Maybe they were, but the shifters were so fast, so intent, it was impossible to tell the breed.

As Beast gave the frontal attacker the mother of all bear hugs, the other two landed, one on his back, claws raking deep, the other slammed into his side. Maybe they expected to topple this mighty oak, maybe they weren't thinking a single thought, merely acted on instinct to stop their prize being taken, but either way they came up short.

The impact didn't budge the man-mountain, but I heard the grunt as he took the hits of the two new attackers before he reached behind and grabbed the dog clawing and snapping at his side and clamped a meaty hand around its neck.

People gasped from the safety of their cars where they'd retreated, I heard them through the windows as Beast squeezed tight around a dog's throat. He looked around quickly—guess he heard the cries too—and rather than squeeze the life out of it he threw it away again. Bones snapped, people shouted, and Beast tore the dog at his chest away. Grabbing two front legs, he whacked it over his head to batter the dog still with its claws sunk deep into his back.

A sickening crunch and both animals went limp, nowhere near up to the raw power exerted by Beast without even trying.

He dropped the inert animal still in his hands then spun and lumbered towards us as Vicky and Sunshine got it together and ran away from the madness.

We met them halfway, trying not to draw attention to ourselves but doing a bad job of it. This kind of thing didn't often happen on British motorways or anywhere else citizens might be. We liked to keep our business private, and it showed just how desperate, and determined, the shifters were to change in public like this and risk exposure. They'd gotten away with it, all people saw were wild animals attacking a very oversized man, but it proved what they would do to get Sunshine, and these were supposedly the good guys.

"Thanks for coming," I said to Beast, slapping him on the back and stinging my hand.

"Anything for you, Arthur, you know that," said Beast, his sweet, gentle voice at odds with his size and demeanor.

"You two okay?" I asked as Steve hugged Sunshine and Vicky tried to straighten her sweater and do her ponytail.

"Fine, just a shock," said Vicky.

"They were going to take me back, hide me away again," said Sunshine before she buried her head in Steve's shirt and began to sob.

Beast raised an eyebrow, even his eyebrows were buff, and I said, "It's a long story."

"Another time," he said, before waving and wandering off.

"Wait, where you going?" I shouted after him.

"I'm still on vacation, going to walk over those mountains." Beast pointed off into the distance.

I whistled. "Other people take it easy, you know?"

"This is taking it easy. But hey, thanks for the diversion, nice to flex the muscles." Beast did a double bicep pose. People oohed and aahed from their cars.

And then he was gone, running off into the hedgerows like the incredible Hulk before he changes back into a regular-sized man, except he wouldn't. He just got bigger and bigger every year.

"Right, to the Wizardmobile," I said, getting my head together.

Wand in hand, but unused, I nonetheless knew the shifters would be healing best they could, or coming after us broken bones and all. I caught sight of two on the hard shoulder in amongst the bushes and knew they'd be up and after us in a moment.

Without further ado, we legged it back to the car and before anyone had chance to say a word I was outta there.

Except I wasn't.

"Arthur, stop. Stop!" shouted Vicky.

I screeched to a halt rather than change up the gears just as one of the shifters ran right out in front of us.

"Goddamn it," I moaned as the man put his hands out in front of him, like he meant us no harm. Guess he didn't, not if we gave him what he wanted.

"Please don't kill him. That's Sam, he's a good guy," said Sunshine from the rear, still nestled in tight to Steve.

"He tried to kidnap you," I said, giving the guy a good scowl.

"I know, but he's read me a bedtime story every night since I was a little girl."

"Wish I had," whispered Steve. It was easy to forget just how hard this must be for him, realizing how much he'd missed out on, all those years away from his daughter, not being part of her upbringing. I knew how he felt, but how much worse was it for him because he knew he had a daughter but wasn't allowed to be a proper part of her life?

"Still plenty of time," said Sunshine, smiling at her dad.

"Too right. I'll read to you until you fall asleep every night from now on."

"Cool."

"Um, what about this guy?" I asked as he stared in at us, unmoving.

"Drive slow until he moves out the way?" offered Vicky.

"I guess." With a shrug, I inched forward until the car nudged against his body. Still he remained. I slowly eased forward, shunting him back slightly as he kept his hands on the car.

"Damn, he's half naked, bet he hasn't got any shoes on. That's gotta hurt." You had to admire his stoicism, or stubbornness, but no way was he getting Sunshine. Not now, not like this. Was it for the best? I didn't know any longer but Steve wanted her with him and she wanted her freedom. It was right and fair, even if it would be bloody dangerous.

I put my foot on the accelerator a little and as the car picked up speed the man finally gave in and moved aside. He banged on the windows as we went past, his eyes full of sadness, pleading with Sunshine to come with him, that he'd protect her. I glanced in the rearview to see Sunshine silently mouth, "I'm sorry."

Then we were past, and leaving the madness behind, if just for a while.

What Could be Nicer?

"Arthur, why don't you let me drive?" whined Vicky, like she was four and I'd promised we could go to the beach but we weren't going fast enough. Um, not that I would let a child drive, of course. Not on motorways, anyway.

"Because if you drive we'll all die and then I won't be able to cuddle up to Penelope. She'd only moan about me being a stinking corpse."

"Don't be silly, I'm an excellent driver." Vicky gave me the evil eye; it just made me giggle.

"Hey, I'm an excellent driver, and what are you laughing at?"

"You, trying to vibe me. I'm immune now."

"I'm not," said Steve from the rear. "It's scary."

"Yeah, very," hissed Vicky, trying harder to get to me.

"Not any more. I'm used to it now, so when you do it it makes me think of you trying to hold in a fart or something." I giggled, which made Sunshine giggle, which made Steve giggle.

"Haha, she does look a bit like that," said Steve. "Now I'll never be scared again."

Vicky turned her attention to her boyfriend, who wilted under her gaze. "You sure?"

"Um, maybe not. Haha, you sure are one ferocious lady. My lady. Now I have another lady in my life too. You wait until you meet Vicky's kids, Sunshine, you'll all get along so well."

Vicky faced forward and I caught the look. I smiled in sympathy. This would be hard for her, hard for everyone. I understood her concerns. Sunshine was wild, dangerous, unschooled in the ways of children, especially those younger and more delicate than herself. Vicky wasn't without her own anger issues, like killing husband angry, not to mention the whole lycanthrope business, but she was still more stable than Sunshine, and a lot more experienced.

There would definitely be several serious talks, and plenty of tears, all of which I planned to play absolutely no part in, if we ever got that far. There was plenty to deal with before any of them got to play happy families, that was for sure.

Speaking of happy families.

Had I called since I took this job? Had I let them know I was well? Had I bollocks. It was a bit late now, better to leave it and give George and Penelope a nice surprise. Hopefully.

Lost to my musings, I snapped back to reality with Vicky shouting in my ear about something or other.

"What?"

"The turn. The turn. Don't miss it." Vicky pointed at the exit, but I ignored her.

"You don't even know where I'm going," I muttered.

"I do too. By that stupid grin on your face a moment ago then I know exactly where you're going. I'm coming too. Just for a bit, then I have to get home. The girls will be missing me. I know I'm missing them."

"What's going on, guys?" asked Steve. "Where are we headed? You got a plan, Arthur?"

"They don't call me The Hat for nothing," I said.

"What does that mean?" asked Sunshine.

"Don't worry, he always says weird stuff like that. You'll get used to it."

"It is not weird," I snapped, replaying what I said and silently admitting it made little sense. But I was The Hat, and I did have a plan, and Steve seemed utterly chilled about the fact he had no idea what to do save go home and wait for someone to come take his daughter from him again.

"Well?" asked Vicky.

"Fine," I sighed, "we're going home. My home." I took the turn.

Just for a While

Peace, that was what I craved, if just for a short while. The problem I faced, along with most wizards, was that I longed for rest and quiet times after a cool fight, or some other derring-do, but when I got it I became antsy and craved action. The curse of the wizard, I guess. First World problems though, nothing to moan about.

I weaved into the city, ever vigilant for homicidal shifters, dysfunctional wizards, indoctrinated Hounds, or anyone else who looked shifty. Everyone was just going about their business as usual, which is a surreal experience when you've had the kind of night we had. People muttered in their cars, tapped the steering wheel, glared at the rear of the vehicle in front, and generally acted the same as everyone else stuck in rush hour traffic with a day of work ahead of them.

We had different lives and lived outside of their world, strangers looking in, and I often found it astonishing that people didn't stare at me and Vicky and point, shouting, "Look, they aren't citizens. They're different. Let's get 'em." But they never did, because everyone was too busy trying to cope with this thing called life, something that takes up all your time and energy, leaving little left over for worrying about strangers in hats or tiny red sweaters.

How did Vicky do it? The school run, parent's evening, sports day, then go home, hack into someone's computer, go deal with the wild characters, and get involved in my nonsense? It was too big a leap from one world to the other. I preferred to remain in a place of magic and mayhem and more excitement than was necessarily good for me at times.

"Here we go," I said as I pulled up outside the city house, as nondescript as always, just another semi in another city drowning in poverty with a veneer of shininess as fake as Vicky's eyelashes.

"It's just a house," said Sunshine. "I thought you said it was awesome, and in the country?"

"Aha, just you wait and see, you little rascal." I winked at her then got out of the car.

Everyone followed and we made it to the door without incident or anyone trying to gnaw our legs off or anything.

Inside, I breathed deep of the faintly musty smell of a house given insufficient airing. It was divine because it was mine, and meant I was one step closer to home and the people I loved.

"Come on, no time to dawdle."

"Can I have a word first?" asked Steve, looking concerned.

"Sure, buddy. You two wait in the living room, we'll be back in a mo." I nodded to Vicky who took Sunshine inside and Steve and I retreated to the compact but clean kitchen.

I closed the door and said, "Take a seat."

Steve nodded and sat at the small table up against a wall. I joined him.

"You sure about this? I don't want to impose, or be a bother. And it's dangerous, we both know that. Maybe we shouldn't come to yours." Steve fidgeted, clenching and unclenching his hands; his foot tapped on the lino.

"Unless you have a better plan?"

"I didn't have one. I just wanted my girl back, didn't think the rest through. You think there will be more shifters after her?"

"I dunno, but those chancers on the motorway probably aren't finished with her, or us. There will probably be more, yes. And others maybe."

"So what should we do?"

"Dude, I really don't know. She's your daughter, so you need to think long and hard about your future. Both of yours. But for now, for today and tonight, you are welcome in my house." I took a breath then said what had to be said. "But I give you fair warning. You need to control Sunshine. She has to behave. No affecting anyone's emotions, making them do stuff they wouldn't normally do. No shifting, and absolutely no killing of anyone."

"Cross my heart." Steve grinned his most handsome of grins and waved his finger about over his chest. "She's a good girl really, just had it hard."

"I know, and I know this is rough on you, but you have to think about the future now. This won't be easy, or quick. She has a lot of catching up to do, a lot to learn, and she's always going to be different. Special. Unique, and a right bloody handful."

"Haha, tell me about it. It's all good, I'll handle it. But I appreciate the offer for today. It'll give us a chance to unwind and get to know each other a little without anyone watching. It's been so hard, Arthur, all these years. Tough beyond belief. What they put in her head is anyone's guess, she could believe anything."

"Then it's your job to set her straight. First we need to let her relax, then we can look into who might be after her. Form a proper plan. Sound good?"

"Sounds awesome."

I went to get the two wildcat women. Oh boy, this was gonna be a nightmare.

At Last

"Do not," I warned, "let go of your dad's hand."

"Sheesh, okay already, you just said that." Sunshine rolled her eyes.

"Because it's important," I lectured. "This is a magical portal, ancient beyond compare, priceless, and it will chew you up and spit you out into tiny pieces if you go through without being linked to me. So, like I said, I'll hold Vicky's hand, Steve will hold Vicky's, and you hold your dad's."

"So, what's really going to happen?" asked Sunshine. "I mean, this is funny and all, but you can't actually travel through space and come out somewhere else, can you?" Sunshine looked at us in turn but nobody was laughing.

Guess it was hard to believe, but you'd have thought she would be one of the first to believe in magic given her abilities.

"It's real, and it's dangerous, so be warned." Without any more faffing about, I took Vicky's hand

and then we all linked up. I nodded then stepped through.

A moment of intense pain and then I was in a familiar place, with country smells welcome after the stench of death I hadn't even realized was lingering, stuck in my nose hairs like death snot.

"That was so awesome," squealed Sunshine as she stared around at the back room of the barn in shock and wonder. Her eyes sparkled, her face lit up with joy, and a slight sheen of sweat covered her pale skin, washed out in the morning gloom of the room with no windows.

"Sure was," I grunted, so used to it now it was easy to forget the true wonder of the Gates of Bakaudif.

I let go of Vicky's hand and led the way into the barn proper. The huge building was ancient, with a vaulted roof made from rough-hewn timbers as hard as nails, criss-crossed with spider's webs and the dust of ages. Motes drifted lazily in the air then danced manically, disturbed by our passage and the hint of magic that lingered. Sunlight streamed through the gaps in the ancient wooden cladding, giving hints of green fields and the blue of the sea off in the distance.

Home. Cornwall. Quiet, with space to breathe. Away from the madness of the city. Far from the amassed crazies who congregated in the cramped places where humanity fed off the energy of others and slowly drove themselves insane.

Sunshine hopped from one bale of hay to another dotted around the edge of the barn, flapping her arms and spinning about, generally acting like a kid for the first time since I'd met her. This was as it should be, what she should be allowed to do, what she needed to do. Steve caught my attention and smiled, then nodded his thanks. He looked so relieved, thankful for the chance to have some down time and feel safe with his girl. Guess he never saw her like this. Free. Free of care and worry, just living in the moment and enjoying her youth.

"Let's go. Maybe we can get a proper breakfast after that crap at the service station. And I can show you my kitchen."

"You really like your kitchen, huh?" asked Sunshine as she hopped down and came close to peer up at me like I was an interesting insect.

"Only because it's awesome," I said, meaning it.

Within minutes we were out of the barn, the doors were closed, and I was driving down bumpy lanes heading to the best place in the whole world.

Home.

Suspicions

"And this is all yours?" asked Sunshine as we stood outside the worn wooden gate, staring at the yard and the old house, deceiving in its simplicity with the barn behind, now knocked through and home to the best kitchen in the universe.

"Sure is. We have fields, there are the stables," I pointed at the block of buildings that housed the scary steeds, "and the house is all done. We haven't been here that long though. A, um, a bomb kind of flattened the old place. But this is better anyway," I added hurriedly, "and nobody will drop a bomb on this one."

"So cool. And you can come and go as you want? Nobody will stop you? What about George, and your wife, do they just like, leave then come back whenever they fancy? What about security, nobody patrolling?" Sunshine searched for men with guns wandering about looking menacing.

I glanced at Steve and Vicky, saw the hurt they felt for Sunshine for the world she knew and how wrong it was. I knelt down and took her small hands.

"It isn't like that for other people, Sunshine. Your mum was protecting you because you are special, but most people don't have security, they come and go as they please. Just hop in the car and go shopping, do chores, whatever. Freedom."

"That's what I want. Freedom. To be normal."

I stood up, as my knees were beginning to ache, and said, "And today you have it. You can hang out here today and tonight while your dad sorts a few things out, and you can see how other people live. I'm not saying this is normal, I am a wizard and there are always bad guys out to get me, so I have magical wards around the property, but yeah, no security patrols, nobody but us here. Speaking of the family."

I waved as the front door opened and George and Penelope came out with their waxed jackets and wellies on, ready to do more chores. George would have already sorted out the horses and Penelope would probably have checked on the chickens always underfoot in the yard, so I forgot about the car, left it where it was, and smiled, my shoulders easing, the weight of the world lifting as I opened the gate and went to have what can only be described as the best thing in the world ever. A cuddle.

"So good to be home," I said as I gathered my loved ones close and hugged them tight. For a moment, all was right in the world as they hugged me back and I took in the scent of strawberry shampoo and the horsey aroma that lingered on George's jacket. It smelled of warmth; it smelled of love.

"I missed you so much. What a night."

"Missed you too," said Penelope as she reached behind and pinched my bum.

"Weirdo," said George as she smiled.

Then I doubled over as Penelope punched me in the knackers and George laughed before pointing at me and singing, "Loser. You so deserved that."

"Where the hell have you been, Arthur Salzman?" shouted Penelope. "You can't pick up your phone? You can't check messages? Why didn't you let me know you were okay? We just got back off honeymoon."

"Honey, let me explain. I'm sorry," I coughed, my eyes watering, my balls aching, "but I've been busy." Damn but this never happened when I was single. It was awesome, in a ball-breaking kind of way. Showed they cared, that was the main thing.

"You can explain later, once you don't stink. Go get a shower, and get changed. Look at your shirt! Is that blood? And your hair is all gross. What are those bits in it? Ugh, you wizards and your games. Always so messy." Penelope pushed me towards the house but I turned to her, unable to stop smiling, and said, "Um, we have guests."

Penelope turned around and saw the others standing there, gobsmacked. Vicky was smiling, Sunshine looked confused, and Steve was enjoying watching the mighty wizard being told off.

"Oh, hello," she said, scowling at me before smiling at everyone. "Arthur never said we were having guests. Arthur never said anything at all."

I smiled and shrugged. "Sorry, still getting used to it."

"It's been months," hissed Penelope.

"Told you," said a grinning George. "He's flaky, and always will be."

"I am not flaky. I was just busy. Anyway, I'm home now, and that's the main thing."

"Idiot," said Penelope, but I saw the happiness she was trying to mask, the relief I was okay, and I promised myself I'd try better to always update her on what was happening.

"Let's go eat," I said.

"Aren't you going to introduce us?" asked Penelope.

"Oh, yeah, sorry. Sunshine, this is Penelope and George. Penelope and George, this is Sunshine. Steve's daughter. She was kidnapped so we rescued her, but turns out she didn't know she was kidnapped but was merely trying to escape where she lived on a boat. There are probably shifters after her, and there are a few other issues too, but that can all wait."

"Just another day at the asylum," said George rolling her eyes then smiling at Sunshine. "Hi."

"Hi," said a suddenly timid Sunshine.

"Hello," said Penelope. "Let's get you inside where it's warm." She took Sunshine's hand, scowled at me then Steve and Vicky too, and led the girl inside.

"Ha! You're in trouble too now," I gloated.

"Am not," said a glum Steve.

"This is all your fault," said Vicky, staring at me.

"Me? What did I do?"

"Shut up."

"Some things never change," said George. "I'll be back soon, just got a few chores to do. Don't go telling all the gossip until I return. No way am I missing this." George wandered off and we went inside to face the wrath of my new wife.

It was awesome to be home.

An Ungodly Mess

"Don't get cross," whispered Penelope, looking anxious as we went from the narrow hall into the cavernous kitchen.

"Why would I get cross? I could never be cross with you."

"Oh, nothing. And that's nice." Penelope smiled and my heart melted.

I loved this woman. How had I got so lucky? She knew me so well, and I'd laid my cards on the table the day we met. I told her who I was, what I was, the kind of man I was. Not always good, sometimes very bad, always in trouble, out at all hours, how I needed magic like I needed to breathe, and that if she stayed with me her life would never be the same again. She accepted it all, and she welcomed it. The madness, the magic, but most of all me. I loved her more each day for that. For all of it.

But I was seriously reconsidering as I stood at the threshold to my kitchen, with its black tiled floor, its waxed beams, its huge island, the shiny taps, the expensive ovens, the gleaming coffee machine, and took in the carnage.

"What the hell happened?" I gasped, trying to get my head around the assault to my senses.

"Don't get upset. We didn't know when you were coming back. We haven't tidied up yet, that's all."

"Is that jam on the floor?"

"Um, maybe."

"Is that flour stuck to the tap?" I asked, squinting to check, hoping it wasn't so.

"Or baking powder," offered Penelope with a smile and a fluttering of eyelashes.

"And is that butter smeared all over the counter?"

"I hope so."

"Dear God in heaven, why have you forsaken me so?" I wailed, stepping gingerly into the room for fear of slipping on something greasy.

"Don't be so dramatic, it's a wee bit messy. We were going to have pancakes. We made batter. From scratch," Penelope added, like that wasn't obvious.

"What, by chucking everything at the ceiling and seeing how it looked when it landed?"

"Hey, cool pad," said Sunshine as she came in with the others.

"It was, now it's a war zone," I grumbled. I removed Grace to rub at my head; it felt fuzzy, like I was dreaming.

"Looks great to me. You want a hand cleaning up?" she asked Penelope.

"Sure, that would be great."

For the next ten minutes we watched, bemused and surprised, as they went to work cleaning up the mess. Sunshine was thorough, bordering on obsessive, which I admired, and Penelope, as fastidious about keeping a clean kitchen as I was, or almost, worked just as diligently wiping up what were admittedly minor spills. I was just being sensitive after the night I'd had. Soon the room was spick and span and gleaming like it was freshly installed.

"Now, who wants pancakes?"

"I do," said George as she returned from her chores. We all said the same so we sat around the table or leaned on the counter and chatted about this and that, filling everyone in on what had happened in a very condensed version.

"You're both welcome to stay," said Penelope. "But no trouble. This is home, sacred. Zero tolerance for trouble. No killing, and no messing with people's heads," she warned Sunshine.

"Deal."

That settled, we set the table and Penelope dished up steaming piles of perfect pancakes with the topping of our choice.

Before we began, I said, "Wait. Can I?"

"Go on then," said Penelope with a resigned smile.

I handed the remote to George—I could never get the bloody thing to work—and she sighed but nonetheless put on a Buster Keaton short.

"It's in black and white," said a shocked Sunshine.

"Yeah, so?"

"Didn't know they made movies in black and white. And where's the talking?"

"Just watch it. It's funny."

"Are you sure?" she asked.

"Oh, positive."

We ate, we talked, I laughed. So did Sunshine.

When we'd finished and the credits rolled, she asked timidly, "Can we watch another one? That was funny. Never knew they had stuff like this."

"Kids," I laughed, stoked she enjoyed something so alien to her generation.

For another ten minutes life was perfect. Lost in the antics of a bygone era where nobody got hurt and danger was always tinged with comedy and the knowledge it would all turn out all right in the end.

Shame life wasn't like that. But I guess that's why they call it an escape from reality.

Sometimes all any of us want to do is escape. Some of us never want to return to our old life. It's easy to understand why. Because often life sucks. Really, really sucks. Not today though, not now, not for a few precious minutes surrounded by family and friends, eating and laughing, the world locked out, everything as it should be.

It made me dread the afternoon.

Weirdly Normal

What I dreaded never came to pass. Nobody attacked, the house didn't burn down, no bombs were dropped. Sunshine behaved, George seemed to like her and showed her around the place, and I got clean along with everyone else. Vicky left late morning to tidy her house and deal with the girls, and once we'd had a light lunch Penelope and I found ourselves alone in the kitchen while Steve dozed on the sofa in the den.

"Sorry about not calling. You know I try to let you know what's happening but it all got a bit mad."

"It's fine. I know what you're like."

"Love you."

"Love you too. Now, tell me what happened. I can't believe Steve's got a daughter. And it's been her all along, messing with everyone's emotions, making us do things."

"Yeah, seems like it." I scratched at my beard.

"What? What is it?"

"Eh? Nothing."

"Yes, there is. You're doing that thing. You get all fidgety when you aren't sure about something."

"It just seems a bit much that Sunshine can have such an effect. I know she's special, and I'll tell you exactly how special in a minute, but to make people act certain ways over countless miles, it seems nuts."

"Guess she's more powerful than you thought."

"Maybe."

I told Penelope everything that had happened, about Sunshine's mum, about the kidnapping, all of it. It was a sorry tale and seemed all the worse when I recounted it. Poor kid was gonna be so messed up from such a life, there was no escaping that fact.

"That's so sad. She's going to have to live with that. But she didn't mean for her mum to get hurt, it wasn't her fault."

"No, it was the others, they got carried away like shifters often do, but still."

"Steve will look after her. It will be tough though."

"Sure will. He's got a lot of trouble ahead, if we manage to keep her safe for the next few days and the heat dies down. I told them they can stay tonight but then he needs to sort something out. We have to think of our family too."

"You're right. People will be after her, but maybe only the ones that protected her, the ones who attacked you."

"Maybe. We dealt with them but they'll be back. I just hope nobody else knows what she looks like, who she is, or that Steve's her father."

"They can't, as if anyone else knew then Steve would have had people asking. More than asking, he'd have been taken so they could get information from him. So, don't worry, it will all work out." Penelope smiled. I loved her for her kind nature. She always looked to the positive. It was lovely, but life didn't always work out like that. Still, it was nice to think that way.

I spent an hour in the Quiet Room topping up on magic I was sure I'd need, and then did chores while Steve continued to sleep.

Afternoon turned into early evening and I headed back to the barn to go through to the city and pick up Vicky and the girls. I soon returned, keen to escape the confines of the car as one Vicky is bad enough, two little clones plus the original is enough to make you hunt for something sharp to ram through your eardrums.

Dinner was raucous, the girls took to Sunshine like a long-lost sister and Vicky slowly relaxed once she realized Sunshine was capable of behaving and wasn't going to eat her children or anything.

Time passed in a haze of noise and cleaning, of running about and playing childish games. It was chaos, it was insanely loud, and it was a lot of fun. Sunshine was like a different child. Innocent, mischievous, delighted to have friends to play with, and constantly amazed that she was allowed free rein of the house, that she could go anywhere and not be supervised constantly. She kept returning to ask if she could do this or that with the girls, if they could go into different rooms, get board games or toys, not quite able to comprehend that these were all things you could do without asking.

Then it was time for the girls to go to bed. Vicky and I took them home and I promised I'd see her tomorrow.

"You okay?" I asked her once we'd emerged from the city house and bundled the girls into her car. They were asleep in seconds.

"Yeah, just worried. She's a nice girl, and I'm glad everyone got on, but what will Steve do?"

"I honestly don't know. You need to have a long talk with him."

"I will, tomorrow. You both coming over after I take the girls to holiday club?"

"Yes, all three of us. Meet us here?"

"Sure. And Arthur?"

"Yeah?"

"Thanks." Vicky stood on tiptoe and kissed my cheek.

"What was that for?"

"For being a nice guy."

"For a change."

"See ya." Vicky drove her children home and I returned to my house.

I wondered what the dawn would bring.

Dying a Little

After removing my boots, I closed the front door and stepped into the hallway. Everything was still standing, nobody was screaming, nothing was on fire, so it was all good as far as I was concerned.

The kitchen was where the action seemed to be, judging by the noise, so I cautiously made my way there to find Steve and Sunshine at the table with a game of Buckaroo all set up ready to go.

Penelope was on the phone, looking stressed as she hissed words I couldn't quite make out.

She frowned as she listened then her eyes went wide, she clenched her jaw, and shouted, "No, and don't call me again." She stabbed a finger at the phone then sighed deeply. Steve and Sunshine spoke quietly, trying not to interfere but as curious as me about what was happening.

"You okay?" I asked.

"Oh, you're back? Yes, fine. No, not fine. Annoyed, angry, disappointed, but I shouldn't be surprised."

"Let me guess," I said, knowing who it was.

"Yes, it was Jake."

"Didn't take him long to get into trouble again."

"I'm surprised it took this long. He wanted money, said he owed some people and he was late paying. They aren't happy, apparently."

"What do you want to do?" I asked, trying to keep the anger out of my voice. He was her family so it was up to her.

"I told him last time, I wouldn't help him again. He's on his own." Penelope sighed then smiled weakly. Jake sure knew how to push her buttons, but after the previous incident she'd vowed never to let him get under her skin again. It had been a wild ride, and he'd shown himself to be a good guy in some ways, not so good in others. One thing he would never be was trustworthy, not unless he got himself cleaned up and stayed that way. Guess he hadn't done too well.

"Are you sure? What if he gets hurt or worse?"

"I can't keep doing it, Arthur, not when I know the same thing will happen over and over. The more I bail him out, the more he'll come to rely on me. He'll get into trouble because he'll expect me to help. So no, he's on his own."

We joined the others at the table and Sunshine asked, "Who's Jake?"

"He's my cousin, but he's a drug addict and he won't stop. He hangs around with dangerous people and keeps getting into trouble. It's how he's chosen to live so he can't expect me to bail him out."

"Oh, okay. We playing?"

Sometimes you have to love the simple way children see life, if only we could be like that as adults.

"Sure. Where's George?"

"Here I am," said George as she came in, the scent of the stables clinging to her clothes.

"Then allow me to show you how the master plays Buckaroo," I said, rubbing my hands together and picking up a tiny lasso to place gently on the saddle of the plastic mule. "Ugh, dammit! It must be broken," I shouted as it bucked and plastic bits went flying.

"Expert! Ha!" laughed George.

We played for a while then George took Sunshine into the den where they proceeded to shoot the shit out of the bad guys for the next few hours while we remained in the kitchen and tried to think about how to get out of this mess and give Sunshine and Steve a fighting chance of making it through the next day.

"Something's missing," I said, exasperated as I leaned back in my chair and laced my hands behind my head.

"You keep saying that," grunted Steve, "but what?"

"She seems such a sweet child," said Penelope. "It's hard to believe she can affect people. Arthur, you mean something else is going on too?"

"I don't know. I just can't shake the feeling that I'm missing something. That we're missing something," I corrected. "She's strong, yes, but c'mon, making people empty of emotion, making people tell the truth, all of it, it's too out there, too extreme for her to do, especially without knowing."

"But that's why she's so special, I guess. I always knew she could do it, but not like this."

We all stared at Steve.

"What?"

"You could have mentioned it, dude. You never said you knew she could do this. How long has it been going on?"

"For always. Ever since she was a little girl. Like, tiny." Steve moved his hands apart a little, showing us exactly what tiny meant.

"And she changed your mood?"

"Sure. When she was a baby if she was upset then we'd get upset. That kind of thing."

"Okay, but this is different, right?" I asked, at a loss as to how Steve could be so relaxed about all this.

"Yeah, very. But maybe she's just growing up, getting more powerful."

"Maybe. Or maybe something is afoot."

"Arthur, you stop that!" scolded Penelope, making me smile.

"I'm not doing anything," I protested.

"You are. You're hoping this is a convoluted conspiracy so you can go running about blasting things and people and getting up to mischief."

"Hmm, maybe. But only if they deserve it." I winked at my wife; she poked out her tongue. Did I mention I loved this woman?

"So what do we do?" asked Steve.

"That, my well-coiffed friend, is an excellent question."

We talked a little longer, going around in circles and getting nowhere. Steve needed to think for himself on this one, and it wasn't easy getting him to focus in any meaningful manner. He liked to wing it, same as I did, but even I knew this would go tits up unless we could face the morning with an idea of what to actually do.

"Let's sleep on it," I finally said as we were all half asleep in our chairs. It had been a long night and an even longer day. Buckaroo is knackering.

We crept into the den but we needn't have bothered. George and Sunshine were fast asleep, curled up together under a blanket.

Steve turned out the light and I pulled the door to. I'd kept my promise, allowed her to play video games as long as she wanted.

Maybe everything would work out fine after all.

A New Day

The mini-death eluded me until the early hours. Despite the love and warmth of my wife, or maybe because of it, all I did was stress and worry through the darkness. Even when I managed to switch off and let my idle thoughts wander by with me paying not the slightest attention, I couldn't find that wondrous, magical state known as sleep.

I was too wizarded up, too hyped on unfinished business, too afraid for my friends and family, and damn annoyed that I didn't have the answers to this sorry situation.

I was kinda miffed too. Partly with Steve for getting us into this, though what are friends for, but mostly because I felt like I was being played somehow, we all were. If there's one thing a wizard of certain years hates, it's not being in control of his own destiny. Over the years, I'd taken enough shit from enough people to do whatever I could to ensure I was in control of my life best I could be, and to never let anyone walk over or manipulate me. That's how I felt, manipulated. I was being screwed with and I did not like it even though I couldn't for the life of me imagine how or why someone was interfering with Sunshine.

Maybe they weren't. Maybe it was merely the unease I felt being around her because she was an unknown entity, volatile yet innocent, dangerous yet only a child, pure but a murderer. Well, we all had that cross to bear. I'd killed plenty, Steve too, even Vicky, but we were grownups so we knew what we did was wrong, not that it stopped us if we felt the situation called for it, or we were having a bad hair day, of which I had many.

Eventually, as the birds began their depressed dawn chorus and the brightness of the previous day was banished like a fading dream, as rain tapped at the window and the dark sky promised to remain that way, I sank into a fitful sleep full of dreams of angry bears chasing me down motorways and being made to tell the truth about what I thought about Penelope's choice in cushions for the den.

"What the..." I sat bolt upright with an ache in my head and a sour taste in my mouth.

"What's going on?" asked Penelope, propping herself on the pillows, her breasts jiggling, which distracted me somewhat from being annoyed about anything.

"Hello? Face, here." Penelope pointed at said lovely face and I grinned as I tore my eyes away from the things I loved best in this world.

"Sorry, but if you will keep wobbling them about what am I supposed to do?"

"Fine." Penelope pulled the covers up and asked, "Better?"

"No, of course not, are you mad? Let them breathe, they need airing."

"I'll air you," she warned.

"I have no idea what that means, but if it's dirty then go ahead, I am your willing victim."

We smiled knowingly at each other as things stirred, but things soon retreated like a tortoise back into its shell as the noise that woke us notched it up several gears.

"What is going on?"

Reluctantly, we got out of bed and pulled on dressing gowns then hurried downstairs with George coming from her room and following.

Judging by the noise, it seemed like a bad idea to go into the kitchen, so that's what we did. We were a family of wizards and witches after all.

"You have got to be kidding me," I groaned, covering my eyes then peeking through because I couldn't bear not to watch even though it was a sight of untold horror.

Rooted to the spot as I was, Penelope and George pushed past me and my darling wife shouted with all her authority, "What is the meaning of this?"

Sunshine froze, frying pan held above her head, ready to throw it at Steve.

Steve lowered his hands and visibly relaxed; the black and white bristles that had popped up all over his face and arms receded as he got control of himself.

The room was in utter disarray. Plates were smashed, pots and pans were dented, spread over the floor, and even the cutlery tray had been emptied. Somehow, there was a fork stuck into the ceiling.

"Sunshine," I said, venturing forth because I was a wizard unafraid of anything, "I don't know what's going on between you and your dad, but you are in our home. You are a guest, and you should know how to behave like one. I told you about this place, right?" She nodded, frying pan still held high, her face still twisted in anger. "You know what it means to me? How it's important, how it's a safe place?" She nodded again. "It's more than that. When I was young, your age, I lived in a poky apartment, we had a small kitchen and my parents never bought food, never looked after me. They were bad people, neglected me, their own son, and I used to spend hours cleaning the kitchen to see if it would make them take notice of me, of anything, and begin to love me."

"That wasn't nice," said Sunshine, lowering the frying pan, caught up in the story despite herself.

"It got worse, they got worse. They did bad things, things I have never told anyone, not even Penelope, and I doubt I ever will. They didn't love me, I don't think they were capable of it. And one day I killed them both."

"You... you killed your parents?"

"I did."

"That's... That's awful. And now you have a lovely home and a lovely family and a great kitchen."

"I do. I know what happened to your mum was an accident, and it wasn't your fault, but I know how much it hurts. But tell me something, do you want to go through life knowing that you killed your dad on purpose?" She shook her head. "And does your dad love you? Does he tell you he loves you? Does he want to do his best, look after you and feed you and protect you the best he can?"

"Yes," she said warily.

"Then stop acting like a spoiled fucking brat and have some respect. For him, for me, for Penelope and George, and for yourself. What are you doing behaving like this? It's shameful."

Sunshine dropped the cast iron frying pan onto the tiles. It split in two and I winced.

"I'm sorry, I'm sorry, I don't want to go. I don't know what to do and I just want it all to end."

Something tore at my insides and before I could stop myself I turned to Penelope and said, "I don't like those new cushions. They're too big and too soft and the color's stupid."

Penelope opened and closed her mouth like a fish out of water and gasped, "You said you loved them."

"I was lying."

"Enough," shouted Steve. "Sunshine, stop that, you're messing with people's emotions, making them change. Stop it this instant."

Sunshine stared from Steve to me to Penelope and George, then burst out crying.

Then she sank onto her hands and knees and changed so rapidly into a fox-like creature you'd miss it if you blinked. Quick as a flash, she shot across the room, leaped onto the counter, and darted though the window always left open to keep the room fresh.

"Shit," we all moaned at the same time.

Some Hugs

Before I had chance to run after Sunshine, or maybe consider getting dressed first, at least some boots, I was enveloped in hugs from my two favorite women.

"Hey, hey, what's all this?" I asked, nonetheless putting my arms around them and enjoying the moment.

"You never said, about your parents," whispered Penelope.

"Dad, what happened?" asked George.

"It's a long story and one I'm not ready to tell. Maybe I never will be. I didn't mean to say anything then, it just came out to show Sunshine what she had, make her realize she had people who cared for her. Plus, I think maybe she messed with me and I couldn't stop myself." I wasn't sure, didn't know if I'd told my secret because I wanted to, or because of her influence. Either way, there was no taking it back now.

"It must have been awful," said Penelope, searching my face as they both released their grip on me.

"Yeah, kinda. But not as bad as it was when they were alive. Not at the end, anyway. Ugh, enough of this, we have to get Sunshine."

"I'm on it," said Steve, who had now returned with his backpack and was standing there stark naked in my kitchen in front of my wife and daughter.

"Dude, not cool."

"Hey, a man's gotta do what a man's gotta do. I'll find her. Sorry about this. She freaked when I said we were leaving today. Said she knew I wasn't going to look after her. Went nuts before I could explain."

"It's understandable, she's been though a lot," said Penelope.

"Yeah, and now she's out there somewhere. I'll get her." Steve strapped the backpack impossibly tight to his back then walked to the sliding glass doors and went outside. On the patio, he dropped down and quickly morphed into a fat badger, all bristly fur and menacing, piggy eyes.

A flash of black and white and he was gone, moving fast across the lawn, the dew disturbed by his passage.

"Breakfast anyone?" I asked, wondering which frying pan to use for eggs now my favorite one was smashed.

"How can you think about food now?" asked Penelope.

"Trust me, this day will be utterly shit, so I need food now because there won't be any more for a while. If I don't call, it's because I'm tied up, hopefully not literally."

"I'll clean up," offered George.

"George!"

"Penelope," said George, "it's just another day in the life of his madness. You'll get used to it. So, what's for brekkie?"

"You pair amaze me," said Penelope. "But I love you both."

So we cleaned the kitchen, got dressed, and had a nice fry-up. What else can you do when the outside world is insane? House guests, eh? They're always breaking your shit and ruining your peace. I decided to turn the spare room into a gym, then quickly changed my mind when I realized I might have to use it.

Boring

We ate, we cleaned up again, we did chores, and generally milled about. There was no sign of Steve, or Sunshine, and by late morning I knew everything had gone to shit. He hadn't found her, and was still looking, that was the best-case scenario. Worst case, they'd both been found by someone else and been taken or Steve was dead in a ditch somewhere and Sunshine was who knew where.

"I'm going out," I said, pulling on my boots, tapping my pocket to ensure Wand was present, and adjusting Grace so I looked suitably wizardly.

"Where?" asked Penelope.

"Dunno, to find them. I'll call if I won't be back for dinner. Promise."

"Have you got your phone?"

I checked my pockets, which took a while, then smiled sheepishly.

"Idiot. I'll get it." Penelope returned with my phone and I took it then kissed her goodbye.

"See you later."

"Be careful. And be kind. It's hard for them both."

"I know."

Outside, I left through the farm gate and tried to think about where they could be. Where would she go, what would she do? Would she stay in animal form? A young girl with no clothes wandering around the countryside was not a good thing, but I guess it was better than it being in the city. Still, if she had any sense, and I knew she did, then once she cooled off she'd want to get dressed. She hadn't come back, she had nothing with her, so that meant she'd hunt out somewhere there were people.

Mind made up, I got in the car and headed to the nearest village. It would be nice to see the sea anyway. Foreign waters are too clean and you can swim in them, I needed the crash of waves and the risk of pollution, even Cornwall wasn't exempt from that.

At the small fishing harbor, I parked the car and walked along the quay, looking for a child running naked through the streets. I encountered hardly a soul, just a few locals, those of an older generation who lived here year round, rather than the majority who were holiday-makers and wouldn't be seen until spring or more likely summer for a few weeks.

The rain came down, the annoying British kind where it's so fine we like to call it drizzle but where it soaks you through and the tiny droplets coat you, sticking like glue. Damn annoying. But today it made me smile, as it meant I was home, far away from the true madness of the city where you could walk for ages under cover in the indoor shopping centers and never see the sky let alone breathe fresh air or get soaked to the bone. I dunno, I preferred the weather to the fakery, but I knew that wasn't the norm.

Through the gloom I saw three figures approaching and my arm twitched, reaching for Wand without me having to think about it.

I tore the Velcro loose and gripped the warm wood tight, the connection between us welcome and instant. Just holding him gave me strength and confidence, not that I lacked either, which often did me no favors, but his power was mine, mine was his, and besides, it made me feel like a proper wizard.

"About time. It's been boring lately," said Wand, his tip shining bright even through the murk.

"You were out yesterday, last night in fact. Don't you remember?"

"Of course I remember. I remember things before you were born. I remember fae dancing around me naked when I was part of the unicorn tree. Young, nubile maidens they were, all bouncy and with golden hair. Faery dust fell like snow and I basked in their goodness, their magic, and they stroked me and I—"

"Yeah, yeah, whatever. Look, just be ready."

"I was born ready. I can handle these guys no problem. You should have let me sort them before."

"It was bad enough Beast fighting dogs on a motorway, last thing I needed was everyone seeing me using you and blasting the shit out of them in public."

"Spoilsport. It wouldn't have mattered. You know citizens only see what they want to see. They'd have convinced themselves you had a weapon, not a stick."

"Yeah, but why take the risk? And besides, it would have traumatized Sunshine more than she already is."

The three men approached, looking bedraggled, soaked through, collars up as if it could stop them getting wet. One limped, one of them couldn't move an arm by the way it hung unmoving, and the other just looked fed up with the weather.

They stopped several paces away and waited, like I was gonna ask if they wanted a coffee somewhere warm. Fat chance, although it did appeal.

"Where is she?" shouted one. "She needs to be with her own kind. With us. We can protect her. We know she's around here, we can sense her."

"Is that right? I don't know where she is. Just having a stroll, taking in the view."

We all looked at the deep cloud obscuring the horizon. Some view!

"She needs to be protected. She has to be. She's special, the greatest shifter for generations."

"And a little kid who wants to be with her dad. Can't you understand that? Leave them alone, she doesn't want to go back to that life. It isn't your choice to make."

"She's too young to decide for herself, she doesn't know what's best for her. We protect her, always have."

"Look, guys, I know you think you're doing the right thing, and I honestly don't want to kill you, but she doesn't want to go back. You don't get to decide. It's her dad that makes the decision, not you. And he wants her with him."

"He can't protect her like we can. He doesn't understand, he's not prepared to care for her, keep her safe."

I sighed, tried to remain calm, but they were doing my head in. "Tough, he's her family, he decides. Not you."

These dudes may have been caring in many ways, looking after Sunshine, but they did it because they thought she was important to their kind, for their own futures, not purely from love, and I sensed the change in them before they even reacted. They dropped as one and were all racing towards me on four legs in a heartbeat.

"Game on," I grinned.

"Woo hoo," whooped Wand as magic fried the rain.

Fun Times

"Arthur, where are you? Thought you were coming over? Steve's not answering, what's happening?"

"Sorry, got sidetracked," I said, putting a hand up to the shifters so they wouldn't eat me while I chatted. It didn't work, and I yelped, maybe squealed a little, then hung up and pocketed my phone, pleased to find Wand had been busy while I dealt with the munchkin.

One wolfhound spun away, yowling as its fur singed down to flesh that turned pink and blistered as Wand yanked my arm sideways and blasted the two coming in for a full-frontal attack. The magic arced, sucking energy from my very core, drawing on my will, my intent, my belief in this unknowable thing called magic and channeling it in a most deadly way.

As the silver energy evaporated the rain and arced, hitting both directly in the center of their foreheads, I got a shiver, a feeling of remorse that sometimes washed over me in times of battle.

What was I doing? Using such wondrous power for such base acts? Others did amazing things with their gifts, used magic to channel energy and mindfulness in wondrous ways, instilling power in artifacts, helping others, conjuring astonishing spells that amazed our kind for generations. Me, I just used it as a weapon most of the time. Sometimes I regretted the path I'd taken, the way I'd chosen to live my life.

But all good soldiers have such regrets, and that's what I was when you got right down to it. A soldier with no army, a loner, unencumbered. I guess many would call me a mercenary. Fighting the good fight, dealing with the bad guys, but damn it was exhilarating. The danger only added to the high, spurring me on to ever-increasing heights of madness in the pursuit of artifacts or cash, of adventure and mayhem.

I smiled as I readied to blast, as deep down I knew I'd made the right choice so many years ago. To be a fighter, to stand up for myself, to not be afraid, to never be afraid. And anyway, it beat stirring things in big pots and chucking stinky herbs in.

The two mutts stirred then sprang to their feet with surprising grace and agility, but one was limping and the other was almost hopping, guess that was the guy with the dodgy arm. It didn't stop them, it hardly even slowed them, and they sprang at me even as their fur burned and their heads weeped thick blood where the warning shot had burned skin but not chewed through bone and brain. They didn't know how lucky they were, that they could have been dead already if I wasn't in such a benevolent mood.

Which one had read the stories to Sunshine? I was trying to be good for her sake, to get them to stop without killing them, but they were trying my patience now and if it came down to me or them then it would definitely be them.

As Wand directed my arm, ready for another more intense channeling of mighty power, I screamed as pain engulfed my lower leg. A quick glance confirmed what I already knew. The damn wolfhound was clamped tight to my shin and shaking its head ferociously, with every intent of gnawing down to the bone and severing the limb. No way. I needed my legs for walking, it would be a right bitch without one. You can't have ferocious wizards hopping about the place, it wouldn't be seemly.

With a well-worn boot, I kicked him in the head but he clamped down tighter, making me sweat and curse. Wand quickly changed course as I focused my will and directed a tight beam of purple energy at the dog's side. The shock of it made the animal yelp and its grip loosened so I kicked him again and he rolled onto his side, a nasty wound burned through flesh his prize for munching on scrawny wizard.

Then the other two hit hard and heavy, right on my chest, bowling me over and sending the three of us toppling into a stack of lobster crates by the quayside. I grabbed one by the throat as vicious teeth snapped at my face, then squeezed as hard as I could but it made little difference apart from to hold it at bay enough for me to get a faceful of slobber.

Panicked, I rolled as the other scrabbled to its feet and loomed over me, ready to tear my throat out. Teeth came down and caught in a lobster pot as I moved just in time and as we tumbled I slammed the dog I had hold of hard against the soaked ground. An audible crack and the animal went limp for a second as light faded from its eyes, but then it regained consciousness and its limbs batted the air. Sharp claws capable of doing real damage scraped against my jacket but caught in the leather, tangling the animal and me with it.

Fed up with this nonsense, I released my hold and grabbed a lobster pot, slammed it down hard over the beast's head, then gained my feet and backed away for a breather.

The dog ran around mewling with the pot rammed tight over its snout, its pointy ears stuck through the sides. I sniggered as I turned my attention to the other dog still battle-ready and let Wand loose with wild abandon. Sigils flared, energy drew down my arm, and I was shunted back under the pressure of the expulsion as magic tore through the beast and ripped away flesh and bone.

The creature screamed, a terrible sound that combined the cries of a human with that of an animal in distress, a sound every animal lover hates. It made my insides quiver and it was all I could do to stop myself moving to its aid. But I couldn't, because this wasn't over.

As the lobster pot smashed, the other dog pounced, uncaring about its comrade when it was so deep into the fight.

I ducked as it leaped high. Its paws tapped on my hat like it was literally raining cats and dogs as it sailed overhead so I turned and punched up with Wand gripped tight, piercing its right hind leg just above the knee. The animal landed with a thud and lay still, panting raggedly.

As I watched, all three returned to human form. They were a sorry sight. Broken, torn, bleeding, covered in bruises. Bone was visible through one shifter's arm, another had a huge wound on his belly, and the third had a nasty, perfectly round hole in his thigh. Was this enough to stop them? How far would they take this?

I took several deep breaths to calm myself and stop the violence escalating, then moved away a little so all three could see me properly and me them.

"I get it, I really do. You cared for her for a long time, saw her grow up, but it isn't right. Maybe it never was, or maybe it was exactly what should have been done, but you don't have the right to imprison her. She doesn't want to be caged, you should understand that more than anyone. She wants to be with her dad and she wants her freedom. She needs it, she craves it, she has the right to have it, and she will have it."

"She'll be taken by others, used and abused."

"Maybe, but that's a risk she's willing to take and so is her dad. She has to be allowed a chance at happiness, at being a little girl, not held captive like a freak. Let her go, let her be. You did your jobs, you got her this far, now let her grow into a woman with a chance at a normal life."

"It'll never happen. You don't know what she can do, what she's capable of."

"Maybe not, but we don't get to decide. I don't want to fight you, but I will. This was nothing, a mere taster. Next time I see you, any of you," I warned, staring at each in turn, "I will assume you are my enemy, that your intent is to steal a child from her father, and I will kill you for that. Do you understand me?"

"It's a bad decision, she won't survive. She needs to be protected, away from others. She'll kill, hurt people, she can't control herself yet."

"My guess is, she does those things because she didn't want the life you all forced on her. Now it's her turn to choose. We good?"

The men looked to each other, undecided, which was understandable. They were in a real quandary and it must have been the hardest decision they'd ever had to make. I'd give them time, let them mull it over, it was that or kill them now.

"You think about it, but don't forget what I said."

I left them to their wounds and their thoughts. Hopefully I'd never see them again.

My phone rang again. Guess who?

More Annoyances

"Why did you hang up?" shrieked Vicky.

"Because I was fighting three shifters who want Sunshine back," I said calmly.

"You didn't let them take her, did you?" came the shrill call of the mini-menace.

"Of course not, you muppet. And anyway, she ran off, so nobody knows where she is."

"You let her run away? Where is she?"

"I just said, nobody knows."

"Then why aren't you looking for her?"

"Vicky, I am. The shifters sensed she was close, they must have tracked her, and they want her back. Or wanted, I'm not sure if they changed their minds. Why did you call?"

"You were coming over, you didn't arrive. Shall I come there?"

"And how will you do that?" I asked.

"Oh, yeah, long drive. Can you come get me?"

"I'm kinda busy. Maybe later after I find Sunshine, and Steve."

"Steve's missing too?" Vicky's voice couldn't have got any higher, my ear couldn't have hurt any more.

"Yes," I replied, exasperated. "He shifted and went to look for his daughter. Look, I'll call you later, okay? Let me find them then we'll come to the city. Not your house though, somewhere else."

"Like where?"

"I'll let you know." I hung up, then rubbed at my ear. Damn but that woman was loud at times. Those times being when she opened her mouth.

I checked over my shoulder but the shifters were gone.

Where to now? Where were they? Close, something told me that. This was all new to Sunshine, she didn't know where she was or where to go, so chances were high she'd stay in the small village while she calmed down. Maybe she'd just return home, or try to, but I couldn't risk her being taken. I definitely needed more information, to know if she'd created a stir in the magical community or if anybody knew or cared about her escape from captivity.

With no idea what else to do, I wandered around the village, marching up and down ancient cobbled streets, admiring the weathered stone cottages, the brightly colored paintwork, the potted plants outside the houses fronting the streets, the mild climate meaning everything was in full bloom already.

The tang of salt does something to you. The promise of the sea, the sense of space and freedom it signifies, opens neural pathways and makes you come alive. The wind blew strong, the waves crashed in the distance, gulls called to each other, and the ionized air made me feel energized and mighty, like I could take on the world.

But my legs still hurt from all the hills, and I hadn't found what I was looking for, so I took in deep lungfuls of air and kept on traipsing in the drizzle, thoroughly soaked but surprisingly light of spirit.

Too Old for This

I wandered, I strolled, I meandered, I loitered, and I even ran, but not very far or very fast, and only because an old woman came out waving a stick at me while I was admiring her geraniums.

What I didn't do is find Sunshine or Steve or even an open cafe. With the village exhausted as a hideout for the wayward uber-shifter, I moved on and drove from village to village up and down the coast before venturing inland and any which way I could think of where there were likely places to hole up and feel safe.

How far could she have roamed? I had to get it out of my head that she was still that fox-like creature. Maybe she'd changed into an animal that found it easy to cover large distances, or a bloody bird. Sunshine could have been anywhere but something niggled at the back of my mind and told me she was still close, that she was scared and lost and wouldn't just run hell for leather as far as possible.

No, she was close, I knew it, and so I continued my search, even called home to report in and earn a few bonus points in anticipation of screwing up later on, which I inevitably would.

Eventually, I was out of places to look so resorted to driving past the numerous remote houses dotted around the landscape. Most were locked up tight against the weather, the owners knowing early summer, even the full height of summer, was often like mid-winter. Smoke rose from chimneys as people hunkered down inside, or battled with the weather to tend farms or smallholdings, distant figures wrapped up in Barbour jackets and high Wellington boots, used to the weather but still preferring to be inside in the warm and so they hurried through their work best they could, dreaming of hot drinks and warm stew.

I found myself near the barn so decided to go in and take a seat where I would be dry but have freedom of movement. As I drew up outside and braced to make a dash for the doors to open up, I wondered why on earth I hadn't thought to check here first. It was only a few miles from the house, and Sunshine knew this place, so it was a likely point to head for. I'd been fixated on clothes, thinking she'd only go somewhere where she could nab something to wear, but what if I was wrong? Then I panicked because what if she thought she could go through the portal? No, she'd listened when I'd told her not to do it without being connected to me, but she was a kid, and maybe she wasn't really paying attention to the danger and the utter certainty of her death if she tried to go through.

Heedless of the rain, my heart fluttering, I ran for the barn doors and opened them up as fast as possible.

Taking no chances, and knowing a few seconds would make no difference if the worst had happened, I drove the car in. I sat in the car, engine off, and braced myself for what I might discover.

After several deep breaths, I got out. The door shut with a clunk that echoed loudly in the silence. There was no sign of her, nothing disturbed, so I marched through to the back room, going fast in case my nerves got the better of me. Senses on high alert, relief washed over me before I even saw the gate because there was no lingering aftereffect of it having been used recently.

Nope, she hadn't gone through, and there were no nasty lumps or bits of child spread about, not that there really would be as she'd be disassembled into tiny atoms and spread who knew where, certainly not onto a straw-covered floor.

A slight rustle sent me running back into the main space although it was probably just a mouse pissed off with the rain same as everyone else. As I got into the room, I caught sight of something furry leaping from one bale to the next, bringing back a memory of the previous day when Sunshine had seemed so happy.

"Haha, just a mouse. Hello little mouse, are you keeping warm?"

Strangely, the tiny creature paused its mad dash and turned to look at me. Weird.

"Hey, little fella, what you up to? Got a nice bed in here somewhere have you? Maybe a family? You storing food for the winter, looking for goodies?" I fished about in my pockets until I found a handful of nuts, always good for an energy boost, and flung them onto the floor.

The mouse looked from me to the nuts then jumped down and scampered across the room. Guess the little dude was hungry.

I watched as it grabbed a nut and began to nibble. Normally, they were timid and would dart for cover, but this was one brave little dude.

Something wasn't right though. The more I studied the creature the odder it seemed. Its mouth was too big, and I swear it had grown a little so it could eat faster. And there was a wisp of pale blond hair on its head, a streak running front to back. That wasn't normal, was it?

"Sunshine?" I asked, squatting to get more on her level.

The creature's ears pricked up, it stared into my eyes, and then it ran away, straight into a bale. Stunned, it shook its head then leaped up onto the top and ran around the edge of the room.

"Wait, it's me, Arthur. I'm not cross, and I'm sorry about what I said. Come home, come and get warm, have something to eat. Everyone's worried about you."

For a moment the mouse seemed to consider my words then it darted down the back of the bales and next thing I knew it squeezed under the gap in the barn doors and was gone.

"Goddammit."

Gotta Try

I knew it was pointless, but I did it anyway, as that's what you do when you want to feel like you gave things your best shot even though you understand you've already lost. I ran after her, flung a door open and bolted outside to catch a tiny mouse in a huge field.

Of course, she was nowhere to be seen, so I resorted to getting down on my hands and knees and running my hand over the grass while I called her name. Nothing, not even the moving of grass to signify her passage. She could be right next to me and I wouldn't see her, so I checked some more, just in case she was, but she wasn't.

I shouted her name, I said I was sorry, and I moved carefully for fear of squashing her tiny form. Nope, she'd scarpered. The grassy field was long and overgrown, left that way on purpose so the place had an air of the abandoned to it, making it the perfect place to hide. For a while, I wandered around calling to her, promising not to shout, telling her again that I wasn't mad, but it was an exercise in futility.

Not wanting to be outsmarted, and being rather stubborn, not to mention wily, I huffed loudly then went back into the barn and slammed the door shut. Quick as I could, I ran to the back and opened a small door and snuck around the side of the building as quietly as the mouse I was searching for. At the corner, I stood still and breathed slowly and silently, watching and waiting for any sign of movement. Damn but it was cold, and wet, and the sky threatened to unleash a deluge of misery at any moment.

Distracted by the bleakness, I looked back across the field to see the grass move in a straight line heading down the hill. A tail poked up above the knee-high grass so she had clearly changed form, maybe into a cat. The tail swished fast as the creature streaked away so I gave chase, no point trying to hide as she obviously wasn't going to suddenly change her mind and come inside with me.

The animal turned to glance at me, the large eyes of a peculiar looking cat locked on mine for a moment then it darted away into the undergrowth and out of sight once more.

"I'll get her," came a voice from nowhere, making my head spin and my system go into instant high-alert.

"It's me, you idiot. Wand," said the sentient stick in my pocket.

"Oh, good. Thought I was being haunted or something," I said, relieved. "I forget you're there sometimes."

"I know, and it's no fun being stuck in the dark. And before you say anything," said Wand hurriedly, "yes, I know I don't have eyes, and yes, I know I should be able to see the same wherever I am, but it doesn't work like that. If it's dark, if you put me away, then I can't see, okay?"

"Didn't say a word," I sniggered. "You can stop her?"

"Sure can," said Wand with utter confidence as I pulled him out and he sparkled with life.

"Don't hurt her," I warned.

"Course not, she's practically family."

"Then go get her." I threw Wand hard in Sunshine's general direction, not that I really knew where she was now, and as the momentum died down Wand straightened out and his tail—yeah, I know, he's a stick—shone fierce red like he was powered up by booster rockets. I sighed, talk about dramatic. I knew as well as he did the light show was just that, a show, that he didn't have to be so OTT, but I guess that's the whole point of magic. Have to be a little bit of a showman now and then as that's what makes it so much fun.

Wand sped forward then dipped low and tore across the top of the grass leaving a trail in his wake as a fine spray of rain was dislodged from the wet grass.

He shot skyward before hanging for a moment high above like a bird of prey riding the thermals and then plummeted as though he'd found his mark and was going in for the kill. I knew he wasn't, but it still gave me pause as he streaked down like a deadly spear.

He hit hard and fast, and I ran towards him as a voice called out, "Get off me, you stupid stick. Hey, let me go, let me go."

Sunshine was curled up in the soaking wet grass, naked and vulnerable, looking tiny and fragile out in the big bad world. Wand had her pinned through one of her hoop earings, and how she still wore them I still don't know, so her head was stuck tight against the ground, covered in mud and bits of grass.

"Don't run off, okay?" I asked in my nicest voice.

"Okay," she agreed, sounding sullen and defeated.

"Wand, good job but you can let her up now."

"You sure? I can keep guard if you want?"

"No, that's fine, but thanks."

Wand pulled out and I hurriedly put my hand out as he sped towards me. I caught him, or he caught me, then I put him back into my pocket and fastened him away for safety, maybe mine, maybe Sunshine's, certainly not his.

"You talk to your wand? Does he talk back?" asked Sunshine as she sat up, legs pulled in tight to her chest trying to hide herself.

"Course he does, otherwise I'd be one of those mad old men who just talks to sticks."

"Um, I think you are," she said, the hint of a smile on her mischievous face.

"Yeah, maybe I am. Come on, let's get you warm and dry." I removed my jacket and placed it over her shoulders then turned away and walked back to the barn, wanting to give her privacy while she covered up, sure she wouldn't run away again.

Luckily, I was right, as no way was I up for more traipsing around in the rain.

A Chat

"You okay?" I asked lamely as a waif-like girl sat semi-naked on a bale of straw, shivering so bad her teeth chattered. Her seat was probably making her bum hurt like hell too. I've sat on a bale naked and trust me, you don't wanna try it.

"Fine," came the morose reply.

"Why'd you run off like that? I've been looking for you for hours. Feels like days, actually." I rubbed at my face; it felt wrinkled. This girl was aging me fast.

"Cause I don't want to go back to how it was before, and Dad said we had to leave. He'll lock me up or give me back to all those freaks who think I'm a superhero or something. I just want to be normal. I killed my mum," she suddenly shrieked, then broke down with a fit of tears and sobs that shook her body more than the cold.

"Hey, don't ever say that. You didn't do it, you didn't want it to happen, it wasn't you." I patted her head, feeling like an idiot, but not knowing what else to do.

"But maybe I did. Sometimes I wished she was dead, and now she is."

"Oh, that's all right then," I said breezily. Sunshine looked up at me with her large, pale blue eyes like I'd gone nuts. "All kids wish their parents were dead at some point. Just ask George. Only difference is, I've died loads of times. Not anymore though, I'm out of lives. Next time I die, I've got to actually be Death, which sucks." I think I was blathering as Sunshine looked at me oddly.

"You're a very weird dude, you know that, right?"

"Am not, you are."

There was an awkward silence and then we both burst out laughing.

"Come on, let's get you home. It's warm in the car," I hinted, wiggling an eyebrow. "And there are clothes at my house, and a lovely kitchen. And hot drinks and food."

"S'pose." Sunshine wrapped my jacket tight around her and I helped her into the car. I turned the heater on full whack until it felt like an oven. Condensation steamed up the windows and it smelled like a wet dog was in there with us, but it was just the lingering scent of Sunshine and her many animal forms playing havoc with my senses. What a way to live, how confusing and strange it must be to change into so many creatures and be assaulted by all those different ways of viewing the world. How did she cope? How did any shifter cope, let alone a child who could be anything, look like anything?

I drove us back to the house; we didn't speak until I pulled up outside the gate.

"Damn, I forgot about your dad. Have you seen him?"

"No, I heard him when I ran off but I've been all over the place, went for miles, and haven't seen or heard him since then."

"Let me call him again." I pulled out my phone and dialed his number. He answered on the second ring.

"Have you found her?" Steve asked anxiously, so far removed from his usual laconic attitude it was startling.

"Yes, just now."

"Is she okay? Is she hurt? Did anyone try to take her?" I glanced at Sunshine then figured it was best to be honest.

"She's fine. Cold, but fine. We're outside the house now. The shifters from the motorway were on the prowl and we had a fight. I didn't kill them but told them to leave Sunshine alone and that she had the right to choose for herself what she did. I told them in no uncertain terms that if I saw them again I would take it personally and assume they were our enemies. They're thinking about it." I nodded to Sunshine who beamed back at me like I'd given her an early Christmas present.

"Awesome. So she's safe, that's the main thing?"

"Yeah, she's fine. Where are you?"

"I, er, didn't find her, and I got lost, then figured maybe she'd headed back to my place in the city, so I'm here."

"What!? Why did you think she'd be there?"

"Just thought she'd come here, to hide out. I hitched a ride and got here quick. Well, not quick, but you know..." Steve trailed off, probably because he realized he was an utter twat. I was about to tell him that when I remembered he was just a worried father and not thinking straight, and also a bit dim when it came to thinking about things logically.

"Okay, stay there. We'll come see you later. Actually, meet us at my city house, just be careful getting there." I thought about what I was saying and changed my mind. "Sorry, no, scrap that. Just stay at yours. We need to keep Sunshine hidden so I'll call you when we arrive in the city and we can meet up. If anyone's watching they'll have seen you alone, which is a good thing."

"Sounds good," said Steve brightly. "And thanks, Arthur, you're a true friend."

"No problem." I hung up then realized he probably wanted to talk to Sunshine. It would have to wait, poor girl was turning blue with the engine turned off.

"Let's get you warm, and dressed," I said softly.

Sunshine nodded meekly before I got out and tried to come up with a plan that would keep this girl safe.

No Rest for the Wicked

Penelope fussed over Sunshine and ran her a steaming bath while George picked out clothes for her to wear and even gave her a swanky backpack rammed full of other clothes so she'd have a few changes and actually have something of her own. The poor girl had nothing personal at all.

We ate a late lunch, had several coffees and hot chocolates and then it was time to go. I loitered by the car while everyone said a teary farewell like it was the last time any of them would see each other. It felt odd because it seemed final rather than a temporary goodbye. Guess we all felt it, that we didn't know what would happen, how this would pan out, so it got emotional and I got grit in my eyes which made them water.

Then it was back to the barn, a quick step through the portal with Sunshine looking freaked and clutching her new bag like a lifeline, before arriving in a small kitchen. The musty smell made it feel even more transient, as though we were strangers, home invaders, and there was no place for Sunshine here.

It was at this moment I understood the extent of my good fortune, just how lucky I truly was. I had an awesome home, large, warm, and inviting. I had money, but mostly important I had a family that loved me and somewhere I felt safe, loved, and at ease. Sunshine had never had that. She had lived a life of constantly being moved around, of no permanent base, just a series of bedrooms and interminable warnings about people out to get her, of being hidden away and always living on the edge.

What kind of a life was that? Not one for a little girl, not one for an adult.

Things would have to change. She needed structure, to be settled, to be calm and to feel safe. To have routine and a familiar face who loved her but who wouldn't lock her up or fill her head with warnings about others out to do her harm. She needed to not be reminded how special she was, but rather to be allowed to forget it and to try to be normal. All impossible, or near as damn it, but she had to at least be given the chance, for Steve to attempt giving her all of that and more. I knew he would, it was clear he loved her, and being as flaky as he was there was no question of her being given her freedom, too much if anything, by a man who lived in the moment and didn't give much thought to the future.

Maybe in time he and Vicky would live together, and Sunshine would be a part of Vicky's family and thus mine. Or was that too much for Vicky? This would surely put a strain on the relationship as there was a lot to consider and it would certainly factor into their future together. Vicky loved Steve, even though they were still in the relatively early throes of their relationship. Not that it had stopped me and Penelope—we moved in together the day we met, but even I knew that wasn't how these things usually worked.

"You really do zone out an awful lot," said Sunshine staring at me like I was a weirdo.

"Do not," I said, smiling.

"We going to go see Dad?"

"Yes, I just need to think for a minute first. Decide where to meet him."

"Can't we go to his place? I haven't seen it yet."

"Maybe later. Best to be cautious first until we know what's going on. Actually, I think we should go see Ivan, he'll know if anyone's heard about what happened, if anyone's after you or if it's only the shifters who looked after you who even know who you are and that you've gone missing. Or," I mused, "maybe we'll meet up with Steve, go get Vicky, and me and her will visit Ivan and you can hang with your dad. No point showing you off just yet, even though you are such a pretty girl. Eh?"

"Me, pretty? You think so?" Sunshine blushed a little, a sweet gesture that brought home how young and innocent she really was.

"Course. You'll have all the boys after you when you're older. Don't touch them though, they're all scoundrels," I warned.

"Okay, I won't," she laughed, pleased to have the compliment.

We got our things together, not that there were many, and I phoned Steve and Vicky with the arrangements I came up with as we spoke.

Then we cautiously left the house, I finally found the car I was currently using after wandering around for a while, and we set off to reunite a little girl with her dad and to pick up my idiot sidekick who was probably foaming at the mouth after missing out on the morning fun.

A Reunion

We met up with everyone at the local park where not so very long ago I had taken up running to get fit and had a few encounters with various bad guys. I recalled the trouble with the old head of Cerberus, and that brought back worries about how quiet they'd been lately. I shook it off; time for that soon enough.

Steve was a wreck and looked awful. But his stress levels lowered when he hugged Sunshine. Vicky was great with both of them as we all stood around getting reacquainted and apologies were given by father and daughter to each other and everyone else for causing a fuss.

I filled the others in on what I had planned and then we left Steve and Sunshine alone in the park while Vicky and I went to have a chat with her brother, the head of the criminal underworld and one of the toughest vampires around. But he was almost family, and sometimes I even liked him, so it was all good.

The sun even came out, the rain of earlier forgotten, and it was with a spring in my step, a feeling of having accomplished something and moving forward, that I walked back to the car with my sidekick skipping along beside me to keep pace. Was this Sunshine influencing me and everyone else in the park who looked decidedly happy? I decided it didn't matter, not right now.

Everything was looking up, and that meant only one thing.

Trouble.

A Realization

"Hi, I'm Arthur." I held out my hand to the woman but she just scowled at me.

"Arthur, this stopped being funny a long time ago," squealed Vicky, jabbing me in my nether regions because she was too short to reach my ribs.

"Huh? What you on about?"

"She is talking about the fact that you seem, for some inexplicable reason, to be unable to recognize me, to remember that we have ever met. That, or you think it is funny to forget you have met someone on numerous occasions. Someone who is the aide to Ivan, who is his girlfriend, and who you see all the time!" The woman finished with a shout, exasperated.

I grinned.

"And what, may I ask, is so funny?" she asked as she stood tall and tried to peer down at me even though we were the same height.

"You, you are."

"Arthur, stop it, you're being so mean."

"Vicky, oh most alive of all my sidekicks, she who has killed me, or got me killed—"

"I said I was sorry."

"—repeatedly, I am not being mean. It's taken me a while to figure it out, but now I have, haven't I? Um, what was your name again?"

"Kim! It's Kim. What are you talking about, you silly little man?"

"Me, little?" I asked, affronted. "Am not. You are."

There was silence, because she wasn't little, but then, neither was I, so what was the deal here?

"What are you talking about?" Vicky tried her glare on me, but I was immune. Almost.

"I never knew what you were both talking about, saying we'd met before, and I honestly don't recall the meetings, not in any concrete way, but I figured it out on the way over. Let's go in, shall we, Ivan will want to hear this."

I barged past Kim into Ivan's swanky place before she could stop me or consider what to do. What was she gonna do, bite me? Yeah, guess she could have.

"Ivan? IVAN? Where are you, dude? I think you need to hear this."

"What's the meaning of this intrusion?" said Kim, her pale neck flushed with either anger or worry.

"You know," I replied, moving from the hall into the library. Damn, but Ivan had made more improvements, turned the place into a proper vampire lair but with nice modern taste.

"Arthur, what are you doing? Stop being so rude. What's all this about?"

"Patience, grasshopper, all shall be revealed. Damn, I actually feel sorry for him."

"Who?"

"Eh? Oh, Ivan, of course, poor guy. Not to mention the girl. Right, Kim?"

Kim's whole demeanor changed, going from cool vampire vibe but with that edge of submissiveness because she was Ivan's aide, to being more of a military bearing, back ramrod straight, face empty of emotion, looking utterly in control and unafraid. I was right, I knew I was. It all slotted into place now, and I hated them all over again, even more than when they blew up my lovely house.

"Fucking Cerberus," I moaned as I slumped into a wingback.

"Indeed," said Kim with a raised eyebrow. "But I do like him, want this to continue."

"How's that gonna happen?" I asked, genuinely intrigued. "And all this current trouble, you think he'll be happy about that? I know I'm not."

"I have no idea. I suppose it shall all end badly. Such is the way of things."

"Yeah, sure is," I muttered, wishing I could kick myself for being so stupid. But then, Ivan hadn't found out, and if anyone had he should.

Why is it when men betray each other they give the game away, but when women do it they are smart enough to get away with it? Not sure what that says about the two sexes, but I doubt it's a good thing for either.

"What's all the noise?" hissed Ivan as he strode into the living room, wearing, and I kid you not, a black silk dressing gown and red socks.

"Blimey, really going for the vamp look, aren't you?" I smirked.

"It was a gift," snapped Ivan. "Hello, Sister."

"Hey, Bruv," said Vicky, standing on tiptoe so she could give Ivan a kiss once he bent down.

"What's this all about? I was busy."

"Busy auditioning for a movie where they want someone to look like a twat," I whispered. Everyone stared at me. "What? I never said a word."

"He is being exceptionally juvenile today," said Kim.

"He is every day," said Vicky, nodding vigorously.

"Am not. You are. Both of you. You too." I pointed at Ivan. Look, it had been a long couple of days, I was running on empty, I still had a lot to figure out, and this wasn't meant to be part of the plan. It kind of just came to me on the trip over, thinking long and hard about Cerberus and their role, or lack of it so far, in all of this.

Last thing I wanted to do was upset Ivan. Okay, I wasn't that bothered as he could be a dick at times, but this involved us all, and I had Sunshine to think about, we all did. She had to be kept safe, that meant Ivan had to give the word she was off-limits, and we had to know who knew about her. More importantly, we had to know Cerberus wouldn't try to take her. I knew that was futile now, but I had to try.

Slumped in my chair, feeling exhausted, ill-prepared if anything went down, and reticent about saying anything but not knowing how else to deal with it, I took a deep breath then said, "Ivan, I'm afraid your girlfriend is a spy. An impostor. Of the worst possible kind."

"Haha." Ivan glanced from me to the stony-faced Kim.

Vicky gasped, ever the drama queen, and next thing I knew I was being shaken by her.

"How can you fall asleep after saying something like that?" screeched Vicky.

"Bit tired. Been, er, saving cats stuck up trees."

"What is he babbling about? Arthur, what are you saying about Kim? Kim, is this true?"

"I'm afraid so. Sorry." Kim smiled weakly.

Ivan's fangs snicked down and he launched at his soon-to-be ex-girlfriend.

More Surprises

Ivan was a tall dude. Some would call him lanky, others would say he looked like a stick insect in a nice suit and that needed to catch a few rays. None would say such things to his face. But when he moved, when he reacted, when he walked, when he attacked you and tried to rip your throat out, he was all fluid grace, no wasted movement. Like an animal, no energy expended unnecessarily.

He had Kim pinned in a heartbeat.

Ivan straddled his girlfriend prone on the rug in what could have been a weird, kinky sex game if it wasn't for the fact he had her arms locked and his teeth were breaking the skin at her neck. He paused as the juices ran down her throat and pooled in that little depression between the clavicles, which there's probably a name for.

Kim didn't move a muscle, accepted the domination and smiled sweetly at her lover as he readied to end her life.

"I think you should reconsider, dude," I warned. "We need to get answers and find out what the hell is going on before you kill her. And besides, you'll regret it as you won't know the extent of her treachery."

Ivan glanced at me and I nodded. He turned back to stare hard into the eyes of Kim before he made his decision and leapt away in a move I hadn't thought possible.

Vicky stood stock still, confused beyond belief and I guess this was a rather sudden revelation. It was a shock to me too, only clicked into place on the drive over, and I wished I'd been wrong about the whole thing.

Kim was not who she pretended to be, far from it. If my suspicions were correct, it went a hell of a lot further than anyone could have imagined. Except me, of course, awesome wizard sleuth that I was becoming.

Kim did this thing where she arched her back then swung her arms and launched up onto her feet in another impressive show of vampire ninja moves. She stood there, staring at us all, while Ivan snarled and bared his fangs. He was angry, pissed off beyond belief, but I saw the sadness, the despair at being betrayed and duped, played like a fool even though he didn't understand the treachery or the game Cerberus was playing as of yet. I knew how he felt. I'd been there myself and it haunts me still.

"Shall we sit?" asked Kim, back to being the formal aide and acting like she wasn't scum.

"Good idea," I said, sinking back into the comfy chair and deciding I wouldn't take a nap even though Vicky had just interrupted some much-needed sleep.

"I want to hear this now," snapped Ivan, brushing a slender hand through his hair as he got himself together and did his best to hide his disappointment.

"Me too," said Vicky, glaring at Kim like she could kill her with a look.

Kim remained cool and impassive, but when she looked at Ivan she smiled weakly and said, "If it's any consolation, I'm sorry. I didn't know it would end like this, that we would become a couple. I was to be your aide, nothing more, so please know that my feelings for you are genuine, nothing was faked."

"But you're a traitor, a spy? You work for Cerberus?"

"I do work for them, I am one of their Hounds."

"A Hound!?" I blurted. "Not the regular type then?"

"You know little, next to nothing about how we operate. You think it's all jackboots and guns? Ha, that's not how organizations like ours work, you should know that, all of you. It's about the intelligence, about the information we gather so we know what's happening and where the artifacts are so we can protect you all, protect everyone."

"Blah, blah, blah," I said, dismissing other words with a wave of my hand. "Heard it all before. So what's the deal? You came to spy on the vampires, on Ivan, so you could keep tabs on what they're up to?"

"That, and you, and the underground as a whole. Ivan is an important man, more important than he realizes, so being here has helped immensely with our work."

"We still beat you though," I said, smirking. "Even with you being his aide, playing the part, we still beat you."

"No, not really. We know what we are doing, Arthur, we know how the game is played. We have, after all, been playing it for millennia. We serve and protect, we know when to retreat and when to advance. I have seen things you can only imagine, been places you would not believe, done things that have saved many lives."

"And you've been screwing with a little girl's life, messing with her head, keeping her locked away and brainwashing her for years. How's that feel, eh?"

"You know nothing of this," snapped Kim, losing her cool. Anger flashed on her face then was gone, replaced with that blank smugness so familiar to Cerberus and their higher-ups. I really wanted to slap her, but couldn't because my chivalrous nature made it impossible.

"What are you all talking about? Who is Sunshine? What is this?"

"It's all just clicking into place," I said, working it out as we spoke, everything becoming a little less murky. I was getting an understanding of the extent of their manipulations and the depths they would sink to.

"First, let me explain something. I couldn't understand why I never recognized Kim, why there was a blank spot when it came to her. Even when we were on our way over, I knew there would be someone here, your aide, but there was an emptiness where there should have been a person. She's a fucking shifter, and not just any shifter, are you, Kim?"

"Arthur, you idiot," said Vicky. "She's a vampire, not a shifter."

"She's a damn sight more than any of us could have imagined," I said. "Right, Kim? I never recognized you because I've spent so many years picking up on the subtleties of the human face and body, the tiny tics and movements people don't even realize they have, that I never recognized you because you were never the same person. You can shift any way you want, change into anything, and this isn't you, how you really look. Every time you take on this appearance, or maybe because you're trying to remain looking like this, it changes a little. Not much, not enough for anyone to notice, but you've been morphing into a slightly different person. Maybe to be more attractive to Ivan, maybe because you can't maintain the look, but it threw me every time because you were just a little different. Oh, and because you screw with people's emotions, make them feel things, and my guess is you wanted to make me feel uninterested, empty of heart when it came to you, but you couldn't quite pull it off because I'm a fucking ace wizard."

I laced my hands together behind my head and smiled, feeling like Poirot after the big reveal.

"Something like that," admitted Kim with a nod of respect at my sleuthing.

"This is making no sense," said Ivan as he sank into a chair and seemed to forget how dangerous Kim was.

"It makes perfect sense. They've been behind Sunshine's upbringing, been controlling her, or trying to, and screwed with her for years. What, you got her mum on side and left them to it, just interfered when you thought it best? Or, ah, I get it, you had your people there too, guarding her. Hounds who were shifters. Damn, you lot have been busy."

"How very astute of you," said Kim, not looking quite as pleased now with me figuring things out. "She's too important to be left without guidance. You don't know what it's like, how hard it is. She needed safeguarding, to be protected until the time was right. Now it's almost ruined, but not quite. We'll get her back you know? Where is she?"

"Like I'm gonna fucking tell you. You bitch. You screwed that girl over. Do you know the kind of life she's had? You were grooming her to become like you lot, make her distrust everyone else and think Cerberus is in the right. You'd say you could save her and protect her but you'd just use her, make her do terrible things. Just because you got treated like that, doesn't mean she should be."

"Will somebody please explain what this is all about? Who is Sunshine and what are you saying? I don't understand." Ivan was losing the plot, gesticulating wildly as his long legs twitched.

"Sunshine is a little shifter girl, Steve's daughter, and she's been kept prisoner since she was a baby because she can shift into anything and she can affect people's minds, their hearts, through the power of her own emotions. And Kim here is the same, to a lesser degree, and was probably brought up in a similar way and became a member of Cerberus. Probably brainwashed as a child. Now they want Sunshine back as we just rescued her. Your people betrayed you, Kim, they wanted a ransom for the girl. She thought she'd got them to help her escape but they screwed you and her both and just wanted the money."

"They weren't our people, our people are dead. We traced them. Our man was still on the boat. It was the others, they had no honor, but this explains why she went missing. No matter, she is close, we will get her. Now, is that all?" Kim looked like she was ready to go, that this was it and she'd just bugger off and leave us to it.

"You aren't going anywhere, you fucking bitch," shouted Vicky, her face almost purple with rage. "How could you do that to her?"

"I was raised like her. It's for her protection, and the protection of others. It has to be like this until she is old enough to know how to control it all. I caused so much damage when I was young, even being kept safe. Cerberus helps people like me, like me and Sunshine, we owe them everything."

"Bloody hell, they did a good job on you, didn't they?"

"They saved me from myself. We help people like me and Sunshine. She can do great things, she can serve. If we left her, she would be a major problem, an artifact of the most dangerous kind. This is our role, to safeguard humanity and stop artifacts ruining our world."

"She's a little girl," I said softly. "You were a little girl. You aren't objects, you aren't artifacts. Sunshine is a child who needs to be loved and allowed to grow into a woman and make her own choices, not something to be locked away like an artifact in your bloody warehouse." The insanity of these people was astounding. I knew they were nutjobs, but this was too much to take in.

Something niggled at my mind and I was about to ask but Ivan spoke first. "So you are a shifter and a vampire, and a Hound? You have been involved in the imprisonment of a small child, done it since she was a baby, and you try to justify that? You know the life I had, the life Vicky and I had, how we were treated, the things that were done to us? That I was a slave for so many years, and you dare," Ivan spat his words, spittle flying, "you dare try to justify treating a child like that? To me!? Me! You were a prisoner yourself and yet you did it to another? Abomination." Ivan flew into a rage I had never seen before. He launched at Kim and I knew this time there was no way he would hold back.

He'd kill her, and we'd never know the extent of their crimes against this girl. Death was too easy a punishment; she deserved much worse.

Should Have Known

Kim, I recalled her name and face just fine now, was ready for Ivan, but I saw the look of hurt on her face, how even after all this she was pained by his words and the action he took. Maybe she truly loved him, maybe she thought their relationship could continue. Maybe she was that dumb. Hey, or maybe they'd work it out and all would be fine. Even as Ivan flew at Kim, I couldn't help feeling sorry for her. If she'd been raised like Sunshine, or much worse as who knew how long ago that was, she'd certainly been brainwashed like the other Hounds, so she wasn't totally to blame for what she did.

It was that same old question that makes dealing with all people difficult. Are they the way they are because that's who they are deep down inside, or are they merely the result of their upbringing? Nature vs nurture.

Ivan grabbed Kim around the throat with fingers boosted by the vampire nature, but Kim was vampire too, and so much more besides. I expected her to fight back, to show how powerful she was too, but instead she took us all by surprise and remained limp, accepting of her fate as Ivan squeezed the life out of her. Kim's face turned puce before the blood drained and she began to turn blue.

"Ivan, stop it!" yelled Vicky as she ran forward and scrabbled at his elbows to get him to relinquish his death grip.

Ivan was lost to anger and betrayal, with a whole heap of confusion thrown in. He'd been given a lot of information in a short period of time.

And then Kim's eyes snapped to full alertness and with a reluctance born out of what I was sure was true affection she nonetheless shot out an arm with her fist clenched tight and hammered into Ivan's chest so damn hard that I heard bones break as he was launched off his feet and flung across the room. He hit the wall hard then dropped into a crouching position.

He took only a moment to recover and then was up and diving for Kim while I grabbed Vicky and yanked her out of the way with one hand whilst I freed Wand with the other. He whooped with delight as he came to spectacular life, illuminating the gloomy room with a light show that was uncalled for but did the job of distracting everyone.

"Everyone calm down or Wand here will start blasting and I don't think he's too bothered about who he hits first."

Everyone stared at me but nobody moved.

"Kim, where is it?"

"Where's what?" she barked angrily, chest heaving, keeping an eye on Ivan.

"You must have a means of reporting in, and I don't mean a phone or laptop. I know you guys, you like your secret shit, and please don't tell me you're just a Hound, I wasn't born yesterday. Who are you really?"

"I'm the one in charge, of course."

"Of what?" asked Vicky. "Like a super secret part of Cerberus?"

"No, you muppet," I told Vicky. "She's the numero uno, the top dog. At least as far as we're concerned."

"But... but she can't be," protested Vicky. "She's..."

"I'm what?" asked Kim, amused.

"She's here, with us, doing all this stuff. Spying. The person in charge wouldn't do that."

"Why not, my dear?" asked a genuinely interested Kim.

"Because you're meant to be all super secret and nobody knows who you are."

"They didn't, now they do. It's for the best, now you know, and I will have the girl. Besides, I'm only in charge of this country, there are others, there are always others."

Then Kim did the weirdest thing. She removed her suit jacket, slipped off her shoes, pulled down her skirt, undid her blouse, and stood there in her underwear.

"You lucky bugger," I congratulated Ivan, ogling Kim's awesome figure.

"He is very lucky," said Kim. "I do love you," she said, regret in her voice. Guess she didn't want it to happen.

"I love you too," said Ivan.

Kim sank in on herself, a rapid transformation from human to animal. A true Hound, an amalgamation of every dog you could think of and nothing like any of them. Huge limbs, short fur, stubby ears, bloody great big paws, and eyes that were all too human. How old was this woman, how long had she been in charge? There was such knowledge behind those large brown eyes, a depth of soul and a fierce loyalty to her true love. Cerberus.

She bolted for the door and loped down the hall, her claws tapping the floorboards.

With a shrug, I said, "Guess we should go after her."

"She's heading to the office," said Ivan, launching himself after Kim but tripping over Vicky who got in the way as usual. "She has access to everything. All of it. The entire structure. The servers," Ivan gasped, panic in his eyes as he tried to untangle himself from his sister.

"What fucking servers? What are you on about?"

"No time. Hurry, she can't get in there. She can lock herself inside. It's like a panic room but much safer. All the information is there, everything. Hurry."

Ivan was a blur as he left us in his wake. I chased after him with Vicky coming up fast behind me.

What bloody servers? Had Ivan gone high-tech? What for? He was a bloody vampire and a gangster, not a man who sat behind a desk pressing buttons and plotting world domination via a computer screen.

Or was he?

Cool Office

Ivan barged though a dark wooden door into his panel-lined office complete with a large oak desk with red leather inlay and a green reading lamp. The usual old-fashioned charm was eclipsed by the sight of Kim back in human form, hurriedly reaching between rows of books. There was a faint click as she pressed a hidden button then a section of the shelving pivoted and blue light streamed out into the room, making me shiver as a cold draft rushed to envelop me.

Kim's bottom clenched and two cute dimples appeared—damn but Ivan really was a lucky dude. Or had been until five minutes ago when everything went to shit.

A freaky silence fell, dulling sound, sucking air out of the office and muting the energy as the blue light seemed to spread and devour life with it. For a moment I thought it was magic, but it was just a typical server room, clinically clean, kept at a constant temperature, and with the peculiar lighting they always seemed to have, probably just because it made everything feel a little more high-tech.

"You had all this and you didn't tell me?" squealed Vicky as drool hung from the corner of her mouth.

"It's business," snapped Ivan. "Private. Hurry." Ivan shot across the room but slammed into the closed secret door as Kim darted though. I caught a glimpse of her standing there, looking regretful, but damn hot too.

"I think I should get a server room for home," I mused. "Then Penelope can wander around in the buff and I can ogle her bits."

"Idiot," said Vicky, eyes twinkling with the excitement. She loved all this, especially if it involved computers and the mysteries of the binary world.

"We have to get inside, and fast," said Ivan, looking about as stressed as I'd ever seen him.

"Chill out, dude, we have her cornered. Man, I can't believe she's one of Cerberus' leaders. Do you think she really is?" I wondered. "They're buggers for telling you fibs and misdirection. Maybe she is just a Hound really."

"I'm more concerned about Sunshine," said Vicky sensibly. "They want her, Arthur, and they'll get her."

"I know, I know, but for now they're safe. Don't say their location," I warned Vicky, just in case anyone was listening in, which was highly likely. If Kim had infiltrated this far you could bet the office was bugged. "But if they didn't pick her up yet then they weren't following us from you know where so they're okay for now."

"You sure?"

"No, not at all. I knew it had to be something, I knew someone had to be screwing with Sunshine for her to affect so many people. They were testing her out, I bet that was it, seeing what she could do now she was out in the world. Or maybe," I mused, "it was to get a location on her. Maybe they amplified her power so they could hone in on it."

"And how would they do that?" asked Vicky.

"An artifact, I assume. They have access to untold items that can do pretty much anything you want. Bound to be something in the collection that would work, boost certain signals, send shock waves around the epicenter, that kind of thing."

"You mean you don't know but you assume that's how they did it?"

"Yeah, exactly."

"Now isn't the time for this. We need to get inside and we need to stop her. I don't understand half of what you two are talking about but this girl is special and so is Kim. She's been spying, she knows my world, she has unlimited access now and can easily steal all the data. We must get in there." Ivan yanked at his dressing gown to keep it closed, probably annoyed he wasn't in his suit for something momentous like this.

"Then blast the bloody door down with your vampire skills," I said.

"It's a steel reinforced door with a lock on the inside. It's designed to withstand a bomb. I can't open it. The floors, walls, and ceiling are the same. It's the most secure location in the city and there's no way to unlock it unless the person inside decides to come out."

"Bollocks," I said, grinning. I'd yet to find a door that couldn't be opened somehow.

"You can't get in," insisted Ivan.

"What's so important?" I asked, unable to understand the urgency. We had Kim, she didn't have Sunshine, and whatever we decided to do with her, there was no doubt that we had ourselves a prized, and hot, bargaining chip. "Maybe the best thing is to leave her inside while we figure this mess out. Unless she can do something to Sunshine. Damn, yeah, you guys reckon she's manipulating her from here?"

"Could be," said Vicky.

"I don't know," said Ivan. "I still don't understand what's happening. This girl is a special shifter, and Kim is too, and she's been hidden away because of her powers? That happened to Kim?"

"Seems like it, that's what she said. So, can we leave her or not?"

"Not," insisted Ivan. "She has access to all the cameras, all the data storage, all the information on thousands and thousands of criminals not to mention the location of every vampire in the country, their personal history, and so much more it's making my head spin."

"You should be more careful," I warned. "Don't trust computers. Why'd you need all that anyway?"

"Because, Arthur," said Ivan in a bloody condescending tone, "this is how you run a business in the modern age. How do you think I control so many dangerous people? Why do you think the other gangsters toe the line? It's because I know everything about them. I have informers, many, and they report back. The information is collected, stored, and used when necessary. It runs smoothly because it's organized, under control. My control. I knew I shouldn't have let Kim take such an active role, she already knows way too much about the business and now she can take all that information. It's invaluable to Cerberus. Get us in there!" Ivan's dressing gown gaped open as he waved his arms around like a manic beanstalk.

"Ugh, dude, not cool." I averted my eyes from the sight of a mostly naked Ivan, and he glanced down.

"Wait, I'll be back. No, get us in now, hurry." Ivan was gone in a blur of movement and I heard him upstairs banging about, the vibrations loud through the ceiling.

"Get ready for some action, grasshopper," I said, smiling.

"This is so crazy. I can't believe all this. Kim's a shifter, was treated like Sunshine. Poor thing."

"Yeah, but she chose the dark side, or was indoctrinated into it. Doesn't matter now, we have to stop her. Ivan's a dick for having all this stuff here, but I guess that's progress for you."

"You are such a dinosaur. How'd you think he ran things?"

"I had no idea. But you didn't know he had this, so nah."

Vicky poked a tongue out at me but we both smiled as Wand was brought aloft and the sigils activated as I focused on the countless spells he held within his tiny form. My will focused as energy built in my system, then the dam burst and a torrent of pure joy was unleashed on Ivan's nice office, soon to be little but rubble.

Awesome!

Stressed Vampires

"Arthur, hurry," shouted Ivan as he paused at the doorway to check it was safe.

"Just about to blast the buggery out of everything," I said with glee as the energy built again, more intense than ever, my arm tingled nicely, and Wand wriggled with excitement.

"I'm getting calls, people are being hijacked, stuff's being taken, others have been eliminated." Ivan's phone beeped and he stabbed at the screen then listened. Then he pressed it again, presumably to take another call, then again and again.

"She's ordering a spring clean, or passing the information on at any rate," I said to Vicky.

"Duh, I get it."

My phone rang and I answered, juggling Wand about and losing my momentum. "Hello?"

"It's me, Steve. What's happening, everything okay?"

"Um, could be better. I told you not to call. You need to get out of there, go somewhere safe. Ditch your phone, they're probably tracking it. Or they will. Is it a burner?"

"Always a burner, mate, you know me."

"Ditch it anyway. Go, um, go to where it all began. Where you saved me that first time. Remember?"

"Yeah, I remember. What's happening?"

"No time, just get out of there and fast. It's dangerous." I hung up.

"Are they okay?" asked Vicky.

"For now. But this is going down and chances are they'll try to pick them up, take Sunshine, kill Steve. We need to do this now. Ready?"

Vicky nodded, worry and excitement combining same as it was for me.

"Do it!" shouted Ivan. "Whatever you're going to do, do it now."

"Fine, I will."

So I did.

Getting Nasty

Wand spasmed and spurted a weak, ridiculous dribble of energy that hardly touched the wall before dying.

"Oops, sorry," he sighed. "False start."

"No, my fault. I need to focus." I let my mind empty, forgot what was happening, forgot the scared little girl, and focused purely on the feeling I had inside, of the magic. Of the things I'd learned, the way to hold it in until the right time. To let it build and the energy to consolidate, how words spoken or thought, some would say spells, can focus you and allow the all-pervading energy of the universe to manifest in such a special way. I was consumed by this energy, felt it become me and me it, and it expanded, grew into something more than either of us, and as Wand shone brightly and the sigils danced crazily, flashing in a very specific sequence like binary code that can become so much more than a series of 0's and 1's, the magic burst forth with wild intent.

I was shunted back, sliding on a rug, as power shot forth. It was all I could do to hold on to Wand who vibrated wildly as he further focused my will and my knowledge into a tight beam of deadly firepower that immediately turned the books and the bookcase to ash, revealing red brick and a wall of steel behind already beginning to melt.

The lights popped and the room was dark for a moment before magic lit up the place like a summer's day as the beam grew in strength and focus as I concentrated on the thick walls behind the molten brick that poured down the wall.

The steel burned red hot then white hot and began to slide like thawing ice. A pale blue light seeped through from the server room as the wall was breached. Darkness consumed us before the blue was replaced with emergency red lights that emanated a sickly, depressing hue, muting my power for a second before I regathered my focus and let rip with renewed purpose now I was gaining traction.

Steam hissed, things burst into flames, and I was vaguely aware of Vicky and Ivan spraying fire extinguishers around the office, dousing flames and coating everything in foam before the fire spread and consumed the building and us.

I left them to it and kept a tight grip on Wand as he shifted left to right, up then down, widening the hole and melting thick steel via directed heat that would incinerate a human in a flash but was so focused and controlled it went no further than was needed, didn't tear into the room, but merely incinerated the walls that nonetheless gave off such an intense heat I had to step back and adjust the power for fear of melting my own arm off.

Satisfied with the size of the hole, but not with the heat and the fact we'd never get through it alive, I paused for a moment, let a different kind of energy take over. My system cooled as the heat turned to cold and the energy became not the fierce intensity of a star burning bright, but of the deepest, darkest, coldest recesses of space. The furthest reaches of the universe where all is dead and empty, cold and lonely.

Blue energy more depressing than the server room coursed through the sentient stick in my hand and the office became an ice box as all heat was vanquished and all fires extinguished. Red turned to white as the steel solidified and hissed, wood became brittle and snapped into jagged shards, the steel likewise.

I shivered. A deep, bone-aching cold took over that made me long for the drizzle and to be standing in a muddy wet field rather than at the epicenter of this utterly bleak, miserable emptiness I had brought to bear to save us from burning up.

And then I was spent. The magic died, Wand's lights went out, and I gasped as the room temperature rose a few degrees, still so cold that my breath was thick in the air, what air was left after being eaten up by the fire.

Without a moment to rest, really wishing for a quick coffee for energy, I ran after Ivan and Vicky who were already through the wall and into Ivan's secret high-tech lair to try to catch the new face of Cerberus and once again do battle with those who would see all magic and wonder banished from the world.

Shame

"Aw," I moaned, as I caught sight of a very annoyed Kim. "You got dressed." She just scowled at me, looking impossibly smart in an almost identical suit to earlier. "Why'd you have clothes in here?" I asked, my inquisitive nature getting the better of me at an inopportune moment like it so often did.

"We, er, used to come in here and..." Ivan trailed off as he put a finger under his collar.

"Okay, yeah, I think I've heard enough. Now, where were we?"

"It's too late, Ivan. I'm sorry, my love, but I had no choice."

"No choice!?" Ivan hissed. "You betrayed me, you stole from me. You used me. Cheated."

"Not really. This is mostly information we already have. You aren't the only one with spies and vast networks. You have no idea how far our influence spreads. But yes, some was invaluable, and things have been put into place. You will find many changes sweeping the country as we speak, if you haven't heard already." Kim seemed way too calm and composed, and the fact she'd dressed was unsettling as it meant she had no plans to shift any time soon. That, or she didn't like old wizards perving over her bottom, which was understandable.

"I've heard," said Ivan as he studied the server room.

I took a look around too, impressed with what I saw. Not only were there banks of caged servers, there were several workstations, a huge wall of screens which I assumed received camera feeds but were currently dead, and there were wires and various bits of gadgetry everywhere.

"This is so cool," lusted Vicky, scowling at her brother for keeping it all secret.

"It was," sighed Ivan.

We all turned at a loud noise but it was just bits of Ivan's office falling down.

"How could you?" he asked Kim. "How could you cheat me like this?"

"I protect Cerberus, I help where I can, and you are an important man. You, and him," Kim pointed at me, and not nicely, "are always involved in our work, interfering, taking things. Destroying. You tried to ruin us, to take what we have spent so long collecting, safeguarding, so we thought it best to keep a closer eye on you. But I took a genuine liking to you, and things became complicated. My colleagues didn't know I had genuine feelings for you, I would have been removed if they did, but I must do my work, it's more important than anything else."

"You can't get away with this," said Ivan as he moved closer to Kim.

"Too late, my dear. Things are changing, you and the vampires have become a concern, more than ever since the incident with Mikalus' ashes. Nobody was happy about that even though it mostly played out as we'd wished, but it still rankled and I was given my instructions."

"And the girl?" I asked. I had to know what they'd done, so we could stop it happening again.

"Ah, the girl. Sunshine. So beautiful, so much promise. We will care for her, protect her, teach her, let her grow and control her gifts."

"Bollocks, she deserves her freedom."

"Freedom! Ha! Nobody is free, everyone answers to somebody else. She belongs with us."

"No way. How did you manipulate her power to change emotion? What did you do?"

"Oh," said Kim, her eyes widening in mock defeat, "is this the point where I reveal all because I believe I'll kill you all so it doesn't matter what you know?"

"Yeah, something like that," I mumbled, feeling like a bit of a dick for expecting her to tell me.

"I'm afraid not. I have no plans to kill you unless you make me, so I won't be giving away all the secrets just yet. And besides, it seems your little reunion has stopped her being so easily manipulated, as our artifact no longer appears to function."

"Because she's bloody happy, or happier anyway. She sees that there might be a chance so she's controlling things a little."

"But we will have her soon," said Kim with a smile, "and then our artifact will function again."

"You will never have her," shouted Vicky as she stormed forward ready to do whatever she could to protect Sunshine. "I trusted you with my kids!"

Kim slapped her hard across the cheek as Vicky lunged. My tiny sidekick was slammed back into a bank of servers before sinking to the floor in shock as much as in pain.

"You bitch!" screamed Vicky as she surged to her feet and ran at Kim.

I caught her arm and swung her in close before grabbing her around the waist and lifting her off the floor where she thrashed about and clawed the air like a tiny, ferocious cat.

"Easy there, tiger, she'll eat you for breakfast." Vicky nodded so I let her down but she instantly shot off at Kim like I thought she might so I grabbed her again.

"Now, it's time to go." Kim smiled weakly at Ivan but he didn't smile back. Poor guy was terribly hurt and yet resigned at the same time. Sometimes life beats you down and it's even worse if you expect it to work out that way. Guess Ivan had had too much pain and suffering over the years to ever expect things to turn out any different.

"Leave the girl alone," I warned, "or I won't stop until I finish off your whole organization."

"Haha, such big words. We have been around for too long and are too vast for one puny wizard to ever stop us."

"Who you calling puny?" I asked, annoyed by her dismissive nature.

But she was gone, the clothes dropped, her form changed into that of a bat, which was clearly just for the vampire drama. She fluttered out of the door leaving us all shellshocked, depressed, and worried as hell.

Moving On

Ivan's phone rang incessantly as he dealt with the deluge of problems Kim's attack had brought to bear. He barked out orders, snapped at subordinates who I pictured quaking on the other end of the line, concerned they were next for the chop. Vicky and I dealt efficiently with any small fires, but I was slowing by the second as the comedown hit hard from magical overload.

My stomach rumbled, my head pounded, and Vicky didn't help by chattering away and gleefully ogling the servers as she ran her hands along the cages. Ivan continued to field calls, getting increasingly stressed as his world came apart and Cerberus took over whatever action they could by eliminating his people or causing destruction where they couldn't step in directly.

He was a grown man and he could handle it, I was sure, what concerned me was that Cerberus had even made such a move. They weren't gangsters, they didn't get involved in this world, so why now? I understood the need for intelligence gathering, for knowing what Ivan was up to, but actively stepping in and interfering wasn't their way. Guess they figured they could control things better like this, but surely they knew they would have a real battle on their hands, that Ivan wouldn't take such a hostile takeover lightly?

Whatever. Let the kids play their games. My concern was for Sunshine and Steve right now, and as soon as I was confident the place wouldn't burn down I was ready to go.

Ivan shouted down the phone then hung up. I took the opportunity to talk even as it rang again.

"We have to go. I told Steve to meet us, and I don't like the idea of them waiting. Cerberus want her, and Kim's pretty fucking nuts. Sorry to tell you that, dude."

"I get it, and yes, she's fucking nuts. I can't believe this, any of it." Ivan looked like he was about to either burst into tears or kill someone, and Vicky and I both unconsciously took a step away from him.

"Don't worry, brother, you still have me," said Vicky with a smile.

We both looked down at her.

"Yeah, you're so lucky," I muttered.

"Go get your friend, I'm fine here," said Ivan as his phone kept ringing.

Vicky and I nodded to each other, she gave Ivan a quick hug, I patted him on the shoulder, and then we left him to deal with his crumbling empire.

All Tingly

The moment we stepped out of Ivan's, I felt exposed. Where was Kim? Were there a hundred Hounds closing in on us now, prepared to do whatever it took to wipe us out? I was next to useless, could have fallen asleep right there in the street, and if it wasn't for Sunshine I probably would have.

This was all such a shock, so sudden and unexpected a turn of events, that I don't think my mind had caught up with what was happening.

And now?

Now Cerberus would go all out to get the girl, no holds barred, no need for secrecy.

Paranoia went into overdrive as I scanned the smart residential street. All was quiet, which unnerved me even more. They could be anywhere, they could be watching via a bloody satellite for all I knew, or Kim could be perched in a tree and just follow us with ease.

"Fuck," I moaned, unsure what to do, where to go, how to proceed.

"Come on, we have to go get them. Why are you standing there doing nothing?"

"I'm not doing nothing. I'm thinking. I'm immobile with indecision," I admitted reluctantly.

Vicky gasped and put a hand to her mouth.

"Drama much?" I asked.

"You... you can't be indecisive. It's you, The Hat, you always know what to do. Or, um, you just do stuff without thinking, you know, like always." Vicky frowned, looking as lost as I felt about this whole business.

"This is important, it's your boyfriend, my friend, and a little girl. Fucking Cerberus," I shouted.

"They want to take her away, and Steve will never see her again," said Vicky, maybe realizing for the first time just how bad this was now.

"I know, that's why I'm not sure what to do. They can follow us, they might be watching. Kim's given the word for Ivan's business to be ruined and they're making their move, and you can bet they are gonna do whatever it takes to get Sunshine. We need a plan."

"A cunning one?" asked Vicky with a smile as she tugged at her tight red sweater and stretched up on tiptoe.

I nodded.

Only problem was, I didn't have a plan, cunning or otherwise.

Decisions

"Screw it, let's go," I said, my mind made up.

"But I thought we were being watched?" Vicky cast nervous glances up and down the street, making me feel even more uncertain.

"What can we do? If they're watching, let them. You hear me?" I whispered to the sky. "Give it your best shot."

I marched with purpose to the car and stood by the door waiting for Vicky.

"Um, it's that one." Vicky pointed to the next car along and I glanced down at the one I was beside. I sighed, it sure was one of those lifetimes.

"Just get in." I shuffled over to the car and tried not to look as foolish as I felt.

The moment I drove away from Ivan's, my paranoia went nuts, and for good reason. At least three cars pulled out of the street behind us, doing nothing to hide their intentions. Seemed stupid, as no way would I lead them straight to Sunshine. What were they playing at? Surely they should try to be covert so I would think we're safe?

Or was this part of the plan? Be obvious so I'd lose them somewhere then think we were okay to get the girl? But they were still secretly following us? Damn, I was getting myself in a right muddle and the longer this took the more Sunshine was at risk. Aha, they were doing this so I wouldn't go to her, so they could find her without my help, being obvious so we'd stay away.

I'd show them.

I floored the car and headed straight for the place where I'd first met Steve, consequences be damned.

And halfway through the city, with the traffic getting chaotic, my mind even more so, I had a change of heart and pulled over to the side of the road right in the heart of the city and killed the engine.

"Let's go," I said as I undid my seatbelt.

"You can't park here, it's double yellow lines. You'll get a ticket." Vicky looked panicked as she scanned for traffic wardens.

"So what? What's more important, Steve and Sunshine or a ticket?"

"They are, obviously, but still."

I felt it too, that deep-seated fear of getting a parking ticket, the anger and vitriol surfacing, the injustice of it all for being fined for parking somewhere you shouldn't. It was utterly without justification, but for some reason it's such a basic fear, the anger every motorist feels towards traffic wardens, that even under such extreme circumstances I was tempted to go find a car park and pay for parking.

"Let's live dangerously for once," I said, then got out.

"For once?" asked Vicky when she was out too and searching for the dreaded traffic warden.

"Come on, this way." I grabbed Vicky and dashed across the road much to the annoyance of the morose motorists.

The three cars following us clearly had the same issues with traffic wardens as they pulled up by our car but nobody turned their engines off. Haha, served them right if they did get tickets.

Across the road I glanced back and saw that the Hounds had made their decision. Three men emerged from three cars, looked worriedly at each other, fear of being fined clear, then they stared hard at me, hatred in their eyes, before we ducked down an alley and ran.

Eyes Everywhere

It didn't take long to lose the Hounds. I knew the city, I knew the streets, I knew the people. A few deft shortcuts, several quick hellos in shops and a nod to the back where we could exit onto a different street, and we were free of our pursuers.

Knackered, stressed, and fearful for our friends, we slowed to a walk as we battled the carnage of late afternoon shoppers panicking they hadn't spent enough money. Now hurriedly impulse-buying so they could get the buyer's high, followed later that evening by buyer's remorse when they realized something was sorely amiss in their lives and the questions rolled around their heads about why they spent so much and how they were going to pay off the credit card before the interest rate charges sank them ever deeper into the pit of debt they somehow found themselves in? Still, they were happy for now as they bought stuff before the shops closed.

Suitably judgmental about other people, and feeling a little better for it, as we weren't the only ones with problems, we walked through the crowded shopping center. A man wearing a raincoat and a nice hat caught my attention. He was just standing there, staring. At us.

I noticed his boots. Black, polished, military. He winked at me, knowingly.

"It's a bloody Hound," I whispered to Vicky, nodding at the guy. She glanced at him then squeezed my hand.

We sped up, moving fast through the crowds.

I caught sight of a woman in an almost identical long coat, with the same boots, again just standing there, watching.

We began to run, barged past people chatting on their phones or just staring at screens as they walked, and the faster we moved the more Hounds I seemed to see. They were everywhere.

Back out on the main street we glanced in all directions, and everywhere I looked there were men and women watching us. All wore plain, unassuming clothes, mostly hidden by long coats, nothing to draw attention to themselves. Nobody made a move to follow us, but as we passed them they spoke quietly as if to the air, our route being relayed to the powers that be, waiting for us to lead them to Sunshine if they didn't just find her anyway.

There was nothing for it, we had to make a dash for it and somehow hope we could get out of this without Sunshine being lost to us for ever.

Faces watched us at every turn, staring without emotion, heads turning to follow our progress, words whispered into the air that charted our path leading Cerberus right to Sunshine and Steve.

My heart hammered, my body ached, my head was thick with indecision even as we ran towards a little girl in need of help. Had they found them already, and were merely keeping an eye on us? Was it too late? Nobody was acting weirder than normal, emotions weren't running high or getting skewed, so did that mean Sunshine was content? Or had they done something to her? Sedated her, used their device to control her emotional influence?

I didn't know and it was maddening.

We ran on, turned down alleys, sped through crowded streets, entered and exited shops and everywhere we went there were faces staring at us. It freaked me out. I felt like a lab rat and we were heading right where they wanted us to go. Only one way out of this maze and the prize was a little girl's freedom. All her hopes, dreams, the chance of a future, were about to be taken from her, and I couldn't do a damn thing but lead her future jailers right to her.

I don't think I'd ever felt so utterly useless as I did at this exact moment.

Closing In

We turned a corner and found ourselves in the back alley that led to the arranged meeting place.

Vicky and I were holding hands and running but we both missed a step and yet somehow kept moving fast as we spied two Hounds coming from the opposite end of the alley.

Why couldn't they leave Sunshine alone? How could Kim do this, knowing the kind of life she would have, having been through it herself? Did she really think their cause justified such a miserable future? I guess she did, otherwise none of this would be happening.

Sometimes I despair of the human race. It's amazing we've lasted this long.

We ran, our breathing ragged, but our steps were certain.

I focused on what little energy remained, channeled my will and my purpose to give myself at least a fighting chance if the Hounds reached the others first. It wasn't enough, I knew this, and I understood the outcome would be my death and the awful fate that awaited me once I did die, but Sunshine's life was more important than mine. After all, I'd had a decent innings, and nobody could ever say it had been boring.

I pushed through the green, freshly painted wooden gates to the back yard. The smell of the large commercial bins was strong, but not as strong as the stench of fear, dread, impending defeat, and despair that filled the air. I was almost utterly overloaded by Steve's emanations.

Sunshine was sitting on an upturned crate, eyes squeezed shut, fists clenched tight in her lap. She looked so frail and small. A thick, oversized coat I'd never seen before was wrapped tightly around her slender frame, making her appear even more tiny.

She was clearly trying her absolute best not to freak out. Maybe this was how she could control the influence she exerted on others, maybe it was just how she stopped changing into something, or someone, different, maybe she was just terrified and didn't want to look.

Steve was beside her, looking a lot less focused. He stroked her head, mumbled words of reassurance, but was far from in control. His hair wasn't his usual slick hipster style, it was wiry and black and white, blending in with a wild beard that ran down his neck and under his shirt. His body was misshapen, the limbs short and stubby, his clothes comical they fitted so badly. And the stink, boy the stink. Not just from Steve though, from Sunshine too. A cloying, sickly sweet smell that did peculiar, unnatural things to your insides. It was both arousing and disgusting, so potent I faltered and stopped in my tracks. Vicky squeezed my hand tight then released it and dashed to Steve.

He seemed to come out of a wild-eyed trance and notice us for the first time.

"Steve, Steve, you okay?" asked Vicky.

"Ugh, yeah, I guess. Hey, babe. You're late, we were getting worried. I wasn't sure what to do, where to go. The bloody Hounds are everywhere."

"Yeah, and right behind us. We gotta go," I said hurriedly, sensing them the other side of the gate.

Steve nodded. Then he grinned. He looked at me with such hope in his eyes that it made my heart ache.

"So, what's the plan then?" he asked, a look of absolute trust directed at me.

"Um, about that." I scratched at my stubble, wishing I had an awesome idea to get us out of this disaster.

"You do have a plan, don't you?" Steve's body quivered and hair grew thick and fast as his limbs shortened further and fingers turned sharp and deadly.

"Yeah. Run?"

"Run," agreed Vicky.

Sunshine's eyes snapped open and she shouted, "No," as Hounds burst into the yard through the gates and others came through the back door of the store. Two more jumped over the fence and landed with a splash.

Then nobody moved, expressions went blank, and silence enveloped us. It felt like being underwater, or having your head stuffed into a large box full of cotton wool.

The sounds of the city, a background hum that's so familiar you don't even notice it, was suddenly absent. There was no chatter from the millions of people, no sirens wailing, no traders shouting about their produce, no noise at all apart from pigeons cooing loudly as though the silence gave them the opportunity to vent their frustrations, to be heard in a city of constant noise.

A wave of utter emptiness washed over me and for a moment I couldn't have cared less about Sunshine and her father. I just wasn't interested, not in the slightest. I understood that I knew them, that I had been helping them, but it all seemed so damn pointless, a waste of time and energy. They could do what they wanted, their actions were of no concern to me.

Then it was gone and I sagged then regained my balance and footing before falling flat on my face.

Vicky grabbed hold of Steve for support, the effects similar for them both, but the Hounds fared worse. This was focused, this was Sunshine actively controlling emotional energy and the field it radiated in. The Hounds slumped, eyes vacant, faces slack, utterly uninterested in her and Steve or anything else by the seems of it.

And it wasn't just them, it was the whole city, maybe the entire country for all I knew. Car alarms sounded, the noise of vehicles crashing into each other replacing the silence, drowning out the pigeons who were once more returned to just another noise in the maelstrom. People wailed, or moaned, or maybe they were just venting their frustration, now angry at nothing, the emotion releasing in a final call for help that wasn't forthcoming. All that remained were four people in a stinking yard in the middle of what I often felt was hell on earth but was drawn to like a moth to a flame nonetheless.

The city was changed, like a new world, reborn without emotion, uncaring, more so than ever, and it felt so wrong.

"Let's go," said Sunshine, standing, looking tiny and weak but I knew she was anything but. She was powerful, dangerous, and super-duper scary.

We walked past the Hounds who either stood, sat, or lay where they were, watching us without interest. Others focused on nothing at all.

Freaky as fuck, I think you'll find is the right way to describe it.

It's the End of the World

Outside the gates was the weirdest damn sight I'd ever seen. Okay, maybe not weirder than that time with the squirrel and the jar of peanut butter, but it came close.

There were a shit-ton of Hounds spread all the way along the alley in both directions, zombies who'd had their fill, alive but unresponsive. Some were lost in intense concentration on scraps of litter that caught their eye as they slumped to the potholed, weed-infested ground, others merely stood there, swaying like branches in a balmy breeze. As we walked, several followed our progress, but it wasn't with the focus of earlier, it was with utter disinterest, a glance and then they couldn't be arsed.

"You did all this?" I asked, my voice a whisper, as if talking loudly would wake them from their stupor.

Sunshine nodded, her jaw clenched. "I can't keep it up, though, it hurts." Sunshine shuddered and her eyes streamed. Steve put an arm around her and smiled, being brave for the sake of his daughter. She smiled back and for a moment I felt the oppressive air lift and heard the moans of Hounds as they emerged from their trance.

"Sorry, Dad, but no cuddles yet." Sunshine shook him off and focused again on her emotional forcefield, as clearly feeling much of anything herself had an impact on how she could deal with this. Her already pale features became almost translucent as she regained focus and the Hounds ahead once again slumped or swayed, uncaring.

It swept across our minds too, but was gone, controlled by Sunshine, freeing us from the terrible grasp of its empty power.

We turned the corner and emerged into one of the main thoroughfares, a place still thronging with desperate shoppers, but they were desperate to buy nothing now, weren't hurrying home before darkness descended, keen to get to the warmth and familiar sights, sounds, and smells.

They wandered aimlessly, stared vacantly at shop windows, bumped into each other but didn't care, merely turned and wandered off in a different direction.

Vehicles were stationary in the road, engines ticking over, drivers and passengers alike sat staring out the windows, oblivious. Nobody cared about anything, had lost all interest. I smiled thinking about how pissed off they'd be when they snapped out of it and realized the damage to their cars so many would have to deal with. I wondered if they'd even remember how it happened. Talk about an insurance nightmare.

We hurried through familiar streets that felt utterly alien without the chaos. This must be what the end of the world would feel like. No noise of other human beings, just alarms going until the power failed and then utter silence. Apart from the pigeons, there would always be pigeons.

Sunshine began to shake really bad and Steve had to catch her a few times when she stumbled. She was losing control and it wasn't just her appearance that made that clear. I became an emotional whirlpool, sinking into utter despair, questioning my life and the choices I'd made, drowning in regret only to surface, feeling buoyant and full of hope, then having to clamp a hand over my mouth before I blurted out truths to Vicky and Steve I knew would hurt.

Then I felt no love for any of them, for anyone, including myself, and you have to love yourself. You're the only person in this world you can guarantee will be a constant companion until the end of your days.

Everyone else felt it too, and noise began to ebb and flow, rippled across the city in waves of joy and anger, pride and pain, happiness and gut-wrenching despair.

The city awoke, and all hell broke loose.

A City Awakes

The noise was astonishing, a cacophony of terror and confusion, anger and hostility, fear and loneliness. In other words, business as usual. It is only when such sounds are removed that you appreciate the true extent of the noise of a city when they return, and boy was it all-encompassing.

People, cars, sirens, shouts, screams, wails, cries, and every other emotion all expressed by millions of people, the distant noises combining with those close by to create a solid wall of humanity's struggle to be heard radiating out from the epicenter. And you are that epicenter, the hubbub filling every available wavelength, drowning out your ability to think coherently.

It was quite nice. Beat listening to the pigeons showing off.

Sunshine fell to her knees and gasped as she scraped skin on jagged asphalt. Steve cursed for missing it and helped her up then had a second thought and cradled her, unresisting, in his arms. She was sweating badly, almost blue, and limp.

But she smiled at her father and whispered, "I did it," before her eyes closed and she slept through utter exhaustion.

"You sure did," said Steve before he looked at me with hope, waiting for me to save the day now Sunshine had got us this far.

"We'll go back to mine, regroup, come up with a proper plan. Actually just a plan will do, we've winged it long enough. These bastards will never let us leave now, not after what they've just done."

"What who's done? What's going on? We had to deal with several Hounds and then we made it to the meeting place but we could sense them closing in. Are they after us?"

"No time, we gotta go," I said hurriedly, aware that Hounds were already back on the hunt and we were sitting ducks here in the shopping district.

"I'll tell you what happened while we run," said Vicky softly as she smiled at Steve then at the sleeping form of Sunshine.

"So let's go." I led the way, jogging past confused citizens who were blissfully unaware quite how lucky they were.

It's Whatsherface

"Oh, hello," I said, smiling at the woman standing in our path. "Um, have we met?"

"You are not being serious? Tell me you aren't being serious."

"Haha, just screwing with you. It's Kim, right?"

As Kim flushed with anger at my antics, I did the only sensible thing I could think of and said, "Vicky, give her a five finger special."

"Huh?"

"Smack her one, really hard," I said, exasperated by my sidekick's lack of action.

"Oh, right." Vicky pulled back her arm to give Kim a whack but to say the element of surprise was lost is like saying Vicky's a tad on the petite side.

As Kim sneered at Vicky and took a sensible step away, I swung out with a much longer range of motion and slammed my fist as hard as I could into Kim's pretty nose.

It went splat.

"Sorry, sorry, sorry. I hate hitting girls, wouldn't normally dream of it, but these are desperate times," I shouted over my shoulder as we took the opportunity to get the hell out of there before Kim overcame the shock of being hit by The Hat.

Hounds gave chase as Kim barked out orders, sounding utterly professional if somewhat nasal.

"You have to learn to act fast," I chastised my dear sidekick. "Smack 'em before they expect it, and make sure it's really hard. Works every time," I lectured as we dashed for the car.

"You could have just said hit her, rather than the five finger nonsense," moaned Vicky.

"Just get in," I ordered as we reached the car.

Steve wasted no time bundling a limp Sunshine into the back seat and hurried to buckle her slumped form up safely.

"Told you," said Vicky with slappable glee as she tore a piece of paper from under the windscreen wiper and waved it about. "You got a ticket."

"Goddammit!" I shouted, anger flaring for having to pay a fine when here I was saving the world from evil and rescuing a sweet damsel in distress. Didn't they know how important my wizardly duties were? I should have a sticker or something so I was exempt. Like police or firemen or something.

Vicky hopped in and I did likewise, then pulled out into the chaotic traffic and scraped past cars and generally drove exceedingly badly because Hounds were already on our tail and I suspected Kim was a bit annoyed with me for breaking her lovely nose.

Vicky waved the ticket under my eyes and I gave her a glare. "Don't know why you're being so smug, you have to pay it," I said.

"Me? Why?"

"Because you didn't hit Kim, so that's your punishment. Ha, who's laughing now, smarty-pants?"

Vicky poked her tongue out at me then we both smiled. The high of the chase was back, tiredness forgotten. I felt pretty good, although a nap would have been nice...

"Arthur, Arthur, wake up."

I shook, then opened my eyes. "Um, I did it again, didn't I"? I asked as I stared out the windscreen at an angry motorist, a burly man in a suit and tie, who stormed towards us, the rear of his car dinged where I'd crashed into it.

"Yes, you did," said Vicky with a sigh.

"Oops."

No Fair

I stuck my head out of the window and shouted, "Sorry," to the angry man before hurriedly grinding into reverse gear and backing up. He stopped dead in his tracks, eyes wide, and put his hands up as he retreated. "Wow, I didn't even threaten him."

"Must be the wrinkles," said Vicky.

"Cheeky bugger."

There was a thud on the roof before a shape slid down the windscreen, blocking the view of the guy as he got into his car and drove off, his exhaust rattling.

"Don't think it was the wrinkles, think it was that." I pointed, not that there was any doubt about what had caused him to scarper.

"Bloody hell," gasped Vicky.

"It's huge," I noted.

"Allow me. Nobody is taking my girl away from me." Steve sounded more like the old him. Unafraid, confident, and powerful.

I turned to see him stripping off even as his body morphed and fur erupted through skin in thick wiry clumps.

The door opened a moment later—how did he do that when he was now a fat badger?—and I turned back to the front to see the very large cat, and by cat I mean a goddamn leopard of all things, hiss and scratch huge welts down to the steel as its eyes widened and it bunched its powerful muscles as Steve, a.k.a Mr. Badger, jumped up without grace onto the front of the car.

"It's like a bloody zoo around here," I groaned, knowing Steve would get a serious badger arse-kicking some time soon.

"We have to help him," said Vicky, unfastening her seatbelt.

"You stay right where you are. We have to protect Sunshine. Get in the back and keep an eye on her. If anyone tries to get in then deal with them."

Vicky clambered over the seat and I pressed a button to lock the doors from the inside. Ha, that'd show them.

"Do you think it's Kim?" whispered Vicky.

"Duh!"

"Arthur, you're so mean."

And then the animals launched at each other.

And then the passenger side window smashed.

And then I took my foot off the clutch by mistake, realized I was still in reverse gear, and the car jumped back several feet. The animals fell off the car, I felt a nasty bump as we drove over something, probably a

Hound's foot, and then a sickening crunch I soon discovered was another Hound crushed between us and the vehicle behind.

Could have been worse.

Somehow.

Then it was, because a rear window shattered and hands reached in to grab Vicky by the throat before yanking her out of the car.

I sighed. Guess I'd have to help or I'd never hear the end of it.

Once More

I entered the fray, weak, sleepy, questioning my life choices, realizing I hadn't called home and wondering if it was dinner time yet and how much trouble I was in.

First thing first, so I yanked out Wand, who was as exhausted as me and about as responsive as a regular stick, but I nonetheless used him effectively by stabbing the Hound grappling with a very wriggly, very bitey and kicky Vicky right in his Adam's apple. It works every time and the guy dropped Vicky instantly as his hands went to his throat.

"No use, buddy, you're already dead," I said, and then he dropped. And he was. Dead.

Vicky kicked him in the ribs before she whirled with surprisingly fast reflexes and booted the guy to her side in the balls before he could grab her.

Not about to be outdone, I jabbed out behind me with an elbow, felt the breath escape sharply from the man about to do something nasty to The Hat, then spun and popped his eyeball with a very gooey Wand.

We hurried to the front of the car as Hounds closed in. The city seemed to hold its breath, and I realized we were making somewhat of a spectacle of ourselves. Everyone was watching, everyone was grossed out, and everyone would be calling the police. This kind of thing didn't happen in the city center, at least not often, and we had to get out of here or one of two things would happen. Either Cerberus would defeat us or we'd all get nabbed by the cops. I wasn't about to hurt the police, they did a fine job, so the only choice was to go, and fast.

Steve and Kim were playing hide and seek around the car, creeping one way then the other, peering underneath the vehicle before launching themselves in one direction or another and raking at each other. Both of their hides were torn and bloodied, but Steve was clearly faring the worst, and as they jumped onto the roof, which was no mean feat for a fat, stubby badger, it was clear Steve would be put down at next contact.

"We have to go, buddy," I shouted above the din of sirens coming from several directions, fighting through the confusion of traffic.

Steve didn't even glance my way, his dark eyes were focused only on the leopard. His muscles bunched, rippled under the stubbly fur, ready to take on a much larger foe once more.

"Hold this," I said to Vicky before I hurriedly removed my jacket, threw it over Steve, bundled him up, heaved the great lump in through the rear window, snatched back Wand, said, "Thanks, now let's go," and scrambled back into the car as Vicky did likewise and Hounds approached from all directions.

I managed to slide cleanly into reverse this time, slammed into the already mushed Hound behind, ran over a few legs and feet, and shunted a car out of the way enough so I could swerve out into the traffic trying to move to make way for the police. We scraped past several vehicles much to the anger of the occupants.

Then we were clear. I stuck to the dedicated bus lane and floored it, swerving this way and that as needed, but I made it away from the scene of the crime with all my limbs intact and I even still had Grace perched stylishly on top of my head.

"That went well," I said, turning to Vicky for approval.

"Could have been worse," she agreed. Her face was flushed, her chest was heaving, she was smiling, and it was unnerving.

"You shouldn't be enjoying this," I lectured. "We could have got killed."

"No way, we're too good. We took on Cerberus and beat their asses. Again."

"Yeah, pretty sweet," I agreed.

There was a muffled sound from the back and I glanced over my shoulder quickly as I hit a straight section of road.

"Oh, shit, Steve."

"Oops." Vicky reached over and yanked several times at my jacket that had Steve wrapped up like a stylish mummy, his limbs all tangled now he had sensibly decided to return to human form.

"That was disgusting," he said, spitting. "Don't you ever wash your jacket?"

"You aren't meant to clean leather," I said. There was an awkward silence. "What?"

"You can wipe it down, use soapy water," said Vicky, giving me a puzzled look.

"Really? You sure? Won't it, you know, make it go funny?"

"No, you dick," said Steve. "It'll make it clean, and stop it smelling funky."

"Oh, right. You learn something new every day. Anyway, how you doing?" I glanced in the rearview so I could thankfully only see the top half of a buff, naked Steve. Vicky was ogling her guy, which was fair enough I suppose.

"Been better. But I've been worse too." Steve groaned as he poked at various wounds, checking them out.

"Sunshine okay?" I asked, amazed she'd been so quiet.

"She's still sleeping," said Steve with awe tinged with concern.

"She's had a hard time of it," said Vicky softly. "Let her sleep."

Steve got himself dressed while I took several turns to ensure we weren't being followed, but it was pretty pointless as no way would this be the end of it. They probably knew where my house was, or could find out easily enough, and they would surely be following. Probably had helicopters keeping an eye on us, drones, some shit like that.

"We'll just have to try to make it to the country house and keep you safe. They won't come there, they know better."

"You sure?" asked Vicky.

"No, but what else can we do?" I genuinely didn't know.

I stopped at a red light, took the opportunity to breathe deeply and calm down.

There was a bang on the roof, making everyone jump, and then a familiar furry body slid down the windscreen and stared in at me with utter malevolence.

Getting Annoyed

"No way, I am not letting this happen."

As the eyes of the cat bored through my skull, I flicked on the windscreen wipers to the setting that also squirted soapy water. That'd teach her.

The wipers were pinned by her furry frame, but the water jets squirted. Problem being, they squirted at the windscreen, so the result was that she got a little damp but I couldn't see out properly. Damn, I thought it was a good idea too.

As the windscreen cleared a little, I revved the engine, looked both ways at the junction, then did a very naughty thing. I floored it right through a red light. I moved up the gears fast, the engine straining, until I hit fifth. A quick glance in the rearview to check the coast was clear and I slammed on the brakes. I grinned and waved as Kim flew off the car and I anticipated the crunching of bones.

Instead, she cheated, and as the leopard sailed through the air it morphed between various sizes of creature before wings spread wide and a bird of prey glided away only to loop up and then turn before landing gracefully in front of the car.

"Fine, be like that," I muttered as I put the pedal to the metal and screamed towards the eagle.

We roared past but I felt nothing hit. "Did we get her?" I asked.

Everyone turned to look behind but there was nothing in the road. Goddamn, where was she?

A large lump splatted onto the roof, denting the metal and forcing the car to slow. "What the hell was that? Can she, um, turn into an elephant or something? A hippo? Steve, could she do that?"

"It's not usual, something to do with physics I think," he mumbled.

"Yeah, physics, I'm sure that plays an important role in shifting from a human into an animal."

"Dude, no need for the sarcasm."

"Sorry, bit stressed."

"That's okay, I understand."

Man, Steve really was a muppet at times.

I drove as fast as I could, then tried the old brake hard maneuver again, but nothing went shooting off. The roof banged harder, another dent, but what could I do? I kept driving and I kept swerving, speeding, slowing, braking, trying to dislodge Kim as she no doubt morphed from this to that to keep her grip while slowly destroying my car.

Sunshine stirred, began to moan, and I knew we had to do something. Last thing we needed was her awake and freaking out, getting scared. She might act rashly, try to help, change into something and get taken or even killed.

"Now," I warned, "this isn't so much a plan as a last resort. When I stop the car, what we're going to do is run away very fast and hope we don't all die. Everyone ready?"

"What? No, absolutely not," said a panicked Vicky.

"Sunshine's still asleep," said Steve.

"Then wake her up now because this is happening. We're close to the house, we just have to get in and... Er, no, wait, I have another idea. Scrap that."

I grinned as I took a left turn and roared through the darkening streets on my way to somewhere wizards were always welcome, everyone else not so much.

Breaking the Rules

"Hey, Turk," I said breezily as we marched through the foyer of Satan's Breath, the sweat already forming.

"Hey, Arthur. Whoa! What you doing? You can't all be in here. Are they women? Is that a shifter? Out, all of you. This is wizards only." The Turk's thick waxed mustache wriggled about like an eel that had been jammed through a pencil sharpener and his stained white vest rode up to reveal a fat, hairy belly as he waved his arms about and did gravity-defying things with his eyebrows. His double chin made his stubble ripple and I swear I saw fluff fall from his belly button.

"Sorry, I know it's against the rules, but this is an emergency. Oh, there's a powerful shifter outside, please don't let her in. Cerberus are on the warpath, have decided to take over Ivan's business, or try, so be warned."

I nodded to the others and before the Turk could do anything to stop us, we darted through the archway then into the locker room.

"If you see an old man with a hair dryer, avert your gaze," I warned. But it was already too late.

There in front of us, leg up on the sink, staring at himself in a full-length mirror, was the same perverted old wizard as always, doing despicable things to his wrinkly bits with what sounded and looked like an industrial level hairdryer.

"I got an upgrade," he said with glee as we hurried past and I put my hands over Sunshine's eyes.

"Was he...?" asked Vicky, faltering.

"Yeah, he was," I grunted.

"Why?"

"I honestly don't know. He says it dries them."

"So do towels."

"I know. Try telling him that. Come on, no time."

We made it to my locker and I opened it up after checking the wards hadn't been tampered with. Everything was as it should have been, the collection of artifacts, cash, clothes and more were all there and behaving, for now. Several artifacts grumbled about being left alone for so long but I ignored them and made sure not to touch them as some had a nasty habit of biting.

I grabbed the infinite bag and with a deep breath said something I thought I'd never say.

"Get in."

"What?" asked a confused Steve.

I opened the bag wider, what appeared to be an old-fashioned, distressed leather doctor's bag, and repeated, "Get in. Hurry, it's the only way."

"It's a bag," said Steve.

"It's my infinite bag," I said.

"What's inside it?" asked Sunshine, peering into the darkness.

"A bit of everything. Try not to touch stuff, some of it's rather volatile. Um, although there should be plenty of space."

"Arthur, is this safe?" asked Vicky. "I thought you said people should never go inside, that it was too dangerous? How will they get out? How will they fit in?"

"It is dangerous, and I don't know the answer to the last but one question yet, but they'll fit, trust me. It's the only way to hide them. So, like I said, get in." I nodded to Steve and a very worried looking Sunshine.

Steve grinned then grabbed Sunshine's hand and before he could change his mind I upturned the bag and popped it over their heads. It swallowed them up like an illegal vacuum cleaner and I turned it back the right way.

"You too," I told Vicky.

"If you think I'm getting into—"

I quickly opened it and slammed it over her head. She disappeared. I righted the bag, shouted, "I'm sorry," into the infinite space inside, then snapped it shut, closed my locker, checked the wards, then ran back out the way I'd come.

"You're seriously deranged, you know that?" I said to the hairy ball-blaster.

"I know," he said with a cackle before returning to his business.

How Much!?

If my math was good, and I knew it was, then I'd timed this just about perfectly. In the archway before the foyer, I opened the bag cautiously and said a silent prayer before I reached in and grabbed something bony and furry that squeaked. I smiled as I pulled out a squirming Vicky by her red jumper then dropped her down and closed the bag.

"Did you say your goodbyes?" I asked.

"I guess. Why did you do that? Why did you put me in there?"

"Because I couldn't face a long farewell and we were, still are, out of time. You got it though? You understood?"

"Yes, this is the end, isn't it?"

"Sure is. For you and Steve, anyway."

A tear fell from Vicky's sad eyes but she knew it had to be this way.

"Come on, there's no time."

We stepped into the foyer and stood the other side of the counter. The Turk was licking envelopes and stamps and placing the mail in a pile next to a worryingly wriggling towel that he slammed a meaty fist down onto. It mewled then was still.

"Got a box?" I asked.

"Got a box? You ask me if I have a box when I have Hounds outside my door and women inside a wizard-only establishment?" The Turk scowled at me then continued to slide out a fat tongue and slurp at the mail. So gross.

"But they won't come in, will they?"

"They wouldn't dare! It would be all-out war. The Turk knows people, knows things, and will have their hides if they dare bother him."

"Then The Hat thanks the Turk and once again asks for a box."

The Turk reached under the counter and grabbed a box. I dropped the bag inside, taped it up, wrote an address on the top, and spun it around to face him.

"Add it to the pile," I said.

"Stamps?" he asked. "You want some?"

"Please."

He placed the box on a scale then gave me a number.

"Bloody daylight robbery," I moaned, but nonetheless said, "Add it to my subscription renewal. Don't have cash on me."

"Fine. So you remember it's time to renew? These lot," he nodded at the envelopes, "need to have it in writing or they'll never pay. Happens every year."

"I know, and it's time for the postman, right?"

"Sure is."

I heard the faint tinkle of bells as the air turned cold. A moment later a fat man with a white beard and an oversized postman's uniform with white trim at cuff and ankle appeared from the back with a large sack over his shoulder.

"Turk," he said.

"Postie," said the Turk with a nod.

"Arthur," said the postman.

"Postie," I replied.

"Are you being a good boy?" he asked.

"You know it," I said with a grin.

The postman loaded the mail into his sack then read the address on the box. He raised a white eyebrow as he looked at me. "You sure?" he asked.

"I'm sure."

He nodded, then dropped the box inside. With a smile, he left. Bells rang out for a moment, almost overwhelming me with the memories they made surface, then the temperature returned to humid, verging on scalding.

"Was that...? That wasn't...?" spluttered Vicky, eyes wide, staring after the vanishing postman.

"What do you think he does the rest of the year?" I asked with a grin.

"No way, you're messing with me, right?"

"Come on, time to go," I said, taking Vicky's hand and heading straight for the front door. At the entrance, I turned. "Turk?"

"Yeah?" he replied.

"Thanks, I owe you one."

"All part of the service," he said, then began folding towels, sometimes thumping them if they misbehaved.

We stepped out into an uncertain future.

Home for Dinner

"And they just let you leave?" asked Penelope as she placed leftover shepherd's pie from our dinner earlier in front of me. Being a wizard is hungry work.

"Thanks. Yeah, it was just me and Vicky, so they either killed us outside or let us go."

"What about Kim?" asked George.

"She wasn't happy, ranted and raved, promised she would find Sunshine, swore she would go in and get them. But by that time there were several hundred wizards outside too. Guess the Turk had made a few calls, so she was pretty much screwed. I gotta say, I was nervous."

"Me too," said Vicky, looking exhausted but jubilant, sad, but relieved too.

"They could have taken you, made you tell where they were," said Penelope, putting a hand to my knee with concern.

"They could have tried, but Kim knows same as everyone else that wizards don't tell. She knew she'd never get it out of me. Nobody ever will. And I mean nobody." I looked at Vicky as I spoke.

"I know, and I don't want you to tell me. Just tell me that they're safe, that they'll be okay, and that's good enough."

"They are right now on their way somewhere far, far away where nobody will ever find them. They will have the chance of a future, will never be found as long as they keep a low profile, and if they play their cards right they'll never have to worry about money again. There's a ton of interesting things in that bag, and I'm sure they can find a way to use them to make a nice life for themselves."

"Good, that's good. Steve was a great guy and I'll miss him," said Vicky. "The girls will too. I'll tell them in the morning. Thanks for letting us stay over tonight."

"Our pleasure," said Penelope.

I understood the pain Vicky was in, but we both knew it was for the best. That they would never have peace if they remained on the radar of Cerberus and the shifters.

"And we made it home for dinner," I said with pride. "Right on time."

"But you never called, you didn't even text," said Penelope, her smile telling me all was fine really.

"Sorry, I'll try better next time. Promise."

"Wait, one more thing," said Vicky. "That wasn't really you know who, was it?"

I ran my fingers across my lips like a zip.

Wizards never tell. They have honor, and they do right by their friends.

Book 11 in the series (and it's the penultimate one!) is Sand Storm.

Get author updates and new release notifications first via the Newsletter at www.alkline.co.uk

Read the Dark Magic Enforcer series for more magical mayhem.

Printed in Great Britain
by Amazon

45018621R00220